The

'Innovative in format a [illegible] multi-layered, challenging and political. It's also full of verve and wit.'

—Monica Ali

'These are stories to savour like the fine food they describe. Sharply observed, funny, sad and entertaining, they leave you more knowledgeable about the world we live in. I loved this book.'

—Paul McVeigh

'Elaine Chiew's short stories are hugely incisive. Here is a satisfying mix of poignancy and humour, light and dark—an unforgettable journey into the hearts and minds of the displaced. Chiew brings original and multiple award-winning skills to great effect in these sparklingly intelligent explorations of identity and displacement. The added charge in Chiew's work comes from her impressive range—her clever, nuanced and varied stories are perfectly balanced.'

—Vanessa Gebbie

'Elaine Chiew's witty stories in *The Heartsick Diaspora* offer us a rich palette of feelings and experiences that often converge: humour, melancholy, rage, and tenderness. Issues of race, ethnicity, and cultural identities are embedded in the everyday—in the kitchen, on the bus, or at school—as characters navigate between connection and isolation, visibility and invisibility, familiarity and distance.'

—Intan Paramaditha

'"Appetites are good," says one of the characters in the title story, "appetites are page-turners". An apt aphorism for this collection peopled with richly imagined characters, whose appetites both literal and metaphorical propel their stories off the page and under our skin. Elaine Chiew's brilliant debut is perfectly poised between playful and serious, and I can't wait to read more of her work.'

—Pippa Goldschmidt

'*The Heartsick Diaspora* is thoughtful, complex, emotionally resonant, both aware of the need to establish its own truth and of the danger that need involves... The stories are as deeply felt as they are, on occasion, playful; there's a kind of impertinence of tone, a creative intelligence that lets Chiew get up skin-close and yet maintain a distance that allows her, and us, to see the larger picture.'

—Charles Lambert

'*The Heartsick Diaspora* is an unflinching examination of the hybrid and hyphenated lives of global nomads, shining a bright light on Singaporean Chinese voices, but also the larger Malaysian and Singaporean Chinese diaspora. It is philosophical and poetic in turns, and stories like 'Face' and 'The Heartsick Diaspora' and 'Mapping Three Lives' are absolutely stunning. Memorably populated with characters who linger in the mind long after the last story ends, this book is a truly impressive debut, full of humour and heart.'

—Dipika Mukherjee

'The characters in Elaine Chiew's wonderful and vibrant collection, *The Heartsick Diaspora,* are drawn with so much insight, humour, and compassion. It is an original and beautiful collection.'

—Karen E. Bender

'In *The Heartsick Diaspora,* Elaine Chiew allows us to visit a breadth of experiences among Chinese migrant communities, both past and present. The range of the emotional worlds of the characters represented in the book is depicted in fragments, echoing the disjointed, often repressed manner in which many of the immigrant families communicate with one another. The stories do an outstanding job of capturing an atmosphere that is recognisable, but presented in fresh tales to engage the mind and heart of the reader, even as they entertain. It is a brilliant first collection by Chiew, marking her as a writer to be watched.' —Shelly Bryant

'A spectacular read! What a handsome showcase of the consummate storyteller Elaine Chiew. Hers is a winning voice, working in pathos with great élan. We become witness to such a rich understanding of human emotion and desire. Elaine lets scene and character speak for themselves, with such self-assured perspicacity.'

—Desmond Kon Zhicheng-Mingdé

THE HEARTSICK DIASPORA

ELAINE CHIEW

First published in 2020 by
Myriad Editions
www.myriadeditions.com

Myriad Editions
An imprint of New Internationalist Publications
The Old Music Hall, 106–108 Cowley Rd, Oxford OX4 1JE

First printing
1 3 5 7 9 10 8 6 4 2

A CIP catalogue record for this book
is available from the British Library

ISBN (pbk): 978-1-912408-36-8
ISBN (ebk): 978-1-912408-37-5

Designed and typeset in Palatino
by New Internationalist, Oxford

Printed and bound in Great Britain
by Clays Ltd, Elcograf S.p.A.

In memory of
my Mum and Dad

Contents

The Coffin Maker

THE INTERPRETER came to the coffin maker's shop in Sago Lane, Chinatown, a few days after New Year's Day, 1945, accompanying a Kempeitai officer. The officer introduced himself as Kanagawa and called her Aiko*san*. During the entire time she translated everything he said into Mandarin, he had his hand on her shoulder. The timbre of his voice was so low that often she had to incline her head closer, and the coffin maker imagined the warmth of the officer's breath misting the helix of her ear. She seemed to speak flawless Chinese and Japanese; she looked Chinese, but the coffin maker could not make out whether she was local Singaporean Chinese.

Standing in the doorway, Kanagawa's head was in silhouette against the late afternoon sun, swathing his face in gloom. The stillness of the head, the almost leonine outline, the stance of the feet planted apart, the hands held behind the back, all of it bore down on the coffin maker. The interpreter said she was working under the auspices of the Japanese military authorities. Kanagawa's mission was to secure a hardy coffin for one of the Japanese commanders who had fallen during a jungle skirmish against the Communists across the Causeway. In the dimness of the shop interior, the interpreter was backed by a halo of light;

it filigreed through her silver-threaded kimono, so that for a moment, the coffin maker imagined she'd hidden flickering fireflies inside her robe. She shuffled in her clogs. The way she moved reminded him of his mother's pigeon gait—his mother with the tiny bound feet that he used to massage at night with Tiger Balm because of the pain. The interpreter's hair, done up in an elaborate bun, was jet-black and with her head bowed, her neck was long and lily-white, just like Mei, his sister. She'd powdered her face so white it made him think of dead maidens and kabuki dolls. Even so, she was the loveliest thing he'd set eyes on during the Occupation.

Kanagawa wanted to know what sort of fine wood the coffin maker might still have in stock. The local Hokkien association had continued supplying him with cheap rubber wood, plentiful from the plantations. Given the low demand for expensive coffins, his stockpiles of Malacca teak were ample, and he hoped it would be good enough for the officer's purposes. Kanagawa tapped and peered inside a casket, fingering the joists and smooth planks, then sniffing and rubbing a hand along his jaw in the same smooth movement, before speaking in rapid Japanese to the woman, who kept her head bowed. He said, 'This is a Chinese coffin, no? You don't have any elm? *Yú mù*?'

The coffin maker scratched his shorn head. Kanagawa had known the word for northern elm in Chinese, had pronounced it with perfect intonation, could be a veteran from a China tour of duty. But northern elm in Nanyang? He snuck a glance at Kanagawa. Was the use of the Chinese phrase meant for him? In the early days before the Japanese came, there were massive drives amongst the local Chinese communities to raise funds to support the Kuomintang's anti-Japanese activities in China. There had been such terrible stories about Nanking, Wuhan and later Chongqing. These stories that swarmed like hordes of angry gnats down the peninsula, funnelled through the local Chinese associations. Then, Singapore suffered its own purges and cleansing. His *shīfù*, the master who took him on as a coffin-maker apprentice, simply disappeared one evening. Anxieties and resentment ran deep within the Chinese secret societies. With the Japanese Administration's control over the dissemination of news, the societies devised their own channels. Secret pamphlets and coded letters were hidden in rice-bins and stashed underneath *samfoos* and sarongs, pedalled and trundled and trucked to the whorls and eardrums of Chinese *towkays*, labourers toiling in tin mines and rubber plantations, and then through to the anti-Japanese resistance in the jungles. The coffin maker did not contribute to these clandestine activities, but still his stomach flipped when the officer came. He hoped that all Kanagawa really wanted was a good-sized coffin.

A fly had flown into the shop and was flitting about.

Kanagawa stroked his moustache. He spoke and the woman translated, 'What is your name?'

'Chin Hsiang,' the coffin maker said.

'Full name?' Kanagawa said.

'Wang Chin Hsiang.'

Kanagawa's eyes had begun watching the coffin maker carefully. 'You have family still in China?'

The fly had landed on the officer's red-striped insignia, sewn on to his olive uniform.

'No, my father was born here.'

'Your mother?'

Chin's mother was a child bride, shipped over from Guangdong Province when his father was ready to get married. There was a hooded gleam in Kanagawa's stare that made Chin's heart-rate speed up. He put a hand out and leaned against the strength of the side-planks of wood he was assembling for a casket. 'She came from China, yes.'

Kanagawa resumed his stroll, this time alongside the casket that Chin had just been sanding. He ran his fingers along the seams, almost caressing. The fly buzzed around his shoulders, attracted by a scent it'd picked up from the uniform. Chin darted a glance at the interpreter, and saw great fear in her eyes.

Kanagawa stopped in his tracks, bent down almost to his waist, and tilted his head to peer inside the unfinished coffin. His hair was sleeked back with hair oil; the fly was crawling up the strands. 'What is this wood?'

Chin stepped a little closer. 'It's very good wood, sir. This is *hé táo,* walnut.'

'Walnut.' He rapped the wood with his knuckles, listening to the stolidity, the lack of echo. 'Well, it's the best one here then, isn't it?'

'It's not finished. I need to oil, then apply varnish.' His last good coffin had just been sold to one of the wealthy local Chinese businessmen whose grandfather had passed away. Chin thought it would be good always to have one solid coffin on show, even if business was dismal. The *hé táo* wood had been bought by his old master before the war and kept in pristine condition.

Kanagawa turned around. 'Well, it will be finished tomorrow.' His words were so quiet that Chin almost didn't catch them.

'I can't do that,' Chin said, 'it would mean sacrificing one of the coats of varnish.'

'It goes in the ground, does it not?' the officer said. One eyebrow lifted, the elegance of it like the beginning stroke of a Chinese radical. 'Now, tell me,' he continued, 'you have sisters?' A sudden fear gripped Chin. Mei and his mother were hiding in a tucked-away Malay village in upper Seletar, up north near the abandoned British naval base. He hadn't visited them in a year; they were not listed on his census card as shop occupants.

Kanagawa wagged his head from side to side. His cap flew off and landed right at Chin's feet. The fly, shaken loose, rose and zigzagged. Its buzzing was strangely loud. It was the movement of a second; it could have been a mirage. With the casual flick of a wrist, Kanagawa pinched the fly from its flight path, caught it in between his thumb and index finger, and put it in his mouth.

Then, Chin watched him chew it with wolfish pleasure.

The requisitioning of the coffin should have been the last of it. But a week later, one of his friends in the Hokkien society sent word that the Kempeitai had 'visited' the village his sister and mother were hiding in. The friend said he didn't know how to say this: Mei had been taken. Eyes were everywhere and tongues eager to wag just for a few extra *kati*s of rice and slivers of meat. The friend was pretty sure it was one of the villagers who told on them. Chin sunk to his knees in front of a coffin. Difficult to stanch the onslaught of images. Mei had never even had a boyfriend, had never so much been courted. The friend said there were many dead, dumped into an unmarked grave, at least Mei was still alive. You're lucky, the friend said, your mother has been spared.

If Mei could just keep herself alive. On a desperate whim, Chin cycled furiously from his shop, first to a number of hangouts of Japanese officers, then to the Bright Southern Hotel, where the Japanese military were known to have their bordello for high-ranking officers. With no sign of Kanagawa, Chin finally cycled to the YMCA Kempeitai headquarters, where many detainees were kept and where Kanagawa had mentioned he worked. Perhaps the interpreter would also be there. It was worth a try, she had looked kind. Easy enough to get the two Giyutai guards at the entrance riled up. Chin simply rode past, not getting off his bicycle as was required. They ran after him, dragged him to the ground and yelled at him to bow. Chin spat at their feet, and for his trouble, the guards proceeded to kick and strike him on the head with the heels of their rifles, like stoving washing in a pail. Call Aiko*san*, Chin kept shouting, holding his arms up against his head, trying to protect his face. 'What's that?' one of the guards jeered. Chin begged, pleaded. He'd do anything, take him instead, but the guards only laughed, 'Go home, Ah Beng!'

'Go home now,' a voice gently echoed. Through the film of snot and tears and sweat and blood that rimmed his face, Chin looked up, squinting. A woman was standing before him, clad in a kimono. Her hair was loose, as straight as a curtain of black silk, but Chin recognised her immediately. Aiko*san*. She gave some sort of command to the guards and they hauled him to his feet. Chin shook his head like a wet dog, but she leaned towards his ear and whispered, 'Go home please. You will not be able to help your sister if you're arrested and jailed.' He looked into her eyes and it occurred to him that he hadn't noticed before how brown they were; the depths now swirled with a message, a dangerous one: *wait for me.*

Croak during wartime, and a few planks of pine or rubber wood nailed together sufficed. None of the informants through the networks of Chinese secret societies could provide further intelligence, although there was plenty of other news: the twists and turns of the war on the European front, the British forces gaining ground with the anti-Japanese resistance in the Malayan jungles, whispers of impending Japanese defeat and the end of Occupation, almost too good to be true.

Then one evening, Chin heard a knock on the wooden shutters of his shop. It was close to dinner time, and the street outside was deserted—no more stray cats or dogs even. Chin opened the wooden shutter and saw a double-container tiffin carrier on the window ledge. With trepidation, he took it inside, lifted off the lid of the top compartment. Inside were noodles—*ramen,* the Japanese kind—together with half a hard-boiled egg and a sheet of seaweed—items not easily procurable even on the black market. In the second compartment was the clear broth, still slightly warm. Tucked against the handle grip and stainless-steel container on the bottom was a note in Chinese: *In Muar.*

Muar was just across the border in Johore. While those two words could mean anything, his heart stirred with hope. The tiffin carrier and the note had to have come from Aiko*san*. She was helping him, enquiring where his sister was. He couldn't stop himself—he slurped the noodles in gulps, his distress dripping into the soup. The noodles were hard and chewy, the broth bland and thin. Still, it was the most delicious thing he'd eaten in years. As he ate, he couldn't help the image of Aiko*san* that came to his mind—her eyes especially, the flicker of brown in them, her lovely long neck. Unbearable hiccups came afterwards, hitching his breath, causing a welcome pain in his sternum. Now he could go see his mother. Now he had some news that could ease her pain.

He couldn't sleep. He lay tossing and turning on his thin pallet inside the mosquito netting. Finally, rising from bed, he picked up a sliver of wood and began whittling. In the past, he used to make miniature animal carvings out of these discarded pieces of wood for fun. To give to Mei. She kept a collection of his miniature carvings on the sill next to her bed; she'd stroke them with her pinky and say that when she had children, she'd give each of them one. 'You plan to have lots of kids then, huh, since there are at least twenty up there?' How Mei had blushed and laughed. '*Ge,* don't tease me. I will give half to my future sister-in-law, for her children.' Then it was his turn to blush and laugh.

By dawn he had whittled a little wooden carving of a *kakatua*, a bird from the Malayan jungles that could imitate human and other animal sounds. He left the carving inside the tiffin carrier, placed the container on the sill, leaving the shutter closed. A *kakatua* to speak for him, to say 'thank you'; being cryptic was perhaps a foil of ambiguity, a test of connection, or maybe just a symbol of muteness.

As dusk fell, Chin opened the window for a breath of fresh air and the container was gone.

His initial relief—*she was alive! Mei was alive*—faded. When it faded, an inner moil of anxiety took root—a furtive, ferrety gnawing that made him feel hungry all the time. Chin began to have strange musky dreams. Kanagawa dressed like a samurai using a Japanese sword to unpick the frog buttons on Aiko*san*'s cheongsam—when Chin woke, he was bathed in sweat and he had an erection. Bile rose in his throat and he staggered to the bathroom. How could he have dreamt up Aiko*san* in a cheongsam? This desire felt gluttonous, vulgar, ridden with menace. He'd only ever seen Mei in a cheongsam.

One weekend morning, he took the bus to see his mother. She came to the door of the ramshackle house to greet him, dressed in a thin cotton blouse and a Malay sarong, something she'd never worn before the war. She'd aged. She was pathetically thin. Her jaw line so sharp it resembled the ridge of a blade. His mother's eyes brimmed with tears upon seeing him. She was trying hard to be brave but her face cracked when he handed her a bag of gula melaka steamed buns.

When Chin came home, he was exhausted. But there the tiffin carrier was again. On his windowsill. This time filled with rough-textured noodles and a side of grilled tenggiri. He didn't like mackerel, but during the war, any meat was luxury. The note said simply: *Sepang*. Possibly, his sister had been moved to a different location. Sepang was further upcountry in Malaya, but that was all Chin knew.

Through discreet inquiries of the Chinese secret societies, Chin learned there was a comfort station for Japanese soldiers in Sepang, and it was a reasonable guess that Mei was being held there.

Chin savoured the small sliver of tenggiri; it went really well with the thin rice-gruel he made for himself. The horrible guilt of being able to eat so well, despite how tasteless his rice-gruel was.

On his way to the market one morning, Chin saw a Japanese soldier beat a pregnant woman. She lay on the ground passively, hugging her belly, neither crying nor begging for her life, and people stood around and watched. So did Chin. He stood, watched, and then cycled home.

In a feverish burst of energy, he built a coffin over the next several days, out of the best wood he had in storage. He shaped the wood with an axe, whittling it till it was level. A Chinese coffin was built using the three-long-two-short principle: three long sides, including the curved lid, and two shorter sides for the head and foot of the coffin. In Mandarin, three-long-two-short, *sān cháng liǎng duǎn*, also meant disaster or death. As he worked, he thought of Aiko*san*, particularly the sheen of her hair, her white-painted face, her soul-cherishing eyes. Most people tended to speed up past the wide-open entrance of his shop, not even glancing in. Bad luck to see a coffin on any given day. To Chin though, a coffin was a beautiful thing; when finished, its wooden gleam and smooth body demanded stroking, its very bulk and stolidity (weighing over two hundred pounds) reassuring as a sanctuary, a place to rest before descending into the seven layers of Chinese hell. When he finished, he wasn't sure at what point—the sanding, the application of varnish?—he began to have a burning desire to see Aiko*san*.

In the end, a stroke of luck. Another tiffin carrier arrived. Inside was rough, stringy tapioca noodles in a simple anchovy broth. But no note.

Chin wrote back: *Please can we meet?*

There was no response, no more tiffin carrier. Chin waited, his heart knocking about in his ribcage. At crazy moments of the day, it would start a sudden patter, skipping almost. He was worried officers would come charging through the door. If she was a Japanese conspirator, why shouldn't she report him?

The thing was, there were comfort stations in Singapore, and it was a mystery why Mei wasn't sent to one of those instead. There was one on Cairnhill Road, an upper-class neighbourhood, where a section of bungalows had been cordoned off with wooden fencing. He cycled there, and this was what he saw: dozens of young Japanese soldiers in a queue that snaked round the fence, soldiers slouching, soldiers playing with their rifles, tapping them against the ground, soldiers ribbing each other and smoking in a cluster, all waiting their turn. On certain mornings, so he'd heard, one could glimpse nude young women sunbathing on the terraces of these houses. He wheeled his bicycle past, and dozens of eyes followed him, baleful, contemptuous, jeering, gazes meant to decimate the soul of the enemy.

But then, another tiffin carrier appeared on his windowsill. Fried yam leaves and bean noodles, and there was an unsigned note. No greeting. Instead, it said: *I began reading* The Tale of Genji *to improve my Japanese. Do you know* The Tale of Genji? *Genji was a deposed prince.* The note then proceeded to say it tells the story of the death of Genji's mother, whom His Majesty, the father, adored beyond what was right for her station as a consort, and his love for her aroused such jealousies and conspiracies at court that the lady succumbed and died. Her death brought such grief to His Majesty that he came to rue his own overwhelming love. There the note ended, leading Chin to wonder if Aiko*san* was trying to tell him something about Kanagawa or about obsessive familial love. Chin had never heard of *The Tale of Genji*. In any case, he wasn't much of a reader. The note, however, left a deep impression, and he found himself at different times of the day thinking about the lovely characters she had used to tell him a story about pain. In response, he sent back a carved wooden figurine: an elephant with one leg missing.

Thus began their volley. Yam noodles with peanuts. *Poems in Genji had an incompleteness to them, a dot dot dot, lovers complete each other's thoughts. See this verse:* 'Bell crickets cry until they fall weary and lapse into silence…' Chin thought long and hard about what she had said about completing poems, and carved Aiko*san* a grasshopper.

Tapioca skin noodles, water spinach, roasted coconut shavings and sambal chili in a salad and: *A light hidden amidst the blades of autumn grass.* Each letter advanced a little further on the story of how Genji was brought to court after his mother died. Chin laughed at the image of the young prince Genji's coming-of-age ceremony, with his hair tied in two ponytails like a girl, to be cut off by the Chamberlain so that he would become a man. And each letter also became more personal. She told him she loved bathing in the river, being neither afraid of mangrove swamps nor crocodiles. She loved eating raw coconut flesh and drinking its sweet juice. She loved the waning moon more than the gibbous, because there is a sweetness to things you see fading away. *When the samurais—the militant warriors—became an influential ruling class, Heian gentility faded away, but I guess one understands Japanese military values better with some understanding of samurai history.* In return, Chin carved her a turtle. To symbolise memory and persistence.

The missives became incredibly dear to him. He didn't always understand the contents, but the days that the tiffin carrier came became brighter ones, as if somebody had come along and opened all the windows to his dark, gloomy shop. Even the coffins, the three or four lined up along one side of the shop, seemed friskier, their coats shinier, ready for occupation!

Next, she sent soy bean cake marinated with shredded forest bamboo shoots, accompanied by a verse: *But when finally glimpsed, how shallow that sweet flag root then seems, shedding its pathetic cries in spite of...* Chin carved her a wooden pillow, so realistic it had crimps and creases, so miniature it was the size of his nail. Root, pillow, these were suggestive connotations, and Chin reckoned he was getting the art of Genji now.

News of the Allied capture of Iwo Jima and Okinawa filtered through. Whispers circulated with alarming frenzy—the end of Occupation was nigh. There'd been no more tiffin carriers for weeks, and anticipation of her letters had him jumping out of bed early in the morning, staring at the shutters while eating his breakfast—a meal of revived coffee and old rice.

Out of the blue, one evening, he heard a rap on the wooden shutters. Flinging them open, he found nobody, no tiffin carrier. There was a sliver of rice paper resting like a leaf on the sill. On it: *The firefly is extinguished by the burn of its inner flame...*

An order for a rubber wood coffin came in, but now was not the time to bury the dead. Chin paced up and down, agitated beyond description, so worked up his fingers trembled. He paced up and down, paced up and down.

Then, spiced papaya soup with a kind of flat pancake: *My heart is sorely troubled for the hagi shoot.* He didn't know what a hagi shoot was, but he wondered if it could be the tiny flower balanced on a thin slender reed she had drawn on the edge of the letter, with leaves edged in green. So, he carved her a water-lily pad with a tiny frog on it and hoped.

Asleep one night, he suddenly woke up. His heart shot up into his mouth: there was a looming presence in his room, an inky silhouette. A hand, warm, pressed down on his chest. His heart sputtered, he grasped the hand implanted on his white singlet, and then he heard a female voice, 'It's me, Aiko. I kept you waiting, I am sorry.' Chin gasped; he thought he would die of fright.

She said nothing else. As his eyes adjusted, he could see she was disrobing. She took out a pin from her hair, and it fell down straight and long. She had turned her back to him, but he could see her sloping shoulders as the robe fell. Then her presence close to him, a knee raised and settled on to his wooden pallet, and her scent came to him, clean and strong, a woodsy, grassy scent. Her long hair brushed his shoulder as her face came near. Chin had never been with a girl before, and he wasn't sure what was going to happen, what he was supposed to do here, but there was also a pent-up urgency, like whispered guidance in his head. *Just touch her*. Her hair now swept the length of his arm, and he felt her pulling at the hem of his shorts, which he gladly shed. His hands went up, like a blind person, and connected with her curves, and he thought of coffins. She kissed him then, but it wasn't really a kiss, more just a rubbing of the lips. Her hand clutched his fingers, and guided them to somewhere warm, soft, moist and he felt himself sinking. Lost within a subterranean cavern. Danger lurking in all dark corners, and all you could do was rush on ahead, heedlessly, frantically. Before time caught up to you.

Afterwards, they had a cup of tea together and it was awkward. Aiko—sitting at his square wooden table, not really daring to meet his eyes. Was this the same woman who just moments before had touched him everywhere? He sat across from her. Both of them nursing their cups of tea, not saying anything.

Finally, Chin broke the silence. 'Why *The Tale of Genji*?'

What was unsaid swam between them—how did she become the Japanese mistress of a Kempeitai officer? Was she a Japanese conspirator? Did she plan to remain one?

Aiko*san*, her kimono robe still slightly untied, revealing an expanse of her lovely, long neck, lifted a hand and tucked her hair behind her ear. 'You don't want to be caught exchanging secret messages through *Romance of the Three Kingdoms*, do you?' Her tone was wry.

Chin bowed his head. 'Will you tell me your real name?'

Aiko*san* did not reply.

She got up, and in tidying herself, Chin saw she was making preparations to leave. Chin became slightly desperate. 'Did you like the figurines I carved you?'

Aiko*san* turned and gave him a lovely smile. 'I adored them. They made me laugh. Laughter is good. It's a balm.'

Chin felt himself turning to mush. What a few choice words could do.

'Can't you stay a little longer?' he said.

'It is very dangerous for us to run the risks we have done, to help you the way I have done.' She came close and he smelt her sweet scent again. Intoxicating. All he wanted to do was to put his arms around her.

'I won't see you again, will I?' He wanted to cry, this horrible bloat of feeling as if he was being abandoned.

Aiko*san* touched his chin with the tip of her index finger. 'You have a small divot here, did you know that? Like in wood.'

Chin bowed his head.

At the door, she turned. 'Your sister will be released soon.

I really came to tell you that.'

Chin's pulse shot up again, and he felt an inner spiral of heat course through him. 'When?'

Aiko*san* said to wait for her further messages. Soon, she promised. If words could be carved out of thin air, he would see those words dance on her exhaled breath.

A lapse in the tiffin noodle delivery; then one morning in May, what arrived was a 'vitamin mixture'—bran, potato peelings, pineapple skins, other ingredients known to contain vitamin B, widely touted by propaganda and sold by the Tokubetsu Shi pharmacy as medicine. His heart thumped as he read the accompanying note: *Hinnam Little Dispensary, Victoria Street.* No precise time nor date given.

Chin sent word to the Hokkien societies; he asked those with shops all along Victoria Street to keep their eyes peeled, to send word the minute they saw a young woman...here his words failed him...a young woman what? But the shopkeepers and their attendants understood. Words meant everything, and words meant very little.

Every day after he closed his coffin shop, Chin cycled slowly down Victoria Street and past the pharmacy. He'd park himself across the street behind a pillar, watching creaking trishaws and passing bicycles, the opening and shutting of *papan*-shutters above the shop, people milling along the five-foot-way. The bottles and ointments displayed in stacks and boxes along the shophouse windows made him think of cemetery stones and memories and suspended time.

Faithfully. Every evening. Time measured by the slow revolution of fans, the slap of pedestrian feet, the closing of shutters.

The tiffin deliveries had stopped completely. His heart too shutting and opening like a bivalve, a foreign organ. Or a

Buddhist receptacle for ashes. On a wooden vase he made, he carved a trellis of the hagi shoot.

The months that followed were long and sweltering. The Japanese officially surrendered in Singapore on September 12, 1945.

On the evening of September 25, slumped on a stool, dressed in a raggedy *samfoo,* her once-long, straight hair cropped to just below her ears, there she was. She was his sister Mei, and again, not his sister Mei. A mirage. He broke into a run. His shout caught in his throat, and what came out instead was a gargled, mangled kind of sound, a murmur, a roll of escaped breath.

His sister remained seated, but her eyes reddened upon seeing him. No tears. She didn't try to get up, but her posture bent in his direction, like a thin shrivelled reed.

Run of the Molars

LILY'S MOTHER arrived on a late October morning when winds were heralded from the Arctic north. Matthew insisted on driving Lily to Heathrow to meet her. Lily had brought Matthew's fishtail parka, which she knew her mother would refuse to wear, but it was cold outside. When the wind blew, it felt like being lapped with an icy tongue.

Lily's mother had a lot of prejudices. She disliked fake Chinese cooking ('chop suey' for example, was not Chinese cooking). She hated going out at noon if the sun was blistering. She abhorred religious pamphleteers, beggars, or people who harassed you for donations on the street. Usual things that most people didn't like—roaches, spiders, crammed buses, having to sit on a suitcase to shut it—were on her shit-list too. But there were an awful lot of things peculiar to Lily's mother, like not minding if her face was tanned as long as her arms weren't, or needing to have a spotlessly clean sink before she could brush her teeth in it, or refusing to drink an imperfectly steeped Oolong or one that wasn't the right tint.

This year, Lily's father had passed away after two years of fighting throat cancer. Along with her two sisters in the UK, Lily didn't manage to make the funeral. The cost of airline tickets was astronomical and her father was buried within two days. 'They sure were in a hurry to get him in the ground,' Lily's middle sister, Ah Won (aka 'Winnie'), said. 'Afraid he would smell,' her eldest sister, Ah Kim ('Maggie'), said.

Although Lily was never close to her mother, she was even less close to her father. He was an intemperate man who often flew into rages over his gambling losses. He spent a lot of time at the races and brooded whenever he was home. When he lost big, he took his belt and randomly chose a daughter to blister. When he died, Lily reflected that there was rough justice, all in all: a man whose 'damn terrible' cussing could be heard three doors down in the terraced housing they lived in was rendered mute towards the end of his life.

With her mother, Lily shared an inherent trait: they could both read faces like tealeaves. Oddly, for all this perspicacity, it hadn't made her mother a more empathetic soul. Lily herself found it a nebulous blessing. It was how she knew, the very first time she met Matthew, that he'd been struck by her and wanted to marry her. It was also how she knew that, while he had married her, he also married an ideological vision of 'her as representing the Chinese race', and yet, paradoxically, it was because he really didn't 'see' race; she understood it was about bridge-building, about wanting to connect.

Neither Maggie nor Winnie was close to their mother, but Lily at least had an uneasy alliance. Unspoken dialogue often bloomed between them when together, interpreting the other's faces, but seldom liking what they read there.

The last time she spoke to her mother was just a couple of weeks ago, when Ah Teng ('Terrence'), her brother, whom her mother lived with in Singapore, was complaining about their mother.

'*Simi tai ji*?' What happened?

Terrence swore in Hokkien. 'Every night she asking for these

Chinese medicinal soups with ginseng and whatnot. Just *si beh* extra, you know. Ah Lan is driven crazy boiling these soups, eh? Who can boil and boil and boil? My poor wife, her face now boiled as red as the top layer of a kuih lapis.'

When Lily spoke to her mother, she found her oddly quiet, not her usual querulous self. This resulted in long lapses on the phone when neither of them said anything, and all that could be heard was the tinselly chirp of some other dialogue interspersing their trunkline. That, and a curious susurration, a clicking like crickets, mysterious and faintly disturbing.

Lily had a strong feeling after the phone call that her mother was having more trouble dealing with her father's death than she let on. Surprising, considering that they stayed together 'only because of the children'.

She spoke to her sisters, a sort of huddling conference held over a potluck that was also a sumptuous feast of eight or nine dishes—kangkung with belacan shrimp paste, curry fish-head, beef rendang, char kway teow noodles, nasi lemak—enough to feed a small orphanage.

The consensus was that they should bring their mother to London for a trip. Just to dissolve tension with their brother, and assuage their own sense of guilt for not making the funeral. Then, the question came up as to who should host their mother. At this, both Maggie and Winnie balked. There was no question of Winnie hosting. She was having an affair with a married man. 'Not like we could go over to his house, eh?' She grimaced, but Lily could see shame etched in the hang of her chin. Maggie demurred: her hours at a Chinese restaurant were close to slavery; Mother would be on her own a lot. Lily sighed, she'd already known it'd be up to her. What would it be like to have her mother stay for a month? The thought made her restless and uneasy. If they couldn't stand each other, she hoped they'd both be able to swallow each other the way one swallowed abominable chicken parts—in one big gulp aided by peristalsis.

When her mother finally emerged from Customs, Lily was struck by how old she looked. Her hair had gone white a long time ago, but now it was also thinning. Her stoop was more pronounced and she shuffled, as if she were wearing cat slippers. Dragging a teal-blue suitcase behind her, she wore a red sweater with pink polka dots and a cyan knit skirt. She looked like an outrageously dressed garden gnome.

'They shouldn't serve fish on a plane,' her mother said, by way of greeting. 'How is it a good idea to serve fish on a plane? I should have flown Singapore Airlines. They'd never serve stinky fish on a plane.'

Her mother's eyes settled on Lily. *You look like crap, Ah Hong,* they said.

And you need to wax your upper lip. 'You must be exhausted, were you able to sleep?' Lily reached out a hand to pat her mother's shoulder briefly. The way one would tap a piece of toast to get some of the burnt bits off.

'A humpback whale on my left and a snoring baboon on the other side.' *Why didn't you book me an aisle seat?* 'And where's Ah Kim and Ah Won?'

Matthew leaned over to take hold of her suitcase, a broad happy smile on his face at hearing the wah-wah-wah of the Hokkien dialect, and Lily's mother finally registered him. 'Eh, he's come, too?' *Look at his big nose,* so kayu, *wooden only.*

'Took the afternoon off work just to come pick you up, Mother.' Lily showed her the fishtail parka. 'It's freezing outside. You need to wear this.'

Her mother examined it as if she'd just been presented with a drift net. She lifted the sleeve and gave a sniff. *What do you cook in your house?* 'No need. Straight to the car, I won't feel a thing.'

'Mother, I insist.'

Lily's mother caught the exasperation in Lily's tone and blinked twice. Her jaw set stubbornly. 'I will not wear that thing,' she said. *It looks like a death shroud.*

On the way back, Matthew wanted to give Lily's mother a drive-around, so they detoured through Shepherd's Bush and Ealing before heading down to Earl's Court. Her mother sat behind her in their old Mazda, shoulders reclined, arms wrapped around her midriff, her big purple leather handbag resting between her legs like a crouching show dog, her eyes swivelling, taking everything in. Lily avoided looking back at her mother's face, she didn't want to know her mother's thoughts as she took in London for the first time. When she was little, her parents talked about the British Empire as if it were the famed Middle Kingdom—all greatnesses hailed from there, including pot pies and the much-coveted Battenberg cake. When Lily got into Bristol University, they were ever so proud, went around telling the neighbours, even though they couldn't pronounce the name—Beh-lissi-towf was the best they could do, and it sounded like a new-fangled way of saying shit tofu in Hokkien.

Although Lily once spoke Hokkien fluently, after all this time the language had receded to the back of her throat, and she found a disconnect between what she wanted to say and the accurate Hokkien words for it. People sometimes asked her what language she dreamt in when she told them her native tongue wasn't English. She'd feel stumped, because the people in her dreams, including herself, were wordless, *sans* language. When she called home, though, she affected the Singaporean intonation and accent of speaking English, but felt fraudulent all the same.

A clicking noise made Lily look back. Her mother was working her jaws, running her top row of molars against the bottom row, back and forth, and the sound was the grind of sliding enamel. A wordless, chittering noise that was ghostly and surreal, as if her mother had been reduced to a sagging sack full of scuttling mice.

Maggie and Winnie came over for dinner. Each brought three Tupperwares filled with home cooking. Maggie even made sambal petai—gator beans, otherwise known as 'stink' beans, stir-fried with stinky shrimp paste. Matthew shrank away after peering at it, and wisely opted for an evening with the boys at the pub.

Lily's mother came out from a nap. Patting her hair, she eyed the Tupperwares like some bizarre line-up of crooks and villains. *I'd rather have steamboat,* her eyes said. A cauldron of hot broth in the centre of the table, into which one dipped and swirled everything one wanted to eat. Cook and eat at the same time, very efficient, which was why her mother loved it. 'Oh, too much food. Why cook so much?' her mother cried.

'We wanted you to feel at home,' Maggie said. 'Has Lily given you a drive-around?'

Her mother sniffed. 'Everything is so old, I thought this country was full of rich people, so why don't they fix up the buildings, huh?' She parked herself in one of the dining-room chairs and her eyes took in the room, from cornice to fireplace to their IKEA furniture, judging, judging. Lily averted her gaze. She concentrated on serving dinner.

'It's full of history. Don't you get history?' Winnie scowled.

'History, my foot. Your father brought back all these photos of Shanghai when he went with that tour group, and you should have seen the skyscrapers. That's what I call a city.'

'This country is older than anything. As old as...' Maggie cast around for comparison, looking to Lily for help.

'It's certainly old. Decrepit.' *Shame on all of you.* Lily could tell Maggie and Winnie felt lumped in with all the *ang moh* Britishers who were responsible for all this decrepitude. They didn't like it either, because they didn't feel they actually belonged. Maggie wanted to retire back to Singapore one day. Winnie didn't know yet what she wanted to do, but she was having too much of a *shiok*! time just now (she and her man loved cosplay and going out in regalia to have English high tea).

And so it went. The entire dinner filled with subtle sniping, like getting your fingers caught in a mousetrap multiple times. Lily had made her mother's favourite e-fu noodles, with straw mushrooms and mangetout and crispy tofu sheets. Out of the nine dishes on the table, that was the only thing her mother ate.

After dinner, Lily made Oolong in a pot. Her mother lifted the lid. *Not enough tealeaves.* 'You can get Oolong here?' she said. She rose from the table and went into her bedroom. The sisters could hear her rustling about inside.

'What's wrong with her?' Winnie said.

'Her usual grumpy self, *leh,* I wouldn't worry,' Maggie said. After the dishes were done, she'd file her fingernails, as if dirt from Lily's house had gotten trapped in the crevices, and then, she'd get ready to leave. When Lily was a university student, she'd worked at a Malaysian restaurant on Wardour Street with Maggie during the summer and term breaks. Everybody was there illegally (lots of Malaysians and Singaporeans) and they all holed up together in one-bedroom apartments around the East End, sharing clothes and food and mobile phones. The atmosphere was so redolent of ethnocentrism and reverse bigotry that Lily felt stifled and depressed. She decided not to return one summer, preferring instead to work at a mani-pedi salon, and because she didn't have a beautician's qualification, she ended up being an attendant, bringing tubs of hot water and washing people's feet. Maggie had argued with Lily about her decision, staring at her like she was one big, festering, recalcitrant molar, denouncing her with, 'What *lah*, you telling me you rather wash stinky feet than get tips bussing tables?'

Her mother brought out decorated tins of Oolong. Six giant tins, clattering on Lily's countertop. 'Two for each of you.'

Maggie and Winnie broke up with laughter. 'Mother, don't be so *suaku lah*,' Maggie said. 'You think this country don't drink Chinese tea?'

Her mother's lips thinned into a straight line. 'How should I know? They kill their own princess and queue up to go to the loo.'

Maggie and Winnie laughed even harder, but Lily could see the spread of an underlying emotion across her mother's brow, something akin to mortification.

Her mother brought her fist up to her mouth and coughed. 'There's something I've been meaning to tell you girls,' she began. Her face became mottled. 'Between Ah Hong and Ah Teng...there was another child.'

Maggie and Winnie stopped laughing. Lily watched her mother, stunned. Her mother's face crumpled, the way paper crumpled into a ball. 'We couldn't afford help, and there were already three of you, all girls. This one was going to be a girl, too, I knew it, the way my belly curved out, same as when carrying each of you.'

They listened in complete silence. The mantel clock on top of the fireplace ticked and tocked, punctuating their mother's Hokkien words. It was rhythmic, and also numbing.

'And your father...you know, he wasn't fond of girls.'

Maggie rolled her eyes at this juncture. Winnie pressed three fingers to her lips. Lily bent her gaze, like bending a steel ruler, and it landed with stretched tension as far as it could out the window. Landed, coincidentally, on two men hoisting between them a cellophane-wrapped mattress and crossing West Cromwell Road, traffic buzzing by in both directions.

Lily's heart rate sped up—the two men's faces were creased with tension. It was almost premonitory.

Everything that happened after that was a blur. A car travelling at speed slammed into the mattress, and first was the sound. It was the sound of exploding plastic. It was the sound of a bomb. It was the sound of the crack of one giant popping firecracker. After the sound, came the silence. One of the men rolled on the road from the impact. The mattress flew up into the air and suddenly ripped foam cascaded and fluttered down from the sky, as if it were snowing. Then, the honks sounded, a shrill jangle of continuous PEEENNNG!! as cars slammed bumpers and wheels rolled on to pavements and dented lampposts, and a dog on a leash began yelping in high-pitched alarm.

'Oh my god! Oh my god!' All of them rushed to the window, their eyes peeled on the commotion outside.

'Is anyone hurt?' It was Winnie, and there was great fear in her voice. Lily heard a noise behind her, and she turned to see her mother still sitting in her dining-room chair, her face as blank and white as a slab of cemetery stone, her mouth agape, so that Lily could see the sliver of chives still caught within her teeth. There was no emotion on her face. Nothing at all. If there was, it was the first time Lily couldn't decipher it.

It was on the news the next day. The name of the mattress company was, ironically, Silent Night. Lily read everything with horrid, perverse curiosity. One of the men carrying the mattress was badly injured. He was Polish, had three daughters, had been in the country two years. 'Now it looks like we have to go back to Poland. How are we going to survive?' his wife wailed.

Lily shuddered. A dank fear gripped her. The accident was so tragic, so ridiculous, that all night she subsisted on a shallow sleep that felt like floating on a thin film of brackish water, so that occasionally she sank beneath the surface and couldn't breathe.

Before he went to work, Matthew asked if she was aware that she'd been grinding her molars. She wasn't. To her knowledge, she'd never done it before.

Her mother came out for breakfast, and Lily immediately saw that she hadn't slept much either. Her hair was mussed, and her pores oozed a kind of old-lady smell mixed with stale Chinese mentholatum oil. Did one pick up one's mother's mannerisms so naturally, so habitually, goaded into becoming one's most dreaded personage?

'Tea?'

Her mother nodded. 'After that big to-do, really cracks your mood.' But Lily sensed her mother was more deeply disturbed than she cared to admit. This was good; Lily felt better about her mother, realising this. And what a secret her mother had imparted, eclipsed by the awful tragedy last night. Nobody picked up again the thread of conversation, they'd simply stood at the window, like standard-issue Chinese busybodies who didn't want to get involved, watching for hours the jack-knifing red and blue police and ambulance siren lights and the pandemonium on the road.

Lily bustled about making tea, but out of the corner of her eye, she saw her mother sneaking glances at the photographs in the paper.

Lily cleared her throat. 'I hope that man doesn't die. He's got three daughters.'

Her mother ran a finger across her upper lip. Back and forth, as if she were brushing her teeth. 'Ah Hong, what I told you girls last night, your brother doesn't know. I hope you won't tell him. He already hates me enough.'

'What are you talking about?' The shame that had leaked

out on her mother's face, unfolding like a dark flower, twisted in Lily's heart.

'His wife hates me too. That old lady, when will she die?'

'Mother, she's not like that. I'm sure...'

'What do you know?' her mother barked. 'Did you see the way they treated your dad?'

Lily bit her upper lip. She hadn't. It was true. She hadn't wanted to know. In her heart of hearts, she felt he had it coming.

'One day, you'll find out what it's like to be old, to be a burden on your family. All you want is a word of kindness. That's all.' Lily's mother bowed her head. 'But maybe, it's justice from above. For killing a child.'

She'd whispered this, knowingly perjuring herself, but Lily felt as if there was an element of drama her mother wanted to produce with the words. A forcible wrenching of pity and sentimentalism from her daughters.

Her mother's unspoken emotional demand squeezed Lily's lungs, made her resistant to giving it. Lily gasped, 'Don't! Don't say that.'

Her mother's eyes brimmed with tears. 'There are ways of paying. Ways and ways.'

Lily turned away. 'Please, Mother. That stuff is too long ago.'

'You don't understand,' her mother said.

'What's there to understand?' Lily said, with a hint of steel. 'It's stuff from long ago.'

The first week, Lily begged off work and took her mother places. They walked around in Piccadilly and went shopping in Chinatown. Her mother became animated. 'It's just like China!' Although she'd never been to China. They had dim sum ('It's just like the hustle-bustle in dim sum restaurants in Hong Kong'—but she'd never been to Hong Kong either). Her mother sneered at the Malaysian restaurants there; she didn't want to touch fake Malaysian food, she said. She refused to travel on the tube or the bus, because she feared the handrails were covered in germs. So, Lily had to drive everywhere, but because parking was difficult and expensive, she ended up taking her mother mainly to the grocery stores, like Sainsbury's and Tesco. Her mother's observation was, 'Giant much better. Sell everything. One-stop shop.'

When Lily went back to work the second week, her mother stayed at home. Lily was the accounts manager for a private medical practice. She'd call her mother on tea breaks and find herself having bizarre conversations. Her mother recounted to her in detail the commercials she was watching. She found UK commercials hilarious.

They chatted about the accident. Her mother wanted to know, blow-by-blow, what happened next. Turned out that because the workers could be considered negligent—parking illegally on the pavement, manoeuvring across busy traffic with a huge object—job insurance might not pay. Her mother was incensed by this. On the bright side, however, the injured man was no longer in intensive care. *The Telegraph* ran a full-length feature about the bright star the elder daughter was in school, which got a lot of important attention from the right sorts. When Lily translated this article for her mother, in her halting Hokkien, she could hear her pause of astonished awe, the click of distinct approval.

An unwitting camaraderie had bloomed between them. Or perhaps it was that window of naked humanity her mother had chosen to reveal. The one that Maggie and Winnie studiously avoided discussing.

Her mother never asked after Lily's job, but in the evenings, she listened with eyes constantly flickering with attention and interest while Lily told about her workmates or the doctors in the practice—one of them was named 'Brer Pitt' behind his back, because he was handsome as Brad but had rabbitty teeth.

Matthew, too, seemed to enjoy having her mother around. The two of them communicated by way of energetic gestures, with her mother shouting at him in Hokkien, as if by shouting, he would peripatetically catch her meaning. Most of their conversations centred around dinner. Matthew would lift his chopsticks, pincer a slice of beef to his mouth, do a thumbs-up sign, or smack his lips for good measure. Her mother would shout, 'I make much better at home. You come and visit, you'll see. This has too much peanut oil. Too much oil will give you colonic trouble.' Matthew would nod, as if understanding. 'Very good!' Watching these interludes, Lily felt a catch in her throat, a gnawing, and for the first time she thought about having children.

What she'd never told Matthew was that she simply couldn't envision raising children here in England. She feared that they would drift away from her, reject her country bumpkin ways as they grew up. Like all three of them had done with their mother. She'd been to a children's birthday party once and had been shocked to discover that even children of three could compare—they'd been given yoyos, but everyone wanted the one with the best rebound. Fighting, screaming, hot wails of anguish, all over a yoyo.

Lily and her mother did have a conversation about children, over the phone. Like many Chinese mothers, Lily's mother did not own tact. 'Are you barren?'

'I am assuredly not barren!'

'It's abnormal not to have children after being married five years.'

'It's a matter of time and opportunity.'

'I don't know what that means. Have you considered a fertility specialist? In Singapore, you could consult Mr Ong.'

'Mother, I just don't feel it's the right time for Matthew and me to discuss the issue of children.'

'Well, why not? What are you waiting for? The buffaloes to crawl home?'

'I'm not having this conversation.' And Lily hung up. But it'd made her laugh.

Strange, Lily reflected, the only reason they could have that conversation was because they'd been seeing each other every evening, forced to spend time together, forced to talk inanities. Something else had changed. A couple of nights, Lily had caught her mother sitting in her room whispering to herself, her fingers working a kind of red bead necklace. When she peered in, she noticed her mother's eyes were closed as she rocked back and forth, soothing herself with words. She tried to listen, but both times, her mother unexpectedly blinked her eyes open and directed a stare at Lily, as if to say she knew Lily was there but chose not to acknowledge her until just then, or that she'd meant for Lily to see her caught in the throes of meditation, perhaps repentance.

Lily felt emboldened enough to ask, 'Are those rosary beads you're praying with?'

Her mother's eyes shrunk to tiny points of light. 'Don't talk crazy. A Buddhist monk gave me these.'

'Buddhist monk?'

'Yes. I recite meditation lines that he's given me. It's supposed to clear my *qi*. It's black.'

For a long time, Lily had felt herself losing confidence. Ever since she graduated from university with her accountancy degree and couldn't get a job in any accounting firm. One of her friends had cited racism as the reason. Another had said, 'It's your accent. You know I go to a speech therapist? You have to whitewash your accent away.' With her mother here, Lily found herself finally admitting her waning confidence problem consciously. She had problems with looking people in the eye. She felt an immediate shrinking of self when someone looked at her too hard or volunteered an intimacy that requested a reciprocal exchange. And now, when she crossed roads, she found herself flailing, hesitating especially on the busy roundabouts London was notorious for, until drivers honked at her. Her faith in the heavenly grace that attended random events had evaporated. She caught herself listening to a woman regretting her abortion on the radio. She caught herself thinking that she and that aborted foetal-sister could have randomly traded places. Sibling order was surely random. But when did this belief in randomness end up as her substitute for faith? How could her parents have so cavalierly decided that a fourth girl was one too many? To terminate because the baby might not be the gender they wanted? What kind of foul reasoning was that? Was it just a stroke of randomness that they didn't decide to terminate at two? It was too horrible to contemplate.

Maggie called to suggest an outing. They could take Mother to the London Eye. 'So she can get a damn terrific aerial perspective of London. Very worth it. Take the hillbilly out of her. Not a city. Pah!' Maggie huffed.

So, Maggie picked them up in her car. Winnie begged off at the last second, complaining, 'I *pengsan* already. She called me to ask why I'm not married yet. I hemmed and hawed, then she accused me of carrying on with a married man. It sounded like her fevered brain conjuring up accusations, except in this case, it's true.'

Lily's mother had bought herself mittens and a scarf from the big Tesco on Cromwell Road. She'd caved and now wore Matthew's fishtail parka. She looked like a giant dumpling or a snowman; children actually swept a wide arc around her, and poodles barked. The wind was brisk, snapping their scarves in their faces like tails. The queue snaked past the Aquarium, and lots of people—tourists, children, vendors—milled about. A Mr Softie van was doing amazing business despite the weather.

When Lily's mother saw the giant cantilevered wheel, she gasped. 'Can you really see all of London from up there?'

'No, we see all of Germany. *Wah lau,*' Maggie said.

Lily shook her head. 'On a day like this—' she pointed up, the sky was overcast and leaden grey, and pigeons dive-bombed among the café goers, splattering the cement with shit '—visibility is not great. We might not see much of anything.'

'Should we still go up?'

'*Arbo*!' Of course.

But her mother balked when she saw the ticket prices. Lily could see her perform rapid mental calculations in her head. 'Almost thirty-six dollars to go up to see something I can see from an airplane for free?' her mother shrieked. So calculating and logical when it came to the inconsequential things, so thoughtless in others. There was no persuading her. She told them they could go if they wanted—*wo bo chap*!—but she was going to sit on a bench and watch the children and the birds in the nearby enclosed playground.

Both Lily and Maggie tried their best to change her mind. 'Damn one kind one!' Maggie fumed. Their mother sat on the bench and swung her heels in mute rebellion. In the end, they sat with her, like the butcher, the baker and the candlestick maker, and Lily translated for her mother from the brochure they picked up. She faltered numerous times, but cracked on. Until Maggie ripped the brochure from her and said, 'Stop, your Hokkien is really fucking *busuk*. It's not a bubble. It's a capsule. Here—' she jabbed the brochure hard '—it's not pillar, it's cable. Six backstay cables. Try saying that in Hokkien, you *goondu*!'

But the language they shared in common from birth had failed them. Neither of them knew the Hokkien words for backstay cables, and neither did their mother. She didn't look like she ever envisioned she'd need a language to transcribe all that she was seeing for the first time.

Every weekend, they had dinner together with Maggie and Winnie. Maggie offered for her mother to come over to stay the second last weekend of her mother's trip. 'At least see where I live,' she begged, and her mother had nodded. Maggie's husband, Tom, was a Malaysian—a big, hearty guy with a bulbous stomach, who didn't speak a lick of Hokkien. He couldn't speak any Mandarin either. This meant that conversations would have to be switched to Malay, with her mother speaking shrill *pasar*-Malay (the Straits Chinese market-place pidgin version she'd picked up since she had no formal language schooling). 'Really *malu, leh*, and damn weird,' Maggie said.

They congregated at Maggie's house in Shoreditch. Maggie's house was narrow and tight, and hot as a furnace, because both Maggie and Tom liked to simulate Singaporean heat.

There was steamboat. Her mother gazed at the broth as if to discern the tidal urges of fate, but her mouth narrowed immediately, and she tucked in her chin. The broth was missing key ingredients, like goji berries, liquorice root, dong quai or jujubes. These were things on her list of must-haves. Their mother was about to leave and all Tom and Maggie had succeeded in doing was climbing on to her shit-list.

True to form, when they sat down to eat, her mother didn't pick up her chopsticks, didn't look at the platters of shrimp, fish-balls, tofu cubes, choy sum, or anything else jostling for space on the Formica-laden table. Instead, she asked for two slices of white bread. 'You have?' she asked Maggie.

Maggie stood up and flung her chopsticks into the corner.

She started cussing in Hokkien. Her eyes bulged like a pomfret. Winnie clapped her hands over her ears. Tom tried to downplay the escalating emotion by shushing Maggie. Matthew stood up as well, but sat back down when he realised there was little he could do. Only Lily and her mother exchanged glances. Her mother's eyes were curiously glassy, a dull flush mottled her cheeks, and Lily could see the gleam of her teeth between the agitations of her jaw. As if grinding her teeth at a succubus over Lily's shoulder.

'Why is nothing ever good enough for you?' Maggie was shouting.

'Everyone please be calm,' Tom said.

'Let's just go get her damn jujubes,' Winnie said. She made a sound like gargling. She began to pull on coat, hat and scarf. 'Who's coming with me?'

'You're going now?' Maggie said.

'Do you seriously see us eating anything while Mother eats two slices of Kingsmill?'

Nobody had anything to say to this. Maggie got up to go amidst Tom's repetitive querying, 'How long is this going to take?' At the last minute, Maggie turned back to lambast Lily with a stare: *Coming or not?*

Lily's heart felt as though it had landed on a pike. She recognised the sisterly call to solidarity, but her mother's face was as pasty as sesame seeds. She remembered, once, her mother had dropped an old hankie during a hospital visit. She'd made everyone search the corridors for the hankie, including forcing a patient to get out of the bed she'd been temporarily using. Lily remembered the blaze of thrill in her mother's face then. How much she'd enjoyed the drama, the voluminous attention.

Nothing like that here, just anxiety—a grinding run of her top molars against her bottom set, as if she were holding in unbearable pressure.

Matthew must have seen Lily's indecision. He volunteered to go.

Lily stood up. 'No, it's my mother. I'll go.'

They tumbled into Winnie's Fiat, but her heart nagged her. Maggie and Winnie carped about whether to go to Lung Fung (a very long drive to North London), or just drive to Chinatown instead. Winnie drove carelessly and attracted a lot of ire from other motorists, especially when circling roundabouts. There was just enough crazy careening in this madcap rush for jujubes and Chinese herbs to make Lily hold her head down in mock despair.

'*Beh tahan*, what?' Maggie said. Can't stand it, can you? Her pupils glowed, little dark pebbles set against a pool of iridescent white, and Lily felt that she'd never understood either of her sisters, that they lived on different continents, could be of a different race, even though physically they lived in the same town and had squeezed out through the same birth canal.

'You know, I think Mother is haunted by the abortion she had,' Lily said.

Maggie snorted, turned her nose towards the windshield as if avoiding a smell. 'Big deal.'

Winnie's brow beetled. 'I don't think it's a good idea to bring on maudlin subjects when I'm manoeuvring London streets, yeah?'

'When are we going to talk about it, then?' Lily said.

Maggie shrugged. 'Why do we have to talk about everything? You're so fierce westernised, just because you've married an *ang moh*. Put you on a couch, Freudy-dreudy, this solves everything, *eh*?'

Winnie's herky-jerky driving almost made them run a red light. Maggie's words hit a nerve. Lily ground her teeth with tension. 'Well, I suppose I should be more like you both. Able to squeeze big TRUTHS into small grid-like cubicles in your head, ice-cube thoughts, like every single fucking repressed pragmatic Chinese person. You guys see a tragic accident but it contains no useful information that impacts your life, so you stuff it into a mental suitcase.'

'Oh, listen to her, with the psychoanalytic mumbo-jumbo. You want black and white?' Maggie began to shout. 'I'll give you black and white. We had an abusive father who tanned us whenever he could. We have a critical, controlling mother. When she had trouble accepting something about herself, all she wanted was to be drama queen. We have a clueless brother. Okay, what more do you want?'

Somehow, it wasn't Maggie's shouting that made Lily really upset. It was her summarisation of facts. What a scattering of taut clichés their lives were. And she was the one who looked ridiculous by wanting to think about things that had happened, words their mother had said, choices that their mother had made. Without even thinking it through, Lily realised, her sisters were happy to live with randomness, to be blown hither-thither like spores, floating along life, occasionally bobbing up for those bubbly bits of potential revelations.

Silence prevailed suddenly in the Fiat. '*Si lang gui,*' Winnie growled. She'd barrelled down Clerkenwell Road on to Theobald's Road, and Lily watched the blur of humanity outside the window, the queue of red double-deckers, bound for destinations spread out like the spokes of a wheel. All these people blowing off in different directions—random multi-cellular gametes just barely grazing each other—without ever connecting, permeating, integrating.

'If you ask me,' Winnie suddenly declared, 'she thinks she's evil to have had the abortion. People didn't do that sort of thing in her time. Dad's death unhinged her—brought home the fact that she's going to die, sooner or later. Death is a resident evil, all that sort of thing. She's looking at all the bad decisions she's made, and guess what, it's like IKEA furniture. Looks good in their showroom, looks cheap in your home.'

They'd turned on to Shaftsbury Avenue by now, and Winnie waved her hand. 'Start looking for parking space.'

Lily felt Winnie's words sink in. The IKEA reference notwithstanding, her respect for her sister had suddenly deepened. 'I'm kinda sad mother is going back soon,' she said, apropos of nothing. 'I feel like I've gotten to know her better during this trip.'

Neither Maggie nor Winnie replied. Then, Maggie bounced in her seat. 'Parking space!'

Winnie expertly drew up beside a blue VW bug. She pulled into reverse gear, hooked a hand over Maggie's seat, then looked behind her. 'Don't you think it's terrible that we wish for different parents?' Her voice was bland, matter-of-fact. 'We do, don't we? Let's face it.'

She backed the car into the spot, her wheel rolling on to the pavement with her misjudgement of distance. She didn't look like she cared one bit. 'I mean, don't you think it's terrible that Mother looks at us and wishes for a different set of kids?'

Lily flushed hotly. Her heart set up a wild patter. 'No, she doesn't. You're presuming terrible things. You're making these horrific assessments because our family has a dysfunctional communication system. But WHAT CHINESE FAMILY DOESN'T?' She didn't know why she'd felt this need to shout. But there it was, she'd shouted, and it felt like relief.

Both Maggie and Winnie now turned towards her, their faces lit with ferocity, and Lily realised that they'd already discussed this, and what's more, they agreed with each other absolutely. 'You're the only one who refuses to believe anything,' Maggie said. 'That's what's so terrible.'

Winnie's face turned still and solemn, her lids heavy with

meaning. 'Don't you think it's terrible that you have chosen to live your life according to a set of false precepts?' She waited for that to sink in, then she rolled up her window, with energy bordering on violence. 'You're not one of us any more, you know? Let's get those damn herbs before the shop closes. Or this Waterloo will never end.'

Dinner ended up balanced on a knife's edge. No one alluded to the conversation in the car. It felt unfilial, like betrayal of a certain honour, to Lily. Yet, the undercurrents of menace ran strong. Her sisters wouldn't look at her. They were conspiring to shut her out. Her mother wouldn't look at her either. Her chin sunk into her chest; it was too much effort holding up the family honour on her own. Lily glanced at Tom, obliviously slushing and slurping his food in big gulps. She looked at everyone masticating. All that could be heard was the massive churning of teeth against mucilage, grinding, grinding. Lily's mother, too, ate with surprising gusto, her chopsticks nimbly splicing cooked meat and dipping it in the spicy sauce Maggie had prepared, grabbing the last slice of thin-sliced beef, sawing through her chestnut mushrooms, her jaw chomping away. Oh, the agony of meat. Lily watched her and wondered if her mother had ever been happy. Even now, with this display of food around her, her mother ate with vigorous desperation, as if it were her last meal. Only Matthew, her husband, looked at her. He looked at her with such warmth and camaraderie.

The rice noodles were the last to go in the broth. Their chopsticks clattered against each other—a drama re-enacted in the fight for food—and only Matthew and Tom talked. 'You don't mix eating and talking,' had been the mantra around their dining table when her father was alive. Talking muddled up things, including sisterhood, digestion and familial relationships.

Lily went to bed that night with indigestion, anyway. She padded through her house to the kitchen to make herself some mint tea, and found herself glancing at the empty bed in the guest bedroom. Her mother had liked to sleep with the door ajar, and in the dark, Lily imagined her sloping shoulders, a shadowy hulk covered with blankets, and the pang of it was strangely welcome and restorative. She actually missed her mother's presence. In her heart, Lily felt that she was right to ask herself questions. Some instinct was telling her that her mother needed her. Perhaps Winnie was right; perhaps Lily had fallen under Western indoctrination, imbibing strange values, like wanting to understand one's parents. But why shouldn't she acknowledge her hurt? To her mother, she'd been just another squalling baby, to her father, just another mouth to feed. Duty. Filial piety. These dratted Confucian values that were forced upon her when growing up; when duty overtook love, did she understand the application of these values? Did her parents? And now, Lily was a disappointment to her mother. Here it was, the judgment: if she had been her mother having that unwanted baby, she'd never have been quite so cavalier about life. She'd have thought about children carefully, as she'd done these five years. Life wasn't random. But they'd been cavalier too. They'd been cavalier about their father's death, and wasn't that just the other side of the coin? These were facts you didn't acknowledge to anyone because they brought such shame. It made her crush the mint leaves into her cup and watch the leaves weep.

Her mother was leaving. Having checked in her bulging suitcases, she sat with Lily at an airport café, her shins crossed under the table, her hands clutching her big handbag. 'You should bring Matthew back for a visit,' she said.

Lily had talked a lot to Matthew the last few days. Told Matthew her mother's secret, told him about the sisterly fight in the car, and it was as if they were discovering each other for the first time. Matthew listened, so closely, his hands clasped together under his head, his eyes speaking to her in the dark with sympathy and the need to understand. She didn't know if he really did, but it made her feel as if they were family unto each other. And wasn't that enough? His relationship with her mother had changed, too—a wariness had set in. She'd not meant to make him think ill of her mother, but he no longer saw her as a simple old Chinese lady who had stale breath and wagged her finger indiscriminately.

'He might like that,' she said. 'Are you glad you visited us?'

Her mother thought for a bit. 'I saw how each of you lived. With these old eyes. Who would have imagined it? Ah, well, I don't know about Ah Won. She behaved so strangely. She doesn't want me to see her place. Don't think I don't know. Giving yourself away like that—to such an undeserving man—it's not worth it. But what do I know? I'm just an old lady.'

'About that, Mother, why did you tell us about that fourth child? Why dig up all that old stuff suddenly?'

Her mother paused. She bit her lip. Her eyes welled up, which surprised Lily. 'I blamed your father for making me abort that baby. I blamed him this whole time. I thought, he made me do it. But that's what marriage is. His mistake is your mistake. You have to share the blame.'

This, from her mother, was such open-hearted, insightful candour that Lily reached out to touch her mother's hand. But her mother clasped her hands together just then, and Lily's fingers tingled from dry spark.

Her mother wasn't finished. Her voice became thin, slightly fevered, 'I was going to tell you. I didn't get to finish. The night your father died, I saw her by his bed. All grown up. She wore a mourning outfit. That's how I knew he was very close to going. She was beautiful. Hair so straight, dark and long. Eyelashes like the barbs of a bird's feather. Skin that was like porcelain. She looked straight at me. Didn't say a word. Just stood there while your father breathed his last. None of you was there. Your brother was travelling in Seremban. His wife was sleeping. No living children, only the dead one. Standing there like a spring sapling, her hair sweeping like a black shroud. You'd think she'd hate me, but no, she looked at me with…Oh, I don't know how to say this. She looked at me, so…so very tenderly.'

Lily gasped, 'Mother!' This—this was family. Her mother's face became as white as marzipan, the old acne scars like the tiny craters of fried egg white in a sizzling pan, but she sat resplendent even so, even grinding her molars together, and Lily thought how indecipherable and contradictory one's parents were—a shrouding mystery of details and autobiography and era and culture. What was random was trying to catch understanding from this morass. The understanding here was as circumstantial as accidental negligence. For a spectral moment though, Lily thought she glimpsed a pipkin of pain skating through her mother's features.

'If she'd lived,' her mother now whispered, 'I'd have named her Ah Chun. Her name—Spring—the way she'd looked, that would have been a perfect name for her.'

Right then, Lily was struck with forcible hope. She really didn't know what to say to her mother now—everything that came to mind smacked of asinine platitudes. Lily's mother looked at her—*I shouldn't have let that one go*—and Lily looked back—*yes, I know.*

Her mother let out a sound, a sound that was a croak.

Rap of the Tiger Mother

Tiger Mothers so gangsta they bring kickass cupcakes
So gangsta their kids can speak five languages
So gangsta they read and write and spell at four
Play the piano like lil' Beethoven. Ms Beatrice, yo?
Tiger Mothers so kool they da first at da skoolhouse door
So kool they drive up in Porsches four-by-four
Juicy J sweat-bottoms rockin' all couture
Tiger Mothers come in all stripes Ms Beatrice-teach
French, Italian, Brit-ish, even Kazakhstan fosho
Ain't just Chinese, nemmind Amy Chua actin' all superior
If Tiger Mothers rule the world, if I rule the world
Our sons will inherit the world, this be the new gospel, y'all.

Ms Beatrice is the Reception Year teacher at the prep school in Belgravia that I send Ethan to. I don't dislike her. She's getting married in the summer, she's probably all of twenty-six. Masses of brown curls, eyes blue as Turkish tiles, if one is in a lyrical frame of mind. This isn't really beef, but she keeps mistaking me with Xu Xuan, the other Asian mother in the class. My name's Charlotte. Hers is Xu Xuan. Do they alliterate? Are they homonyms? Nor do we look alike. I have dyed brown hair; Xu Xuan has jet-black. I dress like someone out of the British countryside: loose cotton shirt, rabbit-fur gilet, jeans tucked in knee-high boots. Xu Xuan opts for Chinese countryside: puffer jacket in a bedspread floral print.

But I get how Ms Beatrice might confuse us. We are both the earliest at the schoolhouse door. Sometimes she's in line before me, sometimes after. She likes to stop me in the corridor to chat. Tells me her son, Viggo (one of those 'double-take' names that makes one too embarrassed to say, come again?), is a music prodigy. Already pre-accepted into the Barbican Junior Musician's programme. Ethan, my angel, tinkles on the xylophone. Xu Xuan is married to a Swedish man with a brow so expansive it could be likened to that of Frankenstein's monster, a manner so taciturn he could be a Nordic crime noir psychopath. But at least she has a husband. Mine took too many business trips with his junior associate and ended up falling for her; with her he was probably higher on the pecking order than with me, or perhaps I fell asleep one too many times watching movies together on the couch after putting Ethan to bed. Now I'm just another clichéd story, a bimbo analogy, a single mother with a *-less* attached.

First teacher's meeting of the year and all the parents are there. The central message is about encouraging our little four-year-olds to learn to tie their own ties and shoelaces. Don't forget your beanie. Don't slobber all over your tie. Try to bring home *your own* schoolbag. We discuss reading next. Ms Beatrice says, 'It's marvellous to see how many of your boys already know how to read.' What, schooled at nursery/Oh, the feeling of inadequacy, descending like wooden blocks on me/Ethan has progressed up to 'f' in his alphabet row/I tell him he's my little Einstein, Ima mould him now.

Next to me—and how I wish she would just find some place else to sit, there are like twenty-six other little wooden tables to perch at—Xu Xuan is beaming. When I came in, she sent me the look of recognition one Asian transmits to another while bobbing in a sea of white. Racial solidarity, it matters more when you number *-less*. Somehow, she has to ask that question (you can literally see the whole room freeze): her son, Viggo, is reading Roald Dahl, and she would like some help with his vocabulary. Because it's tiring having to look up all the unfamiliar words and English expressions in the dictionary. I don't freeze / I grit my teeth / Roald Dahl. Blimey / If he needs to look up words, maybe he shouldn't be reading and learning them words like Twits and BFGs.

How the first term has flown, and it's now getting towards the Christmas holidays. Xu Xuan says they are spending theirs in Sweden. 'Where will you be?'

'In London.' I don't say we have nowhere to go. Not when other mums are bringing their boys to snowy places like Innsbruck and Verbier. 'Will be cold in Sweden,' I say. 'And really dark. No sun. No sun at all.'

Xu Xuan neighs. That's what her laugh sounds like—horsey. Looks like Xu Xuan has finally clued on, I don't like us being seen together.

There are lots of school activities planned before term end, including a Christmas bake sale to raise money for charity, and a Christmas concert, which would be held at the venerable St Peter's Church in Eaton Square. All the boys, Ethan included, have done us proud: they can now sound out their phonics. Ethan brings home assigned reading every day. All about a boy named Benjy and his dog. The boy has lots of adventures; the dog does, too. Hence a whole series of eight-page books. The boy is nondescript, the kind of relatable boy who climbs trees and throws a ball for his dog to catch. The dog has fleas. Ethan scratches himself all over in empathetic suffering. Ms Beatrice says parents are supposed to make notations in a red notebook regarding their children's progress with reading. I thought the little notebook was going to be a dialogue channel with Ms Beatrice. Turns out it's strictly one way. In the end, after reading with Ethan, I made notes like: *All good,* interspersed occasionally with: *Good job, Ethan!* And a heart sign. Ethan gives me a hug after reading.

Then I found out all the little readers are colour-coded. Red dots for beginners, orange for those in the middle, while green is the most advanced. Ethan is still red, many of the other boys are orange; Viggo, well, Viggo is probably off the colour scale.

For the bake sale, I've signed up for the 8.40 to 11.40am volunteer slot to help sell Christmas goodies and baked goods. Been up since 5am baking cupcakes. How ironic, in my investment banking days I used to get up at 5am to fly to America's heartland—the industrial belt, places like Indianapolis, Columbus and Detroit—to conduct due diligence and meet with a company's board of directors and I got paid mega-bucks for it. Here I am deploying the same work ethic—for cupcakes! Many of the mothers in Ethan's class, though, are in the same boat—women who held high-powered jobs but who voluntarily gave them up when they had children. No wonder these children are so precious, as precious as the ambitions, dreams and desire given up. Forget lawnmower parenting, it's lawnmower-*race* parenting, to see whose kid spells faster, reads better, kicks the ball like a footballer wanna-be, saves it like a goalie wanna-be, and they had better show all this potential before Term 1 Reception Year is over.

To my annoyance, the sheet pinned up at the door to the hall shows that Xu Xuan has signed up for the same slot. Not only that, she's signed up for the same table—the cupcakes table. Looking in, I can see her unpacking cupcakes from a very large Tupperware. Hair tied back in a ponytail, skin flushed and glowing. Puffer jacket nowhere to be seen.

'Good morning.'

She looks up with a beatific grin. Vim and good cheer on such a dreary grim morning. Needs shackling. But it's her cupcakes that draw my gaze. These aren't cupcakes. If they are cupcakes, they aren't fit for eating. Xu Xuan has even brought a tiered tray on which she's cupcake arranging. Disney characters imprinted on their faces/Goofy ain't looking hisself, all puffed up and purple/Chipmunks so cheeky they're begging to be cuddled/Cupcake super-achiever, what a bore/Bet the kids will want more/She makes it look so easy it's abc/Acorn does not fall far from the tree.

'Did you do these yourself?'

Xu Xuan nods. 'Easy!' I let out a snort. But she does not elaborate further.

By comparison, my cupcakes are a disgrace. Sprinkles landed haphazardly and several bald patches. Icing not spread evenly and supposed to be swimming-pool blue, now looks electric Kool-Aid green. Just then, another mother joins us. Introduces herself as Esther and says that her boy, Joaquin, is also in Reception Year, but in the K2 section. Esther is an African American from Philadelphia.

'Watch out,' Esther laughs. 'It's gonna be gangbusters here in a minute.'

Xu Xuan looks on with a fixed smile. I compliment Esther on her lovely sweater, she returns with a compliment about my fur gilet.

Our natter turns to reading. Joaquin is improving, but Esther hopes this drill strategy at a London prep school won't put him off reading forever like it did his father, who is Spanish and was sent to a boarding school in England at eight. Esther laments, 'He and Joaquin would rather be out with a ball. It was so cold this weekend, and Joaquin was out in his T-shirt and shorts!'

Xu Xuan says, 'Viggo is reading Roald Dahl.'

A look enters Esther's eyes. 'Well, Joaquin is reading *Green Eggs and Ham.*'

Xu Xuan continues, oblivious. 'Viggo has finished three Roald Dahl books already.'

'Good for him!' Esther says. She turns her body slightly towards me as she unloads her cupcakes, which are just as mangled as mine. Chaos ensues when the four-year-olds swarm in. Little hands everywhere. They get first go since they are the littlest. Xu Xuan falls upon her job like a market peddler, aggressively parting the boys from their allowed fiver—'Oh look, Olaf waves hello. Take him before he melts.' 'Sylvester is mean, eat him before he scrams.' 'You can't take Tom without Jerry.' Her Disney-imprinted cupcakes are disappearing fast. Esther and I exchange a confiding look.

When the shift ends, all the cupcakes are gone nevertheless. Xu Xuan cleans up as briskly as she sells. Within her hearing, I say to Esther, 'Wanna go grab a coffee in Sloane Square after this?' Esther happily agrees. Neither of us invites Xu Xuan.

Esther and I have a lot in common. We both went to college in New England. We both had a career in finance, then quit our jobs when we got pregnant. Our husbands, too, are the kind of metrosexuals who have opinions about everything. 'He insisted on choosing all the cutlery for our wedding celebration!' Esther says. I tell Esther that I'm separated, though not yet divorced. To the other mothers, I pretend Trevor is travelling. School has no idea. The whole sordid tale comes tumbling out. I tell Esther they took too many red-eye flights together to and fro across the pond, was how the affair happened. Esther is sympathetic.

'She's British Asian but with an accent so plummy she could read for the BBC. It's not fair. Also voluptuous. An Asian with curves.'

Esther bursts out laughing, then turns solemn. 'But do you love him still?'

How do you answer that question? *I usedta love him, I did I did I do.*

I change the subject.

Esther also worked on Wall Street after the turn of the millennium. 'Just imagine, we could've passed each other on the street,' she coos. We reminisce about the coffee vendor right outside Bowling Green station. Ay, ay, remember that man they called the charming Iranian/Free bagel on Fridays and hot cuoffee from his van/Blueberry and cinnamon schmear of cream cheese and jam/Too good to be true you know I'm a fan/ Fancy youself an everything bagel all speckled black and tan/ Got that too, even pigeons dig it, this Manhattan.

Esther slaps her thigh.

Or that panini place over at Nassau/shit, that place hot, what's the name again/didya forget same like me shorty got old/Had that tasty prosciutto and basil pesto/Mozzarella slapped in between two focaccia rolls. Sick, yo.

Esther laughs so hard she has to hold her sides. 'Fuck, Charlotte, where you get all that quirk from? I never would've guessed you enjoy rap.'

I tell Esther I wrote bad poems in college—abstract poet incognito, lyrics for a two-person acoustic guitar act. I later dated this guitarist from Flushing, Queens, who stood the idea of ethnic purity on its head. He was of such hybridised ethnicities the highest quotient was a quarter Mongolian Chinese. Wack on rap, he believed that rather than who owned culture, rap was about how to share culture. I got hooked too. Listened to Mos Def, Nas, A Tribe Called Quest, Tupac, Talib

Kweli. Now rap is global.

Before we know it, an hour has gone by and it's lunchtime. The waiter comes by to ask if we will be staying for lunch. Guiltily, we get up to pay.

'We must organise a playdate for Ethan and Joaquin,' Esther says.

We agree it has to be the very next day.

I'm picking up Ethan and Joaquin from school, as we live just a short distance away, in Cadogan Gardens. Esther will join us later for tea. At the schoolhouse door, while waiting for the boys to be dismissed, I overhear two mothers—a British and a French mum—talking. Zoe (thin and bony) and Gisele (graceful as a gazelle). Their sons are in Ethan's class, although these mothers have never bothered to speak to me. They are discussing their boys' football skills, how good a football coach Mr Kerrick is, how both boys have aced their spelling tests this week. Then Zoe says, Viggo, apparently, will be playing the violin for the Christmas concert, which also includes a Nativity play. He'll be the only boy given a solo. Gisele says she understands Viggo is some sort of music prodigy. Zoe says, her upper lip curling a little, the mother likes to make that fact known. Gisele says, she must be a tiger mother. Zoe says, well the Chinese are really good at Maths—Maths and Music being symbiotic. Probably drilling Viggo at the dinner table every evening on his two-plus-two. They giggle.

But sometimes two plus two isn't four. A surge of outrage boils up from nowhere. 'You have been at her dining table while she's feeding Viggo dinner?'

Zoe and Gisele both stare at me.

My voice sounds tubercular and choked up. I hope I'm not glowering. 'Maybe Viggo really has natural talent. Nothing to do with drilling or tutelage or training.'

Recovering her composure somewhat, Zoe speaks up, 'Of course.' She grips her large carryall and brings it to her middle. 'I wasn't implying otherwise.'

'Don't misunderstand us,' Gisele says. 'We meant it as a compliment.'

Zoe nods. 'We are in awe of her parenting skills.'

'You're Ethan's mum, aren't you?' Gisele smiles winsomely. 'I've been meaning to get our boys together. Jonathan mentions Ethan all the time.' I must have looked disbelieving, because Gisele says, 'He tells me Ethan has a fantastic right-kick.'

This is how you win people. I can't help flushing with pride. My little angel.

Zoe smiles. 'It would be so lovely to get our boys together. How about this afternoon? Is Ethan free?'

'Actually, he has a playdate with Joaquin this afternoon. I'm picking both of them up now.'

'Oh, Joaquin is very welcome to come along. I know Esther. I'll just give her a bell. I'm sure she won't mind,' Gisele says.

'But…'

'Do join us.' Gisele tucks her hair behind her ear. 'My housekeeper made scrumptious banana bread and also macarons this morning. I bet the boys would love some after their playtime.'

The boys, just dismissed, come thundering down the stairs, backing into each other at the door to shake the principal's hand grubbily, and, shoelaces untied, ties askew, they launch themselves at us. Gisele and Zoe embrace their offspring with the kind of ebullience usually reserved for airports. I see Joaquin and call to him. Ethan comes down last, dragging both feet and satchel. Once again, he's left his water bottle, and I get a little short with him as I make him go back upstairs to retrieve it. 'Mum,' he whines. Joaquin holds my hand like a pert little prince, his beanie set at a jaunty angle.

While Ethan goes back upstairs, Gisele says it's all arranged. Esther will pick up Joaquin from her house instead of mine and she looks forward to joining all of us for tea.

'That's settled, then,' Zoe says.

I find I don't mind being railroaded; I like this feeling of being included.

Group dynamics and London pavements don't go together. The pavement cannot accommodate, all abreast, four rowdy boys, three mothers, four backpacks, an assortment of sports kits and lunchboxes and shed duffel coats and falling beanies. Zoe and Gisele are already friends. So are Jonathan and Hieronymus. Thus, Ethan falls back with Joaquin. I hold up the rear, loaded down like a packmule. This is a mother's daily battle: which is less exhausting, making the boys carry their own bags to instil responsibility and independence, or watch them like a hawk all the way down King's Road so they don't cudgel others at bag-level and trip up dogs? Some days, it's easier to be the packmule.

I catch snatches of conversation between Zoe and Gisele. Zoe is spending Christmas near Southampton where they have a country place. Sixty acres and there's a watermill. Her two Alsatians get to chase rabbits and squirrels. Gisele, too, has a country place, in Buckinghamshire. They've bought a half-timbered Jacobean farmhouse and are in the process of renovating it. It's not a conversation I can contribute to. My mind drifts and I remember Trevor meeting my mother. Because Trevor and I were both working for bulge-bracket investment banks in New York, and flew back to Singapore just to do the honours, a meeting with the potential mother-in-law had to take place at the formidable Fullerton Hotel. Trevor brought a huge bouquet of flowers, but on my advice, he also brought a box of top-quality bird's nest. My mother didn't say a word to him; she barely even touched her pistachio briolette, her favourite dessert. Trevor chewed his fingernails throughout. Afterwards, my mother asked if Trevor was dyspeptic, chewing his fingernails so much was unbecoming for a virile Caucasian. Trevor was in terror. 'Your mother didn't like me.' How was I to tell him there was nothing he could've done, good or bad? He was simply the wrong colour.

When we get to Gisele's, just around the corner from Bibendum, I'm bowled over by her apartment. It shouldn't rightly be called an apartment because it extends over three floors. A winding staircase connects the floors. Marble tiles. A freaking water feature in the lobby. The private *elevator* opens into the apartment.

Jonathan rushes over to the baby grand in the living room, pounds on the keys in staccato, producing abominable sounds, then rushes up the winding staircase, shouting, 'Last one up is a jumping jellybean.'

The boys get on like a house on fire. When I go to check on them, I see they have begun a roisterous game of dressing up as safari hunters. Lil' bow wows, the lot of them. The bedrooms in Gisele's house are enormous. No clutter anywhere. Plush carpeting, lamp sconces on the walls, and everywhere beautiful paintings. Klimt. Warhol. With a gasp, I run back downstairs, where tea is being set out on the dining table by a housekeeper (of indeterminate Eastern European origin wearing a frilly pink housecoat). Traditions observed.

Tea time is entertaining. Gisele and Zoe are born storytellers. The boys together produce a cacophony of voices. Sometimes, one has to shout to be heard. I learn that Zoe's husband owns the men's fashion house Gieves. Zoe owns an art gallery in Belgravia. They're selling Nelson Mandela's paintings. The one where his hand print accidentally looks like the map of Africa. The auction for it was a riot—someone held up a paddle and bid fifty thousand pounds, while someone else asked in a loud enough whisper to be heard clear across the deck, isn't that just like a child's hand print?

Gisele used to be a runway model. She might not walk the runway any more, she laughs, but she still hand models for Tiffany.

The macarons are all colours all flavas—raspberry, blueberry, pistachio, chocolate, even lavender and vanilla. Earl Grey is served in a teapot and Wedgwood bone-china teacups.

Conversation turns to school and parenting. I let out a sigh. Zoe and Gisele discuss the school Nativity play. There are five key roles: Joseph, Mary and the three Kings. Everyone else is either sheep or a bale of hay or in the choir dressed as angels. Zoe says Hieronymus will be perfect as Joseph. He's been attending drama for tots—well, ever since he was a tot. This is interesting, and we have a fifteen-minute conversation about how successful drama lessons could be if they are this young. To hear Zoe talk, I begin to get itchy heart, I wonder if I've neglected Ethan's talents. I haven't started him on piano, I haven't signed him for the waiting list for Lamda. I haven't looked up maths tutoring. I haven't sent him to a public-speaking course.

Both Jonathan and Hieronymus are already in Grade Two piano. Jonathan is also learning the flute.

'But Mary will get the most lines,' Gisele says. They are back to talking about the Nativity play.

There's some discussion about whether or not Hieronymus would mind being dressed up as a girl on stage. 'He's got quite a childlike high voice,' Zoe says.

'Well, he is a child.'

They both look at me, but don't seem to have heard me. 'If only the choir has a solo,' Zoe moans. 'Hieronymus sings like an angel.'

The talk turns to the infernal topic of reading. Hieronymus really enjoys Nordic myths rewritten for children. 'He believes in gods and goddesses,' Zoe says. 'He writes me little messages in runes.'

'I believe in monsters, too,' I say.

Gisele turns to me, looking at me squarely. 'What about Ethan?'

'Oh...uhm...' The lie trips out without me consciously planning it, 'Ethan reads Roald Dahl.'

It's fun watching Zoe and Gisele's eyes turn as round as pennies. 'Really? Like Viggo then?'

My bluff deflates. Hot in herre. 'No, not quite as good as that. He's just started his first book.'

'And where is he on his maths?' Zoe asks, her hand wandering to stroke her throat.

Ethan is nowhere. He can write his numbers, but even then, they're all crooked. His five looks like a swastika. 'Oh, he's good,' I finish lamely.

'All these Asian kids are simply fantastic at maths,' Gisele says. 'How do they do it?'

The buzzer sounds. Gisele's housekeeper comes in to say another mother has arrived—Esther. The weight lifts and I give Esther a tight hug like she's my sister. Zoe and Gisele look caught by surprise.

But Esther blends in a way I never will. She jokes, nods, represents, tells stories and wu-tangs them. As the playdate winds to a close and the boys have all gorged themselves silly and are as high as if they were on gin and juice, we say goodbye, goodbye, see you tomorrow. Esther and I part on the road, and she says, 'You okay? You were awful quiet in there.'

All I can think of is escape. Trust is a mighty ambiguous thing.

Lo, of all the boys, Ethan gets picked to be Mary. In surprise, I read the note from Ms Beatrice. I tell Ethan he'll have to dress up as a girl to play the part. Ethan, who still loves his fluffy dinosaur and chews on it to go to sleep, asks if he gets to rockabye Baby Jesus. Of course, I say, you're gonna be his dear Mama. He says, cool and runs off to play with his toy action figures. At one time, in high school, I'd toyed with the idea of acting. Even got the lead role in our Drama Club's modern remake of Kafka's *Metamorphosis,* and it being Singapore where roaches are bigger and can fly, my costume had wings. Some of my talent rubbed off on Ethan, I'm thinking.

Just in case though, I ask Ms Beatrice if there's not been some kind of mistake, if the note perhaps was meant for Xu Xuan. Ms Beatrice's eyes meet mine, and her tone is careful. 'No, I meant for Ethan to be Mary.'

His father calls, we try to be civil to each other for one minute, and then, I tell him Ethan has landed the role of Mary in the school play. Trevor's voice positively swells with pride. He asks for Ethan to come to the phone. 'Good man, Ethan.'

Ethan shrugs, says, 'Hi Dad, bye Dad.' *Good man*? In the circumstances, shouldn't it be good humble peasant woman?

Coincidentally, twice I've passed Zoe in the corridors and tried to say hello, but it looks like she hasn't spotted me. I tell Esther the good news about Ethan when I see her at dismissal time. She laughs, 'But that's great! Joaquin is one of the wise men.' She leans in and whispers, 'Instead of gold and frankincense and myrrh, he's just as likely to say, gold and Frank's grandma.'

The rehearsal for the play is calamity personified. Lots of other mothers also volunteered to help out, and their collective voices swell and echo in St Peter's Church, raucous and ghostly, as if an outdoor market has been relocated into a cathedral. General confusion and lack of structure appear to be the order of the day. Ms Conova (the form teacher for the Year Threes and also the teacher in charge of Music and Drama) is waving the script in the air, directing, occasionally raising her voice. These abrupt stentorian bursts startle the mothers, arrest the stumbling sheep. Most of the time, the sheep sleepwalk into the props set up as bushes. Joseph keeps missing his cue, and when told off, he starts howling. The choir is ghastly, off pitch and not at all harmonious. How this will all come together in less than a week is beyond contemplation.

And.

I overhear some gossip.

'Apparently, some of the mothers pressured Ms Beatrice about who gets which roles.'

'Is that so? I heard one mother actually quizzed another about her son's drama school activities during a playdate.'

I frown.

The grapevine shifts to Zoe and Gisele. Apparently, they have had a falling out because Jonathan has landed the part of a wise man, but not Hieronymus.

Ms Beatrice must have overheard too, standing next to me. She points my attention towards Ethan on the stage. In his linen robes, it's hard to discern how he's dressed differently from Joseph, other than the wig of thick braided hair coiling down his back. Ethan is cuddling the baby Jesus, possibly too tightly.

'He's a natural,' Ms Beatrice says. 'A darling, affectionate boy.'

Out of the corner of my eye, I watch Zoe coming into the church, adorned with Birkin bag and court-heel shoes. She pointedly ignores Gisele, who is affixing wings on the choir boys, her mouth full of pins. Zoe sees me, too, and looks away. A deliberate snub. Tea at Gisele's feels as if it's a figment of my imagination. The sneaky thought comes unbidden: was I invited to the playdate so she could suss out what competition Ethan would be, by figuring out how tiger a mother I was?

It's a sickening thought. I find I can't even sleep. I get to thinking about Trevor with his career-hottie and become so worked up I end up baking cupcakes for all the boys at school. I also send Trevor an email: *You better show up for the Nativity Play, or else.*

Two days before the actual play, Ethan wants to quit being Mary. Ms Beatrice takes me aside as I'm about to collect Ethan after school. 'I'm not quite sure what's going on. I'm wondering if perhaps he's...' She pauses, looking nonplussed and embarrassed. 'Shy about having to dress up as female? Perhaps you could have a talk with him. He keeps insisting that he'd rather be sheep.'

On the bus to karate class, I try to talk to my little angel. Ethan is popping raisins in his mouth. He knows he's supposed to have the celery sticks first, but he always zeroes in on the raisins. 'Are you listening, Ethan?'

'The costume is really fluffy, Mummy. Oh, please, please can I be a sheep?'

I pause, thinking hard. 'Ethan, it's really cool you get to be Mary, you know? It's a big responsibility. Ms Beatrice thinks you'll do a really good job.'

'I want to be a fluffy sheep.' Ethan kicks the blue pole of the bus and an elderly passenger sitting in front turns her head to look at us.

'Ethan, don't kick and listen to me. The other boys at school, they're not teasing you, are they?'

Ethan sips his juice loudly. 'They all want to be Mary, Mum.'

It takes a second for this to sink in. 'Did they say that?'

Ethan sucks all the way to the bottom of the tiny carton, then burps. 'I want to be a fluffy sheep. Mummy, look, Winnie the Pooh balloon.' He points to the street where a little girl is walking along, one hand clasped in her mother's, the other holding a balloon. It sails behind her, picturesque and carefree.

Ethan can't take his eyes off her. It's all I'm going to get out of him, I realise.

Trevor is impatient when I talk to him that evening to explain the issue. 'Are they bullying my boy? They haven't been teasing him, have they?'

'I don't know.'

'You should find out, don't you think? Ethan has the biggest role, and why should he relinquish it?'

'It's a Nativity play by four-year-olds.'

'So, what's your point?'

'If he really wants to be a sheep, why not just let him?'

Trevor huffs a sigh on the other end. I hate these discussions with him, I hate the fact that I still have to have these discussions with him.

'I don't need to remind you, Charlotte, but he needs to learn to stand up for himself. This is about keeping what's yours.'

Trevor's words remind me of how he'd coached me while fighting for the promotion at the bank with another colleague. There were rainmakers and then there were rainmakers. We were both bankers in the transportation group; the colleague had brought in Hertz as a client while I'd only managed to bring in mom-and-pop businesses. Trevor told me to use the fact that I was a minority woman to my advantage. The colleague and I used verbal sabotage on each other, and it got truly ugly. In the end, I got the promotion. But then voluntarily gave it up when I had Ethan. I hadn't kept what's mine. Isn't that what being a loser is all about?

I try talking to Ethan again. After a couple more tries, what Ethan says stuns me, 'Mummy, there are too many words. I can't remember them all.'

'But, Ethan, Mary only has five lines. I can help you.'

'Do I really have to, Mummy?'

It's when I am doing the nightly reading with Ethan,

and he's stumbling over reading the words, that I make the connection finally. I look at the spine of the book where the red dot is, and turning to Ethan, I ask him if he knows what those dots mean on the books.

Ethan says, 'It means I read slowly. Guillermo and I are the only ones reading the red dots.'

'No one else?' I ask, a catch in my throat.

Ethan nods, then shakes his head, then nods again.

Somethin' wrong when a boy of four
doubts his reading skills
learns his limits
feels he's behind before he gets through the door
Tiger Mothers all about winning
put in a race where winning is the summit
the ticket, the definition of your core
Right smack in the thick of it
I don't know what values are any more
Fight for your right, do the right thing
right is for those with might
who don't back down who don't retreat
the real crime is done by our parenting
cos we don't know when to call defeat.

In the end, Viggo gets the part of Mary. Xu Xuan is bewildered when I offer for Viggo to take over Ethan's part in the play. I tell her Ethan prefers to be a sheep. It's his choice. Xu Xuan looks at me as if I'm a horned mythical creature, speaking a language not my own. But where are the words for the clash of swords in my heart?

Xu Xuan says, 'He's four. It's too big a responsibility to make him choose. Just tell him to do it. He can do it!'

I've nary a doubt that if I asked Ethan, he would do it. But would it have been for himself, would it have been legit? There are no determined, fixed answers in the 'race' game; middle-class happiness is wrought from the upper cut of shame. His father and I—we end up sparring, blaming, duking it out on the phone. He says not facing your fears is to be a coward, that I'm teaching Ethan the wrong trick. Giving in is giving up. He won't be flying in to see Ethan as a sheep.

Esther doesn't really relate. All I can hold on to as belief is the look of pure delight on Ethan's face when I say he can be a sheep if he wants to. To Trevor, I give a silent 'up yours' from this side of the pond, and though

> I can't say I know what's more right than right
> or what's more wrong, nor what saddens me more
> the loosening of the kernel of worry
> that's wormed into the bridge of Ethan's nose
> or me believing
> that he can face up to his fears
> Role modelling is what parenting is
> He can learn not to be a coward when he's older
> when he has a better ability to see
> how limits are set arbitrarily
> I want my boy to understand, to be able to concede
> that what constitutes bravery is to stand guard
> against the curtailing of different sensibilities.

Chronicles of a Culinary Poseur

On any given Sunday, when business was slow, Kara Hsu got together with her chef cronies for a tipple. Most of them were former classmates from Le Cordon Bleu. Tomasina's Pub in Nolita was a favourite joint. The IPA was on tap, Tomasina herself likely to draw up a chair, offering up free nibbles, and lewd jokes she'd collected over the years from patrons.

One particular Sunday, a food writer from Williamsburg had joined them (a writer always spelled trouble to Kara). She was also a food critic/blogger and she boasted a thirty-thousand following on her blog and an average of ten-thousand hits a day. Bernard Allard was also there. He'd been bugging Kara to hire him in her kitchen at Lumière but she had resisted. He too had studied at Le Cordon Bleu. They even cooked together on one group project, but she didn't like his food—frequently over-seasoned and he cut corners wherever he could (such as, overcrowding the pan with pieces of meat to save time). He was also a womaniser, flirting with anybody who wore a skirt in his vicinity. Luckily, at cooking school, the women wore trousers.

The food blogger's name was Leena Lewisham. Her food

blog, leaning on alliteration as it were, was called *The Lean Pantry*. Leena was telling them how she loved ferreting out the secret ingredients in what made a dish 'divine'. Her blog was all about new, undiscovered culinary gems in the city, value-for-money meals. On the flip side, she didn't mince words. Mince, get it? In her Food Crimes section, chefs too big for their boots were fleeced with regularity and bilious metaphors. As she gleefully boasted, as an example, 'meat so overcooked it was the equivalent of leather roadkill, run over multiple times.'

'Lettuce that limped and onions that singed.'

'The chef seemed to have forgotten which part was the oyster and which the shell.'

Ouch. We get it. Bernard sniggered next to Kara.

At some point in the night, there was a row of lemon drops each for Bernard and Kara. 'Whoever reaches the end of the line first.' Bernard leaned in close. Kara could smell his aftershave. 'If you lose, I kiss you. We'll go on a date.'

Leena looked over with interest. 'Do you two work together?'

Kara ignored Leena, scoffed at Bernard. She hated losing at anything. 'I won't. If I win,' she paused to think. 'Hmm...what do I even want from you if I win?'

Leena said, 'Where do you cook?'

Kara threw back a shot. Another and another in quick succession. 'At Lumière.'

Bernard was following her shot for shot. Leena looked at Bernard simperingly. 'And are you the executive chef there?'

Bernard laughed. Snorted rather. It gave Kara those precious few seconds to pull ahead. She downed two more shots. Liquid seared her oesophagus. She suppressed a hiccup. Kept going.

Leena said, 'I've heard good things. I'd love to come by some day.' The food blogger's way of wangling a free meal.

Kara won. It wasn't even close. Eight shots in quick

succession and her head now felt like mushy swollen fruit. Nausea, which she suppressed.

Bernard's tone was slurred. And sour. 'Well, it's in the red.'

It was true, Lumière was already in debt. Massive capital injection was needed for a restaurant this ambitious. Kara wanted *New York Times* star-review glory. Kara and her sisters had had to mortgage the family home in Englewood Cliffs, New Jersey, sending their dear mother into such harried conniptions she'd flown back to Singapore (where the relatives lived) for six months of passive-aggressive avoidance. Every two days, their mother called to shoot some of her incipient darts of hostility, like an Iban with a blowpipe. Then, a fire broke out in the kitchen during the early days, and Vanessa turned to loan sharks in Chinatown for an emergency loan. The Woon Leong Benevolent Chinese Association (benevolent, my ass) was keen to help. Ever since then, loose-limbed, scary-looking thugs came by once every week to eat and 'keep an eye on things'. What did Bernard know about any of it, but the gossip-monger he no doubt was, he'd probably heard that Kara couldn't pay her seafood supplier this week and had to resort to Chinatown garoupa.

Leena was saying, 'With my clout, I'll have you back in the black with a single good review. Watch me, Handsome. And you can kiss my hand later.' She held out a hand bedecked with fat clusters of jewels. At least she wasn't dressed like a tarot card reader.

Bernard giggled, drunk out of his skull.

Kara tipped her chair too far backwards and fell over.

Leena turned up the very next week wearing a hat sculpture and Jacqueline Onassis glasses. She came with a friend in tow, and her friend too was dressed to the nines, in a taupe silk-satin suit and brown stilettos. Sharks with their gleaming teeth and silky fabrics. The friend glanced around her, making eye contact with the front of house (FOH) staff, to alert them that a VIP had just made her entrance.

Quentin, Kara's maître d', rushed into the kitchen with his usual pigeon-toed gait, all fluttery motions and high-pitched voice, 'Oh my god, oh my god, do you know who that is?'

Halfway through searing a piece of expensive Atlantic halibut, Kara barely glanced up. 'It ain't JayZ, is it?' A ripple of smirks from the line cooks—hip-hop music was banned in Kara's kitchen. It didn't go with French haute cuisine. But it was a losing battle, Kara knew. The machismo and heat and knives and short tempers demanded a channel for release, and rapping seemed to go with the machismo.

'No, it's Leena from *The Lean Pantry*!' Quentin was a very literal person, and he rushed back out to begin his fawning and fussing. He might transmit the mother-hen vibe, but he had an uncanny nose for fawning and fussing over the right people.

Vanessa, obscured by a potted cactus at the cubbyhole desk in the corner, cast her eyes at Kara over her reading glasses. Vanessa was the oldest of the three Hsu sisters. Sensible and sharp as a tack with numbers. She was balancing last week's takings against receipts in the ledger and making annoying, effortful sighs. Kara had told her what had happened at Tomasina's, and all week they'd been wrangling whether or not to call Bernard if Leena did show up.

'Single-Good-Review is here?'

'Don't,' Kara said as she served up the halibut and dinged the bell. Normally, she would be at the pass putting on the garnishes and checking dishes as they went out, but the grillardin hadn't shown up for work, and in any case, there'd been complaints last week about overdone fish. Ramon, her sous chef, was in charge of the pass that evening, one of those 'freebie-honours' Kara gave to her male sous chef to maintain gender peace in the kitchen. Ramon chafed at Kara's authority, even if ethnically, they were on the same level, like that rap parody song Ramon loved so much—'Brown and Yellow'. In French gastronomy, hierarchy was everything. It is instilled in you from the first potato you brunoise.

'What are you waiting for?' Vanessa said. 'Call Bernard.'

'No.'

'Kara, don't be a martyr. Forget you're Chinese for a second. Do us a favour.'

'No.'

Kara sauntered over to the porthole in the kitchen swinging door to peep at the dining room. Who should she see strolling in through the lobby and past the bar but two of the Woon Leong loan-shark goons she owed money to. Pigman and Small Dragon. On first-name basis now, since they came by so often. These two weren't your usual thugs. No shiny black suits and MIB sunglasses. Instead, they wore matching banana-yellow tracksuits. They loped in as if they were animals from the zoo, arms hanging down their sides. They would eat her food as if they were on a culinary pilgrimage, oohing and aahing, licking their thick chops. Kara watched as Pigman and Small Dragon tilted their chins up at Quentin in greeting and sat themselves down at a table. Pigman flicked the Jheri curls on his head with his fingers. Small Dragon caressed the slithering dragon tattooed all over his neck. Kara watched her younger sister, Elvie, up front, pause over the reservation book and gesture with alarm towards her peeping face framed by the porthole.

'Crouching dragon,' Kara called out. These were their code words for when Woon Leong thugs showed up. The more senior ones, the ones who came in wearing mandarin-collared jackets, those were 'hidden tigers'. Kara didn't serve them her expensive halibuts or pigeon de Bresse from the Rhône-Alpes.

No, Kara served them deconstructed lobster noodles. Her sous chef would quickly run down to Chinatown and find the largest lobster dozing in a tank, and Kara would kill, boil, sear, soup-up, sauté, sauce, serve.

'Call him.'

Kara jumped. It was Vanessa. Words advisedly and quietly said so close to her ears they were wraiths of her thoughts. Kara gave Vanessa the stink-eye and called Bernard.

'*Mais oui, mon ami*?' He sounded as if he was grinning.

It irked Kara. 'I'm calling in my win. Here's what I want.'

Bernard listened. Then he chuckled.

Meanwhile, there was the menu to think about for Leena and her friend. Should Kara do their usual French fare, or demonstrate her culinary showmanship?

In truth, Kara had been devising a 'salt-and-pepper' five-course prix fixe. Still on an experimental basis, hence not on the menu as yet. It elucidated the taste of a particular specialty salt, that most lowly of ingredients. So lowly in kitchen parlance it was just referred to as 'seasoning'. It was Kara's way of thumbing her nose at culinary elitism, even though she was part of it. The dishes were all simply prepared, so simple it was akin to pulling the wool over one's eyes, until one took the first exquisite taste. Or so she hoped. That it would be exquisite. No classically trained French chef in a Manhattan establishment had done it yet. Was it too arrogant-cheeky-daring-risky? Who did she think she was?

The thing with being a French chef as a Chinese woman in the battleground of Manhattan could be summed up thus: throw in the towel already if you're going to piss all over yourself before you even got started. But it didn't mean she wasn't assailed with self-doubt. Just don't share it with your male culinary staff. It would be career suicide. What Kara did was to go to the staff bathroom and stare at herself in the mirror for a full minute. A peptalk. Some mindfuck talk. Gah, did Leena think she was testing her? Oh no, the reverse: Kara was testing Leena. Let's see what you're made of, Leena Lean Pantry. A true food connoisseur would be able to suss out the secret ingredient without an explanatory spiel from the food runner or server.

She came back out, tightened her apron by pulling the tie straps round to the front and double knotting. 'Quentin!'

'*Oui,* Chef!' He materialised like a convivial genie.

'Ask Table 26 if they are happy to have omakase. Chef's choice.'

'Right away, Chef!'

Elvie bustled into the kitchen all in a tizzy, making the swinging door flap. 'Pigman wants moo goo gai pan and Small Dragon wants General Tso's chicken.'

Kara swore. Only dim-witted gangstas would stroll into the epicentre, no scratch that, the *temple* of French gastronomy, and ask for Chinese take-out fare. 'Tell them to get the fuck out if that's what they want. Go down to Mott Street. Five restaurants there will serve them that.'

Elvie looked at Kara uncertainly. '*Oui,* Chef.'

For Leena and companion, omakase it was.

The menu started off with a simple tomato soup garnished with basil and seasoned with smoked sea salt and Tasmanian pepper. This wasn't just any old tomato soup. The tomatoes were heirloom, specially chosen for their sweetness and flavour, each gently roasted by hand over a stove fire and skin peeled, seeds removed. A laborious process that no worker in the kitchen charged with making the starter dish could shirk or shortcut. Simple tomato soup. At the same time, it paid homage to a glorious cultural past in French gastronomy—from Vatel to

Escoffier, Guérard to Bocuse, a tomato was treated with more respect than the batterie and brigade de cuisine.

Manuel was her trusty commis, who prepped all the ingredients for the hot appetizers station. 'Manuel,' Kara gave a holler. 'Soupe à la tomate!' Kara had just gone over the experimental menu with him last week.

'*Oui*, Chef!' came Manuel's answering cry.

Elvie came back bearing a basket of bread with a splayed Swiss penknife embedded in one of the rolls. The penknife's wine corkscrew, protruding at the very top, was missing the screw. The handle was embossed with a golden dragon, its spinal plates looking like tongues of fire. 'Um...Chef...they insist,' Elvie squeaked.

Kara adjusted her toque, then caved. Fine, moo goo gai pan it was, that simple dish of chicken stir-fried with mushrooms. But she was going to Frenchify the hell out of it. Kara had cremini, chanterelle, morel, shitake and even wood-ear in her dry goods pantry. A wild mushroom medley risotto style, and sitting in pride of place would be a square slab of chicken cooked three ways—poached, lightly smoked, and then skin deep-fried for crunch. The smokiness of chicken augmenting the woodsy taste of mushrooms. Served in a balsamic-garlicky glaze. Perfect. The mushrooms, luckily, had been prepped earlier and were ready.

Quentin came back in to report that the crouching dragons had moved tables and were now ensconced back to back with Leena and her friend. 'Bad joss!' Quentin muttered.

For his interview for the job, one of the first things he did to prepare was read James Clavell's *Tai-Pan*. Kara had informed him, 'Different region, yo. My family background is third-generation Singaporean.' Quentin's face crumpled so comically Kara decided to hire him anyway. Now Kara looked at Quentin. A mind-meld passed wordlessly between them. To prevent the goons from fomenting further trouble, Kara dished up the remaining tomato soup as amuse-bouche. 'Table 28! Pronto!'

Quentin didn't even wait for the food runner. He bore the two shot glasses of tomato soup himself on a tray and sailed out through the swinging door.

The soup platters came back empty and Tómas the plongeur gave Manuel the commis a high-five. Next up on Kara's salt-and-pepper menu would be Malpeque oysters with zucchini tagliatelle and Hawaiian red clay salt. It was meant to amp up the 'chic' level. The tagliatelle was gently poached in Kara's trademark chicken court bouillon. Kara immediately gave orders to her garde-manger station for prepping zucchini tagliatelle. No such thing as a mandoline or V-slicer in Kara's kitchen. You had to demonstrate serious knife cojones even to be a prep cook. Long strips of zucchini, cut uniformly, each three cm in width and ten cm in length.

Bernard breezed in, looking like a Grecian god. Tousled hair, six o'clock shadow, open-necked white shirt and jeans. The line cooks wolf-whistled. Kara growled without looking at him. 'Go suit up!' Then she sniffed. 'Are you wearing cologne?' Bernard grinned sheepishly. Kara shook her head. Another demerit in her book where Bernard was concerned. Okay, he was a little sexy but such unprofessionalism.

Kara watched as Ramon wiped off the tiny specks of vinaigrette on the plate of Malpeque oysters, but her mind was already turning to General Tso's chicken. General Tso was likely an amalgam of a couple of infamous generals. One version had him as a Qing dynasty general from Hunan Province; another had him as a Kuomintang general who later immigrated to New York to start a Chinese restaurant. Whichever version, Kara suspected it was a name, or names (at different points, they were called General Ching, General Chai, General Mao), given to dignify a humble peasant dish of sweet and spicy deep-fried chicken, to elevate the 'plebes' because they dined on fare worthy of a famed general. She slid the plates over to the runner and thought she would do exactly that—elevate the humble chicken so that its essence, its *jouissance,* was revealed and celebrated. Instead of deep-frying, she would coat the chicken portions in a blitzed peanut and parsley panko, then roast it inside a brown paper bag—chicken en papillote. It would be accompanied by sautéed vegetables in a fiery ginger and coconut emulsion. She didn't have an actual coconut, so concentrated coconut milk would have to suffice. General Tso might raise an eyebrow or two at how he'd been diaspora'ed south in Asia then vectored to the Western hemisphere.

Bernard was back. He tied his apron, rolled up the sleeves of his chef digs. He clapped his hands. 'What can I help with?'

Kara ignored him. The problem with too many off-piste items is that it buckled the firing line and upset the timing. The dining room wasn't completely filled, even so, she could see that the orders were piling up and the ticket printer was chattering. She set about prepping the ingredients for moo goo gai pan and General Tso's chicken herself. For Leena, the fish course would be grilled Atlantic salmon on parsnip mash with a fennel butter sauce served with Maldon sea salt flakes. A dish Kara concocted during a three-month stagiaire with two-Michelin-starred Bloom in London. She'd fallen head over heels for parsnips. Her parsnip mash melted in the mouth. But it was the rub she'd made for the Atlantic salmon that was the trade secret. No one knew what ingredients and aromatics she'd put in it.

Quentin came back in, his eyes shining with excitement. He said Leena was busy scribbling notes at the table, and over her shoulder, he saw the word 'Omakase' and a string of punctuation marks. Never had the coupling of an exclamation point and a question mark been so telling, so eloquent. Another empty plate. Another good sign.

After the soup, Kara sent Pigman and Small Dragon a trio of sashimis—tuna, salmon and kona kampachi. Any French restaurant worth its salt would have a well-stocked fridge that would always include sashimi-grade raw fish—it's what you use for tartare, after all. She served it with a simple cucumber and lemon vinaigrette. Bernard was making a general pest of himself, chatting with Duet and Minuetto, two of her line cooks, disrupting their flow. Quentin came back in, looking stressed. He reported that Pigman and Small Dragon seemed to be developing rapport with Leena and her friend. They were comparing notes and Leena was asking too many questions: What did Pigman do for a living? Wasn't it wonderful that a French restaurant had this contemporary twist and Asian influence? Did Small Dragon know who the executive chef was? Lumière didn't seem to have much of an online presence. It said it was started by a consortium only three months ago. It was one of those times Elvie's tardiness in getting their branding and online marketing going was actually turning out to be a boon in disguise.

It was during the fourth course that the mix-up happened. For Leena and her friend, Kara had planned a sous vide pork tenderloin with a quince compote. The salt-encrusted crispy skin of the pork tenderloin produced a satisfying crunch even as the tender meat melted on the palate. Somehow, the two food runners—Piper and Crosbie—ended up serving the deconstructed moo goo gai pan and westernised General Tso to Leena and her friend, and the sous vide pork to the Woon Leong goons. While the runners had been instructed not to reveal what the secret specialty salt was, it was ordinary protocol to 'spiel' what was on the plate. 'Deconstructed what?' Leena had said, quirking an eyebrow.

Terrible as her Chinese was, there was a Chinese saying Kara knew that went something like this: *shuō Cáo Cāo, Cáo Cāo dào.*

Speak of the devil and the devil comes. Tso, *cao*, it was courting trouble and no two ways about it. Quentin came bustling in saying that Leena had asked to meet the executive chef.

'Bernard!' Kara yelled.

'*Oui, mademoiselle.*'

'It's Chef to you, you fuckwit.'

Bernard gave her a megawatt smile. Nothing fazed him, that bastard.

'Come with me. I do the talking, you do the nodding, you got that?' Kara snapped. Bernard nodded. Brown limpid eyes, docile like a child.

Off to the dining room they trooped, Vanessa and Quentin trailing behind. It hadn't occurred to Kara then, group dynamics and tell-tale body language not being her forte, but a quartet of culinary staff showing up at a patron's table was a sure signal something was afoot. To Kara's horror, Leena and Pigman were sharing morsels from their entrées with each other, passing a plate back and forth. Just sacrilegious.

As they rocked up, Leena paused mid-spear. 'Wow, what an honour! The sous chef and the executive chef, too. Nice to see you again, Bernard.' She held out her hand. Small Dragon was picking his teeth with the end of his Swiss blade.

Bernard was the only one of them with the presence of mind to behave normally. He shook Leena's hand. Kara and Vanessa and Quentin all looked at Leena, flummoxed and tongue-tied. Leena caught Kara staring at the half-consumed General Tso's chicken on her plate. Her eyebrows rose into the tinted bangs sweeping her brow and then fell. Her mouth wriggled slightly, impatient.

'This was your idea, wasn't it?' Leena said, her eyes hooking squarely on to Kara.

Nobody else spoke. A few immediate explanations rushed to Kara's head.

Leena continued, 'I thought I sort of detected a theme behind all the dishes. They're simply constructed, I mean, tomato soup, I wasn't quite expecting that. But it was heavenly.' Leena paused dramatically.

Both Pigman and Small Dragon were taking an unnatural interest in the drama unfolding at Table 26. Small Dragon sucked his teeth, Pigman draped his elbow across his chair and leaned over.

Leena was saying, 'The five-course taster is structured around a single ingredient, isn't it? I can't quite put my finger on it yet, but I will. It all seemed coherent until this dish. The server tells me this is deconstructed moo goo gai pan? That's just bizarre. You had something to do with this, didn't you, Kara?'

They all froze. 'What?' someone spoke.

Leena snapped her fingers. 'I've got it. The secret ingredient is fungi. Am I right? It's a celebration of fungi. How brilliant—' here, she turned to Bernard '—that you allow such freedom of experimentation in your demesne. We all know how important mushrooms are to Chinese cooking. But to zero in on its essence and its complementary relationship with chicken, and to whizz it around so that it's French, but also Asian. Bravo!' She clapped. It wasn't at all clear that Pigman and Small Dragon understood the torrent of English, but no matter, they joined in the applause.

Leena's friend spoke up, 'You are the executive chef here, aren't you, Bernard?'

Bernard looked at Kara. Kara looked back.

'But, of course,' he said. 'Do you doubt it?'

'I suppose I did,' Leena said with a little wry laugh. 'All these Asian notes in modernist French cuisine. I hadn't expected that. I looked up the restaurant's website.' Leena actually began tapping on her phone, then scrolling and reading from it, as they stood around, trying to peer over her shoulder, trying to act nonchalant. Their supernumerary encircling of one table was beginning to draw attention from all the other diners. 'The Hsu Consortium. Isn't that your last name, Kara?'

Vanessa let out a small gasp.

'If I were to put two and two together, it looks like you have a hand in the ownership of this restaurant, don't you, Kara? But Bernard, your leadership is phenomenal. At first, omakase threw me. It's a Japanese term, and I wasn't sure where that came from. But now I see how open-minded you are. You are a trailblazer, Bernard.'

Kara opened her mouth and would have spoken if not for Vanessa's quick restraining hand on her upper arm.

Bernard bowed. 'Actually, the secret ingredient is salt. The artistic vision you see here is nothing short of gourmet pioneering. A spectacular display of culinary pizzazz. A healthy, intrepid exploration and respect of nature's bounty.'

Kara narrowed her eyes at Bernard suspiciously. How did he know this? Had Duet and Minuetto said something to him just now?

Bernard's tone grew expansive. 'Even an ingredient as menial as salt has a role to play. Here, we have chosen to spotlight it. Because salt is actually the essence of life. Our bodies by weight are composed of 0.15 per cent salt. Homer called it a divine substance. Lot's wife was turned into a pillar of salt for looking back at Sodom and Gomorrah. Jewish culinary custom spells out that a loaf of bread piled with salt on the dinner table is a sign of hospitality. The act of sprinkling salt anticipates the taste of the food it's paired with. It's the art of enhancement—sour with salty, sweet with salty.'

Leena, her companion, Pigman and Small Dragon were listening to Bernard all agog. He had them in the palm of his hand.

'Salt is associated with fertility, sexuality. It plays a part in ceremonies, rituals and covenants. The Romans called a man in love *salax*, a salty state, where the word salacious came from. Just think about all the things salt can do: it brightens the colour of vegetables being blanched; it pickles and brines and enables us to keep food longer; it gets more heat out of boiling water; it removes spots on clothes, puts out fires, keeps cut flowers fresh, kills poison ivy, and melts ice.'

They were all staring at Bernard. Kara's jaw dropped. Then she remembered. This was straight out of Dean Kastner's lecture at Le Cordon Bleu. Bernard, this copy-catting proselyte, had simply memorised it.

'Stupendous. Sensational. It's genius,' Leena gushed.

Then the injustice slammed Kara. She couldn't believe her ears. Bernard was stealing all her credit. It was Chinese salt history that had inspired Kara, factoids that now swam up from her subconscious as unverbalised repartee, factoids she'd picked up while researching her menu and that had given her a strange moment of recognition, a sense of an almost prodigal return: the Chinese were the first to evaporate ocean water through the boiling method and make salt crystals; Emperor Huangdi had the dubious honour of presiding over the first war fought over salt; the state monopolies of salt and iron became a major constitutional issue during Confucian times on the duties of good government. These factoids demanded that Kara open her mouth and speak. Instead what came out was: 'You'll find that even dessert is served with salt—in this case a terrine composed of poached pear, a pinch of kosher salt, champagne-soaked flan, as well as a further verjus sorbet served with pineapple caviar and kala namak, Indian black salt.'

Leena didn't reply. Her eyes took in Kara's expression. Quentin and Vanessa froze. Pigman interrupted, 'Roast pork also Chinese.'

Small Dragon said, 'Yeah. Very good here. This dish very good. I come back. Mouth, tongue, belly, everything happy.'

Bernard said, 'The dessert is all Kara. And it is sensational. Sensational does not begin to cover it.'

Kara frowned.

Leena said, 'Well, I look forward to it.' This time, she held out her paw in such a way it was clear what she wanted. Bernard stooped low, bending over her hand, and kissed it. Kara stomped back to the kitchen, followed by Vanessa and Quentin.

Quentin was releasing little hot puffs of air. 'Oh god, that was close. We are out of the woods, I hope?'

The review came out the next day. It said, 'Chef Bernard Allard's new restaurant, Lumière, is luminous.' It said, scintillating, titillating food. It said, Asian accents that hinted at a bold, intrepid spirit and an all-encompassing culinary gestalt. It said, the salmon rub was enigmatic and captivating, like Chef Bernard. The roast pork tenderloin produced instant, mind-goggling drool, like Chef Bernard. This was ironic, since it wasn't what she was served. Also, Leena the mean, lean, metaphor-churning machine had produced not a single metaphor.

But the damage was done. The phones began ringing incessantly, the reservation books were booked solid for the next three months. The salt-and-pepper prix fixe went on the menu. Pigman hadn't cottoned on to the deception while Leena was quizzing them, but when Kara called to beg him not to reveal the truth, it all clicked. Pigman sounded pleased. 'You owe me a favour.' Favour was such an ominous word.

And Bernard? There was the rub. Kara had to hire him as sous chef and put up with his incessant flirting. He too claimed to have done her a favour. When clientele demanded to meet the executive chef, he fronted for them.

How long this house of cards would stand was anybody's guess. A simple, allowed misunderstanding had somehow ballooned into all-out public deception. In her quieter moments of reflection, Kara was filled with twinges of guilt and misgiving. And yet, amidst all the trickery and fraud, Kara had never been more undilutedly herself: with the restaurant as full as it was every evening, Kara cooked, expedited, garnished and *seasoned* like a maniac, as only she could. When their mother called, Elvie happily chirped, 'be satisfied, Ma. Ka-chink, ka-chink.'

Face

'WHY SHOULD LULU know how to roll spaghetti with a fork? We're not Italian.' Karen bangs the saucepan on the stove, because this is how some Chinese people take out their frustrations—by abusing their cookware.

Yun sits at the kitchen table and follows her daughter-in-law's movement, always a fraction of a second behind: when Yun registers Karen at the stove, she is already opening a tin with energetic cranks of the can-opener; by the time Yun makes out the writing on the tin—*Pitted Black Olives in Brine*—Karen is at the sink.

'What three-year-old can roll spaghetti with a fork, you tell me?' Karen demands. She pours in chilled carrot and coriander soup to heat. She turns around; her glare is not directed at Yun, but it lands on her nonetheless. Karen speaks to her in a mixture of Mandarin and English, her Mandarin being stuck at third-grade level. Yun herself speaks little English; she tries to learn by reading words on tin cans and turning on the captions for the hard-of-hearing on TV.

'"I don't know what you serve her at home." In *that* tone.' Karen takes a dishcloth and swipes at the table. Yun removes fingers in a hurry. 'As if all Chinese people eat only with chopsticks. We wouldn't know how to use a fork if you poked our noses with it. Racist, I tell you.'

Yun glances at the shamrock walls, the track lighting, the shining copper pots that pan back her glinty reflection. When she looks at her daughter-in-law, she sometimes looks at the space and the objects beside Karen more than at Karen herself. It gives her a momentary relief.

'I know you probably don't understand,' Karen says. 'Mama, London isn't just Wardour Street and Queensway. Can't simply interact only with other Chinese people.'

Yun looks at Karen, spooning out the soup, putting a couple of mealy saltines on the side. Chinese people do not eat like this. Karen sets the bowl in front of Y un. She herself eats a store-bought salad, full of artichokes swimming in oil, and the greasy olives, the pits dotting the enamelled basin later like watchful eyes.

'*Wǒ xiǎng huí jiā,*' Yun says. I want to go home.

Karen stops chewing mid-bite, a sprig of rocket protruding between her lips. 'But who is going to take care of you back in Malaysia? You might fall down, or worse, die and get half-mauled by a farm dog before anybody discovers you.' Karen eyes Yun steadily. 'Why are you bringing this up suddenly? It's not about the bladder issue, is it?'

Yun sets her mouth in a stubborn line. 'At home I can pee whenever and wherever I please.'

Back in Malaysia, Yun had owned a chicken farm, before she'd had to sell it when Zhi Wei died suddenly from a heart attack. Those halcyon days when her Buff Brahma chickens laid a dozen eggs a day, her Cochin another even dozen, her Grey Shanghai at least eight on a good day, when they weren't fluey. She'd totted up the numbers in columns in a blue notebook. Here, in London, she twiddles her thumbs, locks eyes over the dinner table with her granddaughter who complains to Karen, 'Why does Nai Nai smell like wee?'

Free medical care, her son, Qiang, has said—for her urinary incontinence. Karen took her to a GP, but had to come into the consulting room to act as translator. The doctor gave Yun some vaginal cones, a series of small weights to be inserted like tampons. When Yun finally understood how she was supposed to use the cones, she cringed. *Tiān ah,* how could such womanly matters be discussed so flatly? How could the doctor, an elderly woman herself, not understand this?

In the car, afterwards, Yun asked if Karen knew a Chinese herbalist.

Karen cast Yun a sideway glance. 'I don't. Will you just try? It'll give you more freedom of movement.'

'I simply won't go out,' Yun had said.

Karen twisted her lips into a moue—a disagreeable expression that altered the flat contours of her face. It conveyed her dissatisfaction about many things Yun could only guess at, but there was a sedulous concentration on her mother-in-law living with them. 'You're going to lock yourself up in the house? How is that going to help?'

'I won't embarrass you, at least.'

'Please don't talk like that. I don't want Lulu to learn this kind of self-deprecation.' A pause. 'At your age, exercise is really important, Mama.'

Yun fell silent. The conversation was often like this: she meant one thing, but her daughter-in-law took her to mean another. She felt like a suitcase of discarded things. Should be donated to Oxfam down the road. Somebody else might have a use for her. Qiang should just let her go home. Wang *Daifu* in the village will prescribe some Bu Zhong Yi Qi Wan for the incontinence. None of these cone-like things to attack one's sphincters.

Once back in the beige-walled, temperature-controlled bedroom she sleeps in, Yun tried to nap, but could only stare at the shape of those cones in their waxy-white packaging. Yun overheard Karen relating the episode to Qiang. *Her generation, no way is she going to put things up her whoopee.* What is whoopee? The shrug in Karen's tone. *Rather piddle her trousers in Waitrose.* Piddle. Nice word. Yun liked the English words with double Ds and Bs in the centre. They sounded kind; they sounded as if they would tickle.

The cones reminded her of Ben Wa balls. Back when Zhi Wei was alive, he'd bought a box as a gift for her once. Came home and proffered it with a snaggletoothed grin. She'd opened the silk-covered box and gasped. Watched the double ceramic balls roll in their divots as Zhi Wei leaned down and said, 'Want me to pedal you up the road?'

They did. The most incredible experience she'd had, jouncing behind Zhi Wei on a bicycle up those potholed rugged road tracks, her hands lightly clasping his waist, her eyes rolling milk-white, her breaths coming in short spurts.

He, gone too soon, and she, demoted from Ben Wa balls to vaginal cones.

Maybe it's the soup she's had, but Yun feels a churning of discontent in her gut afterwards. There is much she wants to say to Karen. Karen, who was born in San Francisco, with eyes pebbly dark, and flawless skin that she rubs with expensive lotions containing sea algae. Karen, with her Colgate post-braces teeth, so westernised underneath her Chinese skin. Karen, whom Yun wants to talk to about the loss of respect for elders. Karen, from whom Yun is learning so many things. The other evening, at dinner, Karen said, pass the broccoli. At her look of incomprehension, Karen explained it's what you do when the dishes are too far to reach. This is Chinese eating culture in the West? Instead of proper placement, main dishes move around the table like mobile units? In Yun's growing-up days, family dinners were boisterous affairs: grandparents, parents, children, cousins, everyone helping themselves, and the noise was a wacky symphony of clicking chopsticks and conversation fragments layered on top of each other. If you were unable to reach a dish, someone would notice and surely slip a slice of meat or a morsel of veg into your bowl of rice. By contrast, Karen's dinner table clatters with spoons. Spoons everywhere. A serving spoon for every main dish. Oh, so many spoons!

But mostly, Yun wants to talk about the other day on the tube because she's tired of carrying all this weight. Coming back from Wardour Street on the Piccadilly Line, a lanky, young man wearing a hooded sweatshirt, a ring through his nose, had sat on her. Sat on her as if she were a foam cushion.

Yun herself is heavyset—her thighs are thick joints, her stomach weighs on her like a bulbous cantaloupe. By contrast, he was so thin that when he squashed himself down, she could feel the bones in his ass.

His friends stood around, their greasy hands clutching the blue pole in the carriage, smirking, reeking of alcohol. Yun, too taken aback, could not speak.

The boy squirmed and ground his frame harder into the fleshiness of her lap. Then, he turned around and spat, his voice a low hiss, 'Go back to where you came from, you mook!'

Yun didn't know what a mook was. But there was no mistaking what one of his chums said. Leaning in, the girl peeled her top away from her chest, and said, 'One pound, wash shirt!'

Her companions and the boy sitting on Yun laughed uproariously.

Yun, throttled with rising anger, felt herself dampen with sweat. She poked the boy in the armpit. 'Get off me!' she shouted in Chinese.

The girl leered, 'Ching chong chunga, eh!'

'Speak English, you bamboo witch,' the boy said.

Yun felt herself disengage—as if she were watching

something on telly. She placed both palms flat against the boy's back and shoved. The boy fell off her lap with such force that his head thwacked against the metal pole his friends had congregated around. A collective deadening gathered, the air thick with pockets of clammy and sour mustiness, while the other passengers simply stared. No one came to her aid; no one said anything at all.

The next station came up. The doors opened with a hiss. Yun felt as if someone had smacked her with the paddle of a ping-pong bat. She watched them lope off, the boy and his chums, and only then realising what the girl's green mascara and spiky, pink-dyed haircut reminded her of, she shouted after her, 'You, dragonfruit!'

The incident now feels grafted as invisible weight on her back, mushrooming like a smelly fart, and no matter where she goes, she feels tense, teetering on the edge of perennial filthy exposure, as if people everywhere in England were liable to come up to her and rip off her face. In terms of keeping her at home, it beats urinary incontinence.

Karen has a favour to ask. 'Mama, you pick up Lulu from school. She likes the nursery rhymes you teach her. That way she can learn some Chinese.'

Yun looks at Karen neatly plaiting Lulu's hair into two pigtails before the mirror. Lulu purses her lips at having her hair yanked every which way. Yun shakes her head. 'I don't know the way.' She suspects this isn't a favour to Karen, as such, more that Karen has discussed with Qiang the problem of his mother not venturing out of the house at all, and how the lack of exercise will increase her obesity and exacerbate her other attendant physical illnesses.

'This is not a prison,' Karen laughs, but Yun thinks she detects intent behind it.

Afraid I'll become twice the burden; a spike of spite rises in Yun's throat. Deep in her heart, she suspects she's becoming hysterical.

When she first arrived, Yun had brought White Rabbit candy and haw flakes for Lulu. One look and Karen snatched away the candy and said it'd give Lulu cavities, her granddaughter's bereft expression notwithstanding. Haw flakes? Look at the nutrition label. Full of processed sugar. Yun doubts she has anything else Lulu will want to have.

'I'll show you a couple of times and you'll have no trouble.' Karen pats her on the arm.

'Not a good idea. What if I get lost?'

'I don't want Nai Nai to take me,' Lulu pouts.

'What if I have to talk to the teachers? My English isn't good enough. I'll never be able to relay any of the messages.'

'Don't worry, they'll just hand you a note. They don't have time to speak to so many parents and carers.'

'Karen, please don't ask me.' Yun tries to keep the fear out of her voice, but it snakes in, making her throat convulse and quiver.

Karen gives her a sharp look. Yun blinks rapidly. Her saliva tastes of bile.

'It's only a small thing I'm asking,' Karen says.

Qiang comes home from work and enters Yun's bedroom. Her son has aged beyond his thirty years. A degree from MIT, and here he's just another computer geek, a lowly peon in a major investment bank. The cold damp, the fogginess, the leaden skies of England seem to have seeped into the crags and pores of his skin, giving him an eternal greyness. He even moves with slower speed—his ankle suffers from a traction deformity where the Achilles tendon pulls against a sliver of heel bone, and as a result, he walks as if he were bouncing on air pockets.

'Are your feet giving you trouble again?' Yun enquires.

It isn't often that Qiang comes into her room for a chat. Yun has an idea what this is about, but still, it brings a frisson of delight and pleasure to look at him—the way he smooths back the wingtips of hair behind his ears as he sits down beside her, the way he lifts up his chest as if he's in a declamation contest. This last thought brings back a memory of Qiang as a seven-year-old, having won third place in an elocution contest. So proud of himself that for days afterwards, he'd recited, as loudly as he could, to anyone who would listen, the poem he had used—Zhu Xi's 'The Boats are Afloat'.

'Mama, give us a hand.'

'You talked to Karen?'

'To be honest, there's a yoga class Karen would like to take. She's still self-conscious about her weight. If you pick up Lulu, it'll also give you a chance to bond with your granddaughter.'

For an instant, Yun wants to quibble: I tried with haw flakes. She wants to tell Qiang about the boy on the tube. How she thinks about that boy all the time and how she tries to rationalise what he did—of course, the alcohol was responsible. The boy probably didn't even remember what he'd said. What swims up in her memory, though, like a film of greenish scum, is the way those punks walked off the tube, their backs jostling each other. This kind of casual hatred she'd never encountered. Hatred binds you—she'd never be able to forget that boy's face, or the girl's either, but she has a feeling that if she were to run into them on Shaftesbury Avenue or Wardour Street, they wouldn't remember her at all. This kind of hatred is so anonymous it has no face.

'It's not that I don't want to help,' Yun begins, but she sees Qiang's eyebrows tighten, his cheekbones draw together. 'All right,' she sighs. 'I'll try.'

The first afternoon she's supposed to pick up Lulu, Yun keeps one eye on the mantelpiece ormolu clock, the other on the telly. Twenty to one, Yun is all dressed, pink scarf wound round her neck, bottle-green puffy jacket on. She sits on the couch and watches the second hand tick in circles. Her black brogues lie side by side, waiting for her feet. If Zhi Wei were here, he'd be sitting side by side with her on the couch, waiting patiently, like that commercial for flu medicine—the one with those Mongolians packed close together on a couch, sneezing with cold, waiting for steaming yak dung to clear the nasal passages. It only takes five minutes to get there, but Yun wants to give an extra half hour leeway, in case anything should happen. Her heart thuds unevenly, her skin flushes hot and cold, and her bladder is burning.

She goes to the bathroom again, adjusts the stay-dry pad that Karen has bought for her from Boots. Douses herself in lavender talcum so Lulu won't complain about her BO. She parts her lips in a silent whinny, examines her teeth for food residue, rubs a pointer over her gums and smacks her lips a couple of times.

In the hall, after she slips on her shoes, she sees that she's missed her intended departure by five minutes. She takes the house keys firmly in hand. Just as she's about to open the door, she thinks, did she leave a fire on; are the windows open? She makes a quick inspection of the house: the stove is unused, as vacant as a keeled-over boat; the drapes are pulled, the air circulating the house is musty.

Yun pulls open the front door. The hallway outside is dark, the stairwell echoes hollow with the sound of an apartment door closing on one of the floors above. A tinny voice wafts somewhere below, and a gust of wind, from nowhere, blows in her face, bringing with it a sour, heavy smell—something fetid, like alcohol. Yun pulls the front door closed. She locks it. She steps away. Her glance falls on the clock face. The second hand is blurring.

The phone is ringing like an alarm; its shrill jangle arouses Yun from her stupor. Did she fall asleep? She draws the drapes. Paltry sunshine palliates the sullen greyness outside. Two birds alight on the bare branch of an elm—thrushes, or that's what Karen has told her they're called.

Time has slipped by, and the phone now stops ringing.

Yun returns to the couch.

This is how Karen finds her when she walks in with a panic-stricken Lulu. Karen's face is as puffy and mottled as a red bean bun.

'What happened? The school called me, some school secretary being all snippy with me on the phone because no one came to pick up Lulu and it's an hour past home time. Are you okay?' Then, she slowly takes in the scene—Yun sitting demure on the couch with jacket and shoes, her face fallen into a kind of comatose immobility. 'Did you hear what I said?' Karen shakes Yun's shoulder.

Yun jerks upright. Her right eyelid feels congealed so that she sees her daughter-in-law through a one-eyed squint. Karen's pupils are black and dancing with rage, and she seems to be trying to control her words with effort.

'What's the matter with you?' Her hand grabs Yun's, crushing the fingers. 'Lulu was scared half to death, thinking I'd forgotten to pick her up.'

Her granddaughter does seem diminished somehow, flatter in the jaw, her shoulders squared tightly around her frame. She's had a scare and it's all Yun's fault. Tears well. Lulu looks away.

'Well?'

The silence dips and swells. It has its own presence.

Karen's face gives way at last to her inner rage, turns

disbelieving, then scornful. 'Wait till Qiang gets a load of this.' She drags Lulu with her. 'Come on, sweetie, let's get you changed for ballet.'

Hours later, when Qiang gets home, Yun is lying on her bed, still in jacket and shoes. She hears Karen's rabid English wittering away, and Yun turns over to face the window. The thrushes are still on that branch, pecking at their feathers. Or maybe they've gone and come back. They've flown their little trips, circumnavigated the neighbourhood, alighted on other destinations, all without the slightest effort.

Qiang knocks on the bedroom door. 'Ma, *nǐ méishì ba?*' There's nothing wrong with you, is there? His tone is not belligerent. In fact, it stays casual, emotionless.

Her gaze still on those thrushes, Yun says, so softly that she wonders if she means for her son to hear it, 'On the double, bibbidi bob.'

From behind the door, Qiang's knocking pauses. 'Did you say something, Ma?'

She doesn't answer. He stands there for long minutes. Finally, she hears the soft click when he releases the door handle, his tread as he turns away. This is how a Chinese person becomes invisible, not because she is rubbed out by society or the racial elements in it, but because her face is no longer familiar to her loved ones.

At dinner, Qiang turns to her quietly. 'Just tell me why. I want to understand.'

How to explain that paralysing heaviness that began to creep up her legs that afternoon? How to explain that moment at the door—it wasn't as if she actually made a decision, a choice to abandon—no, a kind of momentum tipped her backward, an action that was as verb*less* as a Chinese person without a face.

Qiang stabs an asparagus head with his fork, waiting. His

mouth hovers above the spear, opening. And then, the moment to reveal anything is gone. His lips grip the stem. The teeth sink down, it disappears. How discombobulating a mouth can seem, as if to spite the face.

Lulu comes in to say goodnight, breath minty fresh, wearing eyesore pyjamas with a busy print of princesses and frogs that she's buttoned all the way to the neck. Yun feels awful about earlier, but Lulu crawls into bed with her, blithe and carefree. She's never wanted to do this before. Is it that the memory of the young is short, or that Lulu forgives easily? A sharp stab in her heart as Lulu says, 'Nai Nai, tell me a story.'

Yun pats Lulu on the head, clears her throat. Proceeds to tell her the beginning of the story of the Monkey King and the *Journey to the West*. But with the cacophony of foreign Mandarin syllables she's not used to, Lulu is fast asleep before they even get to the monkey emerging out of his stone-egg. Qiang comes to carry Lulu back to her own bed.

The need for Yun to communicate with her son suddenly courses through her like wild desire, the way Zhi Wei's Ben Wa balls had once inflamed her—molten, searing heat that blazed through her innards. 'Do you remember the poem that won you that contest when you were seven?'

Qiang blinks. 'What?' Her son appraises her. Seems to draw a kind of conclusion. 'Ma, talk to me. You do remember what happened today, don't you?'

She isn't going loopy, if that's what he thinks. She tries again. 'You also really liked Li Bai's poem. Do you remember this one?' She begins to recite the eighth century Poet Sage's famous poem about homesickness:

Chuáng qián míng yuèguāng
Yí shì dì shàng shuāng

Qiang interrupts her, 'Ma, did you hear me? I asked you what happened today.'

'*Zhēn de xiǎng huí jiā.*' I really want to go home.

'But why?' Qiang's face elongates. 'Why do you want to live alone? Who will take care of you back home?'

The words settle into her bones like weight. It's hot in the room, and her feet lie sunken in the bedspread. Her son wants logical answers. Logical deductions and logical reasoning. Is this really where understanding begins?

She hears the words. Do they think she can't hear or understand the words? In the dark, light from passing cars outside strobes across the ceiling, a pattern so precise it mesmerises her. A horn bleats, pedestrians chatter on their way home after a night out; an inner hum along her veins, and those words, like black bats, fly around the room.

Words she can't understand, but that she knows are about her all the same.

She hears the words 'hospital' and 'money'. She hears Qiang's frustrated sigh. She hears him ask what the relatives at home would think, that he can't even look after his old Ma?

It's not like that. Yun wants to comfort him. I know you care about your old Ma. I know you do.

She can't sleep. It's deep in the night when she hears Karen and Qiang making love, the creak and groan of the bed, their sighs and quiet enjoyment. Their quiet talk in the bathroom afterwards, the toilet flushing, the tap running.

She rises from her bed, struggles with the bedcovers, her voice lifting like a thin shredded cry from her cracked throat—words she's learned from the telly, 'Need to get to your mate's weddin'? All out of dosh and feel like sweaty vermin?'

Finally, it comes. The silence of the household—the stopping still of all motion.

'Get yourself a deodorant/an anti-perspirant of superior quality/your mum's tights have chafed your skin.'

The pausing in the flapping of lips. The foot half-dangled in mid-step. The door not yet closed. Are they finally listening now? Yun spreads out her fingers. Her face breaks with jagged lines, splintering like a saltine.

A Thoroughly Modern Ghost of Other Origin

ASIAN PEOPLES have colourful ghosts.

Here are some facts about the *pontianak,* a female Malay vampire:

- As a human, died during childbirth, and as a result, wants to prey on the blood of men and other helpless folk.
- Pale-faced, dressed in a long white smock smeared with blood, long black hair, red scary eyes.
- But can also be a beguiling beautiful woman, before tearing your intestines out.
- Attended by the fragrant scent of plumeria, a white flower that is most scented at night, but has an undercarriage like decayed rotting flesh.
- Sniffs out her victims through the scent of fresh laundry. As my mother would say, leave your undies drying outside at night, and you *kena*.

An *èguǐ,* by contrast, is Chinese, literally meaning hungry ghost. Actually, it's like a super-ghost, because the Chinese believe all souls are ghosts, but an *èguǐ* is a soul reborn as a hungry ghost, destined to wander through limitless lifetimes in search of release. Here are some facts about the *èguǐ*:

- Long, thin neck like a needle, distended belly—Yama's rotten idea of a funnel.
- Can be male or female. Mouth issues torch or flame, or tiny vile creatures. Pick your poison.
- The crowd-starter is every seventh month of the Chinese lunar calendar, when the gates of Hell are thrown wide open and they stream out and roam around in the realm of the living for a month, giving 'raising hell' a new window-dressing.
- Singing ghost songs—in Singapore, we have *getai* performances—can help appease their spirits.

The creature I met at the laundromat one evening could be one or the other. In the last few months, I've been having a tussle with my libido. In order for my mother not to discover how frequently I come in my underpants (or there will be hell to pay), I take them to the laundromat in our block late at night. The uncle there sometimes gives me coins to feed the machines, in return for closing up shop for him.

I was taking my wash out and had discovered I'd left a bar of chocolate in the pocket of my beige trousers. Streaks of brown criss-crossed different items of clothing, like mud tracks. Shit, I said. No kidding, she said. I snapped my head round—there she was, sitting on top of a dryer, her thin blue ankles crossed, her long black hair in dreadlocks. Her eyes were red and bulgy, her mouth also a garish red, except she had a couple of lip piercings. Her smock looked like the tribal one with tassels my sister also wore, from H&M.

Shit, I said again, not now.

Here's the thing. Ghosts have appeared to me in one form or another throughout my life. I'm that kid from *Sixth Sense*—I *oso* see dead people—except I live in a Housing Development Board flat in Singapore with a grandmother, my parents, and two brothers and two sisters. Also, one Indonesian helper. I'm the youngest—small and gangly for a sixteen-year-old teenager, but it's still pretty cramped in our three-bedroom apartment (my grandmother sleeps on a canvas cot in the living room, and the helper sleeps on the kitchen floor). You can't get a cup of hot water from the boiled water thermos without banging elbows with the hanging wok or brushing against the dried squid Mother has strung up along the kitchen tiling.

Feed me, the ghost said.

This too is not new. They always appear before me starving. It's a miracle I still have my kidneys and intestines intact. Where am I going to get food this time of night? I said.

Feed me, or you die.

I laughed. That not even scary. What kind of ghost are you?

She scrunched up her eyebrows, which had the distinct effect of making her red eyes look pinched, like a red dot sighting from an EOTech shooter on *Battlefield 4*. I lie, I do get scared shitless still. I started humming Ed Sheeran's 'The A-Team'. She looked like a modern ghost, I thought she might appreciate a little Ed Sheeran, or maybe One Direction?

I get the feeling I've been here before, she said. Like I've been wandering around for a long time.

I swear I've never seen you before. Are you a *langsuyir* or a *núguǐ*, a *pontianak* or an *èguǐ*? Or a *bhoot*—an Indian ghost?

The ghost pondered this for a moment. I guess I don't know, she said.

When you live in a multi-racial place like Singapore, you're defined by your ethnicity, even after you're dead. I ask, What were you before you died, C, M, I, or O—Chinese, Malay, Indian, or Other?

For the life of me, I can't remember.

That's funny...life of me...anyhow, I have some leftover *kim zua* I can burn you.

Kim zua?

Joss paper food the Chinese burn during the Hungry Ghost Festival. If you manage to receive it, that could mean you're a Chinese ghost. You can follow me home if you want.

Aren't you scared? Most men I show my face to crap in their pants.

Ah, well, I do other things in mine. Follow me.

On the balcony, I took out a used Milo tin, lit up a McDnalds (correct spelling, yo!) with a single strike of the match—a veritable Mickey D's with French fries, double cheeseburger and a McNugget meal. The ghost told me she felt a hollowness in her belly that gnawed and she had a feeling it wasn't just hunger. She said she felt incredibly tired, a fatigue that ached deep in her bones. She must have been travelling for a long time. She turned up the soles of her feet and I wished I'd never asked—they were filthy and covered with pustules—they looked like the floor of a chicken coop.

She said, I think I'd like to retire from being a ghost. Either get reincarnated, or be put out of my misery with a stake in the nape of the neck.

I took a look at her neck as she parted her hair. No hole. So maybe not a *pontianak*.

I said, I've never met a ghost with amnesia before. You don't even know what race you are. That's really blur as a *sotong*.

Still hungry, she said.

I found leftover paper effigies of a half-torn sushi platter and steamboat feast and burned that.

Still hungry.

The hungry caterpillar can't hold a candle to you, but I've got nothing left. Come back tomorrow.

Give me some of your blood.

Straight away, balls dropped and blood curdled. I hurried over to the fridge and found my mother's Tupperware container of congealed pig's blood. Mother puts it in zhuzha tang, pig-offal soup, along with pig bones and pickled mustard. Don't ask me why there's always a container of it around, we don't eat zhuzha tang that often. I emptied the container into the Milo tin and set it on fire. Hey, I said, you have a name you can remember?

No reply. Ghost happy, ghost gone. But stinky smell.

Just in case she shows up again, I do some grocery shopping. The *kim zua* shop is also in the same HDB block as the laundromat, and the auntie there likes to sit behind the counter fanning herself while watching Korean dramas on a TV screen screwed to the wall above. It gives me the creeps, looking at all these things for the dead, but I guess the Chinese dead are also particularly enamoured of progress, because there's an iPad, the latest iPhone and Samsung Galaxy, even a Google Glass. Not to mention a red Ducati and, fuck me, a Joe Rocket leather motorcycle jacket to go with.

The auntie looks at me askance as I pile my shopping on top of the counter. Did someone die in your family? she asks. Your grandmother kicked the bucket?

Nobody died, I say in a low voice. I just like this stuff.

The auntie's eyes bug out, which she tries to hide by bagging everything double quick. I know she thinks my family is weird. My mother collects kitschy Chinese icons—pink-faced Laughing Buddha figurines now adorn every available surface. My sister Bee Lian is in her Goth phase and often dresses all in black, with heavy mascara and purplish-black lipstick, when she goes out. My other sister, Bee Khing, sleepwalks and has, more than once, scared the urine out of our neighbours by showing up in her long white nightdress at the void deck very early in the morning while old men are doing tai chi. The boys in our family, with me the exception, are totally normal, though. Both my brothers are gregarious and well turned out—both work as salesmen, one sells mattresses and the other sells portable toilets. My siblings can't stand to have me around, on account of I see dead people, but nowadays I keep mum even if I do see one. Mother, despite her lazy eye, used to bring out her feather duster—this thing with cockerel feathers on one end and a long, hard rattan handle on the other—and use it on me, not on the ghost. For a long time, I was prohibited from going to funerals, just in case I attracted more ghouls than need attend.

I don't know why I attract ghosts. I'm not particularly bright or angry or resilient or tough. I'm not anything. Other than the fact that I see ghosts, I don't stand out in anything. I come last in the one hundred-metre dash; I long jump like a cricket, while my best friend Hamid long jumps like a puma; I don't even have a particularly large appetite, unlike all my friends who are still having frightening growth spurts—Chee Kin's chest size has ballooned out into a Dwayne 'The Rock' Johnson, and he weight lifts in the sixty-nine kilo category. Meanwhile, this weird libido I'm struggling with—I'm terrified I'll get found out and be humiliated.

Later that afternoon, ghost shows up more ravenous than ever and almost makes me drop my bubble tea with her 'boo'.

Look what I got you. I show her the ten-course variety meal I bought that any Chinese banquet would be proud of: paper abalone and a medley six-pack of Heineken, Corona, Guinness.

Bee Lian pokes her head round the door, her eyes narrowed with suspicion. *Si lang gui,* who are you talking to?

Nobody, I say, trying to look guileless. It's kinda funny my sister has just uttered the swear words 'dead people ghost' in Hokkien which literally describes the situation in the room.

The ghost breathes near my ear, tickling my earlobe. I swat and Bee Lian yells, Mother! Seng Huat is at it again. I can hear Mother yelling from the kitchen. You best not let me catch you with a ghost, HUAT! or I surely throttle you.

I glance at the ghost's long, thin neck, a referencing gesture. I say, If you don't have a name, how about 'boo'? It seems apt.

Boo shrugs. Call me anything you want. Even I don't know what I am. I was at the cemetery this morning, the Muslim cemetery in Kubor Road (I give an involuntary shiver—its translation is Graves Road, JC!) just to see if I got some sort of pang or quickening, and nothing. Zilch. Nada. It's really very depressing. I can materialise before you, but with others, they can't even see me. I'm totally invisible to them. It feels like shit to be ignored like that. I got on to the No.16 bus heading for Bukit Merah and danced the Soulja Boy, and nobody clapped. *Benci lah.*

Is that a swear word in Malay? And *Muslim cemetery*? Scratching my head, I say, You don't seem like a *pontianak* to me; I've never met a *pontianak* who can dance the Soulja Boy, not that I even know what that is, and besides, there's no sound of baby cries or fragrant scent. You have a thin neck, but not a distended belly, and the lip piercings are total red herrings.

Huat! Mother is yelling again, Are you talking to the ghost? I told you not to talk to the ghost.

But a *pontianak* has more currency somehow, I say. You can be a marker of Singaporean diversity. But Mother shows up in my room with a flyswatter. You best skedaddle, I shout as I get up in a rush, darting out of the room, trying to avoid Mother's amblyopic aim, but she still manages to clip me on the shoulder.

I rub my elbow and shin, where I have a few bruises forming. One of the disadvantages of living in a cramped HDB flat is that when your mother aims to give you a hiding, the ancestral shrine also gives you a knock on the head, the sideboard gives your hip a wallop, even the footstool joins in on giving your toes a few stubs worth all the trouble.

A few pop-up ads on my computer showing scantily-clad manga girls rattle me and I can feel the rise of that niggling urge, although knowing a vampire might show up any minute sure dampens any joy.

It's getting towards midnight, and as soon as Mother turns off the light, Boo appears. Your mother still beats you, even at your age. That's humiliating.

Okay, Boo's comment stings. Rapidly, I blink to hide my hurt. You want to eat now?

You can just give me some of your blood and I'll leave you alone.

I don't respond but head out towards the balcony.

After the ten-course meal, Boo says, What *lah,* no dessert?

I draw a Japanese mochi for her—even fill it with red bean paste—then burn it. She says it doesn't taste like mochi. It tastes like paper.

I don't draw so good, I mumble.

Does your mother hit your other siblings too?

I shake my head. I'm jinxed. I give my mother the heebie-jeebies. Even funeral directors avoid me. Mother thinks the only profession I'm suited for is a Chinese funeral priest. If so, there's no point even studying, is there?

Boo shrugs. Maybe I can help you?

And how will you help me?

In reply, she climbs on top of the bookshelf, positions herself astride Dickens and Asimov, her heels thumping the spines of *The Book of Bunny Suicides* and my two favourite manga comics—*Hayate the Combat Butler* and *Gin Tama*. She says, Why don't you ask her why she hates you?

I glare at her. She doesn't hate me, it's called tough love.

Boo rolls her neck and it actually makes a 'pop' sound. All right, man, it's your funeral.

I tell Boo how I once overheard my mother and grandmother talking about me: my grandmother thought maybe I was possessed and needed an exorcism, but Mother said, 'Born like that *lor*. The first day he came out he used to stare off into the distance even when drinking his milk. Lucky he isn't the eldest son.'

Boo doesn't say anything. I guess there's nothing much she can say. Then she pipes up, Wanna play rock paper scissors?

I have a better idea. Let's play chess.

I can't move the pieces, she says.

No problem, I can move them for you. Just tell me what to move.

She adds, Not having a body certainly has benefits, no one can give me a thumping.

I look at her. Don't know when to stop, do you?

She smiles. Just saying. When she sees me look stricken, she says, Oh lighten up, will you? She giggles. Lighten up, get it?

If the deaf and dumb tend to be clumped together, the ghostly and the astonishingly libidinous must make a right pair. I don't see Boo for weeks and just when I think she's figured a way out of her dilemma, she pops up as I'm cleaning myself with a wad of tissue.

Whatcha doing? she says, right in my ear.

I yell, practically jumping out of my skeleton, scrambling to make myself decent. Don't you knock?

She laughs knowingly. You're looking huat, Huat!

Leave me alone.

I brought some friends, she says. She puts two fingers to her mouth and wolf-whistles. Four other ghouls pop up. I'm not really able to give justice to any description of these girls—they are a potpourri of scary:

- one has a javelin or spear driven into her intestines; her chain of guts looks like a string of pork sausages, and it's dripping;
- one wears a bridal veil, but is eating a packet of Khong Guan lemon puffs;
- one is completely wrapped in a shroud, must be a Malay *pocong,* except for the Kancil car key dangling from a raffia-loop belt around her waist;
- and finally, a Chinese hopping vampire, although she's dressed in a white smock, her eyes are blood-red and her fangs are curved scimitars.

Don't tell me you all have confused identities too, I mumble.

Feed us, Boo says. It's almost 5pm and Mother is at the wet market and Grandmother is sunning herself out on the balcony. I make my killer emoji face—upbeat positivity in the face of absolute grimness. Where will I find food for a cadre of ghost women?

Feed us, or we'll have your blood, they chorus.

Alamak, I have no doubt they will.

I've had to do this on one other occasion before, steal from Mother's grocery money, which she keeps in a Jacob's cracker tin in the drawer next to the hob. Two hundred dollars rolled up in fifty dollar bills—take one hundred dollars, roll up the other two fifties multiple times to disguise number of folds, can borrow from Hamid tomorrow to cover.

The owner of the *kim zua* shop eyes me and then my pile of shopping and spits her seeds into a newspaper. Ostentatiously, she pulls out her temple charm—I suppose it is one of those that wards off evil—and places it carefully on the surface of the counter.

That's no use against five of them, you know?

She swats her hands at me. Curse her ancestors a thousand generations, this *ajumma* is meaner than a hopping ghost.

Singapore has all kinds of litter laws (hefty fines and potential time in the lockup if caught) and thus, receptacles for burning *kim zua* are provided, usually somewhere in the vicinity of the void deck, but old uncles often sit in the square scratching their balls and playing mahjong.

You will all have to come back after 10pm, I tell the girl-ghouls. They go berserk. The wailing, ululating, clap of thunder, veritable lightning light show, flying around—it is all very crouching what hidden what, and I hide underneath my bed with earphones on, terrified out of my skull. Girl ghosts, friends or foes? Mother, when she comes after me, love or hate?

I don't hear the call for dinner, buried as I am under a caterwaul of hard rock and electronica. And then I see my sister Bee Khing's face peering at me from her crouch beside the bed. You're in for it, she says solemnly. The *kim zua* auntie downstairs called Mother just now. You know Mother doesn't like you consorting with ghosts.

I roll my eyes. Dense as a cement truck, she is.

This has happened once in the past—a tanning so bad I ended up in the hospital with bruised ribs, and the doctor asked how it happened and I lied that I fell down the HDB stairs.

Bee Khing says, Come out willingly, or she will haul you downstairs.

When fear clamps down on you real hard, this is what I discover—something in you cracks wide open and you literally float out of your body, like in virtual reality, as in your body is not your body, so you can get blitzed and feel no pain. Everything is sharp and vivid and glitters, but your senses have actually shut down.

In fact, afterwards, Bee Khing replays for me how I had

refused to come out from hiding, so Mother came in, got out her feather duster, dragged me out by the curved rattan handle, and lugged me downstairs to the cement pavement in front of the block; in full view of a row of eateries, she whipped me. This will teach you to play with ghosts! And people stared while sucking on their chilli crab legs.

You good-for-nothing, you think I don't know what you do with that thing between your legs?

Something fluttered overhead, a light breeze. I felt wet all over.

Nobody will want you, she cried. Who would want you?

The quintet of ghosts, arms interlinked in a row, were swaying kumbaya underneath the drooping banyan in the square, and I fixed my gaze on them. It seemed the only thing I could do. Bee Khing said one of the customers at the eatery had intervened then and called Mother some choice Hokkien swear words.

Over the next few days, the whole thing became a scandal. There was an article on us in the *Straits Times* and Mother had to write an apology for publicly caning me. She didn't talk once about ghosts there; instead, she blamed my 'fornicating habits'. It opened up a public discourse, and one comment from another mother said: It's quite right that a dirty-minded *lan jiao* boy like that should be adequately disciplined.

I refuse to eat for a while and my weight drops down to thirty-five kilos and I have to be hospitalised and put on a drip. On the bright side, my bruises fade quicker than I expected; so do the ghosts. Or maybe they don't know where to find me, or are too *pai seh* to look me up. While in the hospital, I have a lot of time to think about the girl-ghouls' predicament. Confusion can really fuck you up, and then I have another thought: maybe those ghosts are confused because they are basically hybrid-beings, like a sphinx or Garuda or a minotaur? Or maybe

Peranakan—half Malay, half Chinese? Love, too, is a hybrid thing that contains endless possibilities of twinning with hate.

I find myself missing the ghosts, especially Boo, I was just getting to know her. We could've played Monopoly in the ward, I bet she'd pick the boot as her playing piece and she'd chuckle when I stomp her boot for her all over the board. A correlation occurs to me: when they leave me alone for a period of time, my 'fornicating habits' taper off too. Or is that due to my drastic weight loss?

When Mother comes to get me the day I'm discharged, she shoves a plastic bag containing three manga comics in my direction—I glance at the covers and realise I've already read them, but I take them anyway. Mother doesn't apologise to *me*, not that I expect her to.

As I get in the car, I notice one of Mother's new collectibles on the dashboard. Flesh-coloured this time, to join the other two kitties in black and white. Grotesquely, automatically waving their paws up and down, on account of the strong sunlight powering through the windshield. Their grins are supercilious and smarmy. I feel it then, my overwhelming sense of shame. It makes me break out in sweat, cleaving my thighs to the fake leather seat and making it squeak. I look across at Mother, wearing her polarised sun visor even in the car, to protect her 'important neurons', as she likes to say. Her Lacoste T-shirt. Her granddad shorts. It's as if I'm seeing her for the very first time. An overwhelming love for her swamps me, making it difficult for me to breathe, because I am so angry.

She feels the intensity of my stare. *Kuai simi?* What you looking at?

When I don't answer, she looks at me again, not keeping her eyes on the road. She makes a *tch* sound. You know I just want you to turn out well, Huat. Be normal.

Be normal. Two words that don't trip up the tongue; even

the rounded vowel in 'nor' is easy to trot out.

Tears spring forth automatically, hot and stinging, so I turn my head to look out my side of the car instead. Can I go to 7-Eleven to pick up a slushie? I'm so thirsty.

Mother taps her fingers on the steering wheel. You're a smart boy. If you will just try harder, you can be so much better.

Boo would be proud of me if she were here to witness what I trot out instead.

Cannot.

Cannot what? Mother asks, looking in the rear-view mirror, changing lane aggressively.

Girl ghouls might show up again and it's not my fault. But when the moment of truth arrives, why does it feel that the truth won't be enough, that it won't save me? I wish, though, that Boo could see the way Mother's mouth falls open when I say: Ma, you look ridiculous and you collect solar meows.

Confessions of an Irresolute Ethnic Writer

'He who is willing to work gives birth to his own father.'
– Kierkegaard

THE ETHNIC WRITER was a somnambulist, also a whiner. He should be writing, but spent many hours thinking about consistent narrative voice and examining every zit on his countenance, or simply gazing at his own visage in the mirror and making faces. The Yellow-Peril Face. The Fu Manchu Face. The Charlie Chan Face. The Fresh-Off-The-Boat Face. The Model-Minority Eager-Beaver Face. Which one was his True Face?

When he couldn't sleep at night, he padded around his apartment in flip-flops and ate Maltesers. He was garrulous, accustomed to pulling his lower lip in a rant of one kind or another. He was a doodler of Disney characters and Goofy was his best imitation. When he couldn't write, he blasted Bruce Springsteen very loudly and used his wireless mouse as a microphone in off-pitch karaoke renditions. His invocations for his muse were alliterative jingles: *Moose for a goose, how about it? Shitty Chinamen in cities shine your shoes.*

Garuda arrived early this morning, swooping down on to the windowsill like a dark angel, the turtle and the elephant in his talons tired of squirming, lying limpid with staring eyes. Garuda, himself a hybrid being—half man, half eagle—had been watching the Ethnic Writer. It was hard to fathom the young man. He didn't look very chewable or appetising. He ranted about political fiction and the limitations of fictional frameworks, and this made Garuda think he might taste leathery. Although the Ethnic Writer was not bad looking—full head of black hair, nice sloe eyes (the Ethnic Writer was having an internal wrangle over whether to use that description, even if in ironic jest)—Garuda suspected he might be bony and full of cartilage, given his sparrow ribcage and muscley thighs. Was the Ethnic Writer possibly a Brahman? Must not on any account eat one of those.

It felt like yesterday still to Garuda, in a timeless out-of-time kind of way—his encounter with his father, Kasyapa. Wasn't it just like fathers to be prescriptive without being helpful? Kasyapa had told him to seek out the elephant and turtle quarrelling in the lake and to go eat them on Rauhina, the Tree That Could Speak. Kasyapa hadn't provided directions or sonar navigational tips—how was he expected to locate Rauhina, this old friend of his father's? Garuda billowed out his wings and launched himself into the skies. He flew thousands of leagues. It was all very tiresome, because the skies were leaden, filled with sulphurous, dense clouds. Periodically, he flew through ionic patches and got zapped. Then, without warning, he must have flown into the eye of turbulence—he felt weightless, without any sensation of his extremities, and then that drop of vertigo, *oh what a rush,* like that infamous girl in literature with the pinafore and that rabbit tunnel! Darkness all around, with the occasional twinkle of lights in outer perimeters. Wind tore at him, lashed him and spun him about. He fell out of the sky and his bottom hit a slushy element, something moist and soft. The king of flight, what humiliation! People who own dogs should be more responsible.

Where was he? It was early in the morning. The elephant and turtle had both got bonked on their heads in that crash landing and were swooning. Then Garuda saw this blazing square of yellow light, in some kind of schmaltzy apartment complex, where the inhabitants dumped their garbage in Tesco plastic bags to be later scavenged by errant foxes and mongrel dogs. Here he'd been, until the Ethnic Writer roused from his onanistic reverie.

Upon noticing the outsized shadow grazing his wall, the Ethnic Writer emitted a yelp, then said with great tone control, 'Em...who or what are you? What are you doing on my windowsill?'

Garuda shook his blue-black wings and folded them. His claws gently pushed elephant and turtle over to one side. 'Ka,' he said.

'Ha?' the Ethnic Writer sneaked a look at his own face in the mirror, and the wide panic in his eyes made him self-conscious.

'I'm hungry and looking for something to eat,' Garuda said.

This seemed to scare the Ethnic Writer out of his wits. 'Are those an elephant and a turtle you have there?'

Garuda shook his feathers impatiently, which made a horrible rattling sound like swords. He was a God and yet, still he had to suffer an ignoramus of this particular variety.

The Ethnic Writer shook his head as if to clear it. 'All I have are Weetabix and Greek yoghurt. If you want, I can rustle up an egg. But the pan is gunked up with charred stuff and I'd rather not have to wash it.'

Garuda frowned. 'Have you a tree anywhere in the vicinity?'

The Ethnic Writer was used to non-sequiturs, being a writer. 'I have a ficus that's dying in the kitchen. Will that do?'

They repaired there, where the Ethnic Writer got out two melamine bowls and cups. 'Coffee?'

Garuda examined the ficus. It was dry and crackly, and the minute one of his claws touched a branch, it snapped off, which filled Garuda with foreboding. The Ethnic Writer poured milk on his Weetabix, shoved in a mouthful and started grinding his molars. The sounds he produced were so much like the crunching of bones that Garuda looked at him with new respect. Perhaps the Ethnic Writer was very lonely, perhaps he'd been too marginalised, or perhaps he was exercising his imaginative capabilities, because he didn't think there was anything odd about having a creature of Buddhist and Hindu mythology sitting in his kitchen, clutching an elephant and a turtle that were Lilliputian. Or perhaps he was possessed of great presence of mind by virtue of having to dance on his toes around the perimeters of exclusion/non-exclusion.

As if to demonstrate this particular virtue, the Ethnic Writer asked, conversationally, 'What brings you to town, or specifically, to my window?'

'What is this land?' said Garuda.

'Em...Fulham.'

'But you're not from here. Where are you really from?'

The Ethnic Writer became visibly agitated. 'Does it matter so much? I'm here now.'

Garuda told the Ethnic Writer about his mission to bring *soma* to liberate his mother from slavery.

'What's soma?' the Ethnic Writer asked.

Garuda was shocked. 'You don't seem to know your mythology. Are you not from the third world?'

The Ethnic Writer blanched. 'So?'

Garuda nodded sagely. 'You know Beowulf? Odin? Soma is a drink that marked the passage from nature to culture. You know it as mead.'

'Of course I know mead,' the Ethnic Writer said tersely.

Garuda explained the rivalry between his father's two wives: his beautiful mother, Vinatã, and her sister, Kadru. Kadru asked for one thousand snake sons, while his mother only wanted two. The eggs incubated for five hundred years, but when Kadru's eggs hatched first, his mother became jealous and impatient, and broke his brother Aruna's shell before it was time. Aruna had emerged only half-formed and, angry at being called prematurely to existence, he sentenced his mother to be Kadru's slave for five hundred years. Soma would set his mother free. And where was his father all this time? Off levitating in the forest.

The Ethnic Writer listened avidly, drew a breath and experienced a mini-epiphany. 'Are you my reflection in mythology? Are you, like, the embodiment of allusion and allegory?'

Garuda was puzzled by the Ethnic Writer's obsessive mulling of his writerly existence. Nevertheless, Garuda talked about his search for his father and wanting to know more than the circumstances of his birth. As he talked, Garuda felt pain and anguish and desire build within him, reaching such a high-water mark that a wracked caw broke out from his curved beak and rattled the windowpanes. This awed the Ethnic Writer, whose mocha-brown eyes became wide and round with wonder and mystery. 'I see. Love, honour, pride, pity, compassion, sacrifice.' He gave a self-deprecating laugh and flicked his boyish hair back. 'I get it, it's all about the father of literature.'

Garuda shivered. The Ethnic Writer's apartment was cold. Again, he wondered if the Ethnic Writer could possibly be a Brahman. He stretched his wings. The dark violet curtain of them rose up like a shroud.

The Ethnic Writer had a lot to say. His father had wanted him to be either lawyer, engineer or doctor. Never on any account one of these ambiguous titles with no discernible boundaries and no upward mobility. He had defied his father's wishes because he didn't believe any of those professions, so against his natural inclinations, would help him contribute anything substantial to mankind. Filled with delusions of grandeur and strangely diffident, he too was in search of *His* voice.

Garuda thought the Ethnic Writer was one very lost boy. For someone with no voice, he sure talked a lot. The muscle ticked in the Ethnic Writer's cheek, beating like an avaricious pulse. Garuda wondered if the Ethnic Writer, with his power over words and syllables, could help him steal the soma to free his mother. There was so much Garuda wanted to know. Why couldn't he eat a Brahman, his mother's edict? Why was his father so distant? But even the few times that he'd located his father deep in a mediaeval forest, Garuda had felt tongue-tied, unable to make his mouth form the words that contained the meanings of what he sought. What deep irony from he who was himself composed of syllables, the metaphor for rhythm, sound and metre.

'The power of words is in sound.' The Ethnic Writer's eyes had turned defiant. 'I used to know this.'

'I don't mean to be rude and interrupt you,' Garuda said, thinking, perhaps I won't eat you after all, 'but I really must get on. Perhaps you might like to come along? I promise I won't eat you if you help me find soma.'

The Ethnic Writer rushed to put on his Birkenstocks and retrieve his satchel with Dictaphone and notebook. How often he'd wanted to travel beyond himself, to escape the confines of his own skin. Now was his chance. He clambered up on top of Garuda's shoulders, and really, he'd never imagined that the triangular scapulas riding each side of Garuda would feel so much like camel humps.

'I might die doing this,' he screamed against the gales of wind as they coasted up and up on pockets of air currents. 'We are on an odyssey, aren't we?'

Garuda enjoyed listening to this tortured soul produce a stream of words that reflected an inner perverse logic. The Ethnic Writer was introspective in a way that Garuda felt himself to be when he was in flight.

They flew beyond the perimeters of city blocks and electrical power lines. The roads snaked and crossed in cloverleaf patterns. At some point, the landscape changed: patches of floret-like greenery were interspersed with wide, open fields and rolled hay and blue hills.

The Ethnic Writer waved his hand about as if he was riding a bronco. 'Yeeha! We're the new global nomads!'

They were now flying over golden wheat fields, dotted with farm machinery crawling slowly like individual black ants against counterpanes of yellow. On the top of a brown, low-slung hill stood a lone, tubular tree, spreading its shade along the ground with its leafy branches.

Garuda's stomach growled. 'Mind if I make a pit stop?' He swooped down low. The dip quite took the Ethnic Writer's breath away.

They landed in a field where bales of hay rolled up here and there looked like giant curlers on blond hair. A red-roofed barn tilted in the far distance. The Ethnic Writer dismounted. Garuda flew up and alighted on a branch. He was famished. The elephant and turtle cast their surrendering eyes at him, and he opened his beak, revealing a great maw of darkness, fathoms deep. But despite their sacrificial expressions, Garuda felt an instinct bubbling within him—that it was wrong to eat them now. There was a time and place. With a rumbling hiss that seemed to emanate from the acids in his stomach, Garuda sucked the air, and the worms, squirrels, bugs, beetles and other creepy-crawly inhabitants in the trunk of the tree were vacuumed up into this black cavity and extinguished.

The Ethnic Writer said, 'Holy shmoly, how'd he do that?'

Garuda was still hungry. He looked around for something else to eat. The leaves of this particular tree—an oak or something—looked dusty and twiggy, and he remembered the thousand coiling black snakes around Kadru, his mother's sister. Those coiling black snakes were his half-brothers, but damn, they looked plenty savoury. He looked down at the Ethnic Writer and was tempted. The Ethnic Writer started babbling.

Put-putting up a dusty road-track fenced on both sides with stiles was a farmer in his tractor. Garuda immediately inclined his head that way. He eyed the farmer. He eyed the tractor. The Ethnic Writer took a comb out of his satchel and began to toy with his hair like a 1970s movie star in extreme nervousness.

Garuda lifted his wings. To see him launch himself airborne was a magnificent sight—the giant brush and collaring of his wings, his arms and legs curled up underneath, the swift descent, the sudden darkening, the farmer's turned-up face frozen in fright, the fraction-of-a-second disappearance of farmer and tractor, scooped up like a ball of ice cream.

Now that Garuda was sated, they took off again, passing fields, stiles, hay bales, sheep and cows, brown-roofed barns and houses. The edges of a forest, like a child's irregular pencil markings. It could be a fairy tale. It was a long while before the Ethnic Writer could speak. He craned his head and looked down. The elephant and turtle had dozed off, as stiff as carcasses.

They crested a hill—its summit fashioned with a craggy outcrop of rock. A sun haze around it created a perturbation of the air, which they did not perceive until they'd flown straight into its maelstrom. It was like flying into the glow of a fire, one moment cold, the next piping hot. A detectable shift in the wind. Garuda's giant wings flapped once, twice, and then hovered—he'd felt a gentle sucking resistance, as if he were being palpated by a mouth and then spat out. With determination, he beat his wings, and the air-rush underneath propelled them up twisting, twisting, piercing this imperceptible membrane, and all at once, they felt that everything was different, although the scenery hadn't changed at all. Yet, the gradations of colour were more vivid somehow, the river glinting beneath the dappled leaves more scintillating, the blades of grass all various hues of green. Was this what it was like when you entered an alternate reality? the Ethnic Writer thought, life became more compelling, more digestible with every in-drawn rasp? The temperature had distinctly risen.

Far below, sitting on the riverbank, was a balding man in a dhoti. He looked like a mendicant, as perhaps he was. Garuda made a beeline for this quarry.

'Please don't eat him,' the Ethnic Writer begged. 'Are you going to eat him?'

'Why would I eat him? He's a sage, we're here to consult him.'

'Oh, good, my shivery unconscious can't handle another wanton killing.'

The mendicant looked up as they approached. His glasses and bald pate glinted in the sunlight. His cheeks were round and doughy as dumplings. The mendicant reminded Garuda of his father, and this filled him with a pang of longing. Guilt. Foreboding.

'It's a curse that such a great one as yourself should be yoked with someone so puny,' the mendicant shouted to Garuda. His voice was phlegmy, his eyes rheumy and vacant as if he were doped up.

The Ethnic Writer rolled his eyes.

'My son, I have a message for you. You have deviated from your one true path.' His milky gaze roved over both of them.

'Are you referring to me?' the Ethnic Writer shouted, but even so, his words were borne away willy-nilly by the moderately violent wind.

'All you have are words. You have not carried out one jot of your mission. You have shown neither passion nor compassion.' The mendicant picked up a branch from the ground. He swished it about, producing a *whap, whap!* as if against the hide of an imaginary buffalo. Garuda hung his head, ashamed. The Ethnic Writer felt his cheeks reddening with defensiveness.

'Waste no more time. You are to go north. Find ice. Find snow-capped mountains pockmarked with caves. That's where you can finally dispose of the elephant and turtle.'

'I need to explain to Father,' Garuda said.

The mendicant pursed his lips. 'And what good will that do?'

There was no answer for this. None that would satisfy. Garuda knew this.

'If you want to have hope of penance, read the Vedas,' the mendicant advised.

'What about me?' the Ethnic Writer said.

'What about you?'

'What's to be my fate?'

'How should I know?' The mendicant turned his head towards the wind. Tufts of hair around his ears ruffled in the breeze. His dhoti curled around his legs, sinuous.

A voice spoke up, 'Were you not born in a third-world developing country?' The voice was coming from the tree, and its hollow echo sounded as though it was issuing from deep within its trunk.

'Not that, again,' the Ethnic Writer said.

The mendicant smiled into the wind. 'Child, is the diaspora

not within you? Do you not contain multitudes? Trust in the ineffable, the invisible. The voice will find you.'

What a lot of rot, the Ethnic Writer thought. So much for Hollywood's idea of the magical, brown guru. And the guy had cribbed from Whitman.

'But whatever you do, do it also to locate compassion, heal the heartsick, provide dignity to the living. Our collective mission is to rise together. But you can't do that if you don't first—' the mendicant coughed '—love yourself.'

'Is that from a pop song?' The last word ended on a falsetto, as if the Ethnic Writer were revisiting puberty. He was beginning to feel like the faithless, ever suspicious of all forms of knowledge.

The elephant and turtle had woken up. One trumpeted meekly and the other waddled its legs. The Ethnic Writer felt sorry that they would die an ignominious death.

'Get lost.' The mendicant coughed again. 'I mean, get lost more often.'

In the north, a diffuse light was growing, and a smell of turpentine wafted from somewhere. Garuda felt the plangent call of his mother. *Garuda*. He flexed his muscles, fluffed his feathers, stiffened his spine, sniffed the air.

'What's happening?' the Ethnic Writer stood up.

'It's time to go.' Garuda bowed to the mendicant. 'No time to lose.'

The Ethnic Writer wriggled his eyebrows. He was feeling lots of abstractions at the moment. Illusion and fantasy. Image and Significance. Art and life fusing together. In Search Of.

'Coming with?' Garuda lifted an eyebrow.

The Ethnic Writer took one last look at the world he knew as he climbed on to Garuda's broad back, and wondered, life being circular and all that, if the end of something could also mean the beginning of something else, and what that could be.

For eight days and eight nights they flew north. The air progressively became colder and felt like knives. The sky turned a bruised purple. The elephant and the turtle rode on Garuda's back, and at night, the Ethnic Writer snuggled in with them for body heat. His heart surged with tremulous hope. He'd never seen anything so beautiful as the sun rising over the horizon of water and sky. The half-light cast a bluish tinge over the sea they travelled above. The sun was a bright orange fireball. The winds combed his hair and clothes back in powerful gusts. The more he looked out at the vast expanse of rippling blue, the more he couldn't fathom where the ocean ended and the sky began. Perhaps this was what the inside of an eggshell looked like, vast and limiting. Beyond it the universe was unrecognisable, unknowable. He tried to make out the inner lining of the horizon. It was a thin, concave, blue line. The sky looked peaceful, a carapace for the ravaged sea. He experienced a series of small epiphanies, like body-tremors, and ideas began to form in his head. He started scribbling, stopping occasionally to eat or to shiver when the air became so cold that the muscles in his hand seized up. And then he employed his Dictaphone, speaking far into the night in a low murmur. To Garuda, it felt like a kind of meditative chant; it almost put him to sleep. Sometimes, the Ethnic Writer would shout with joy, 'Too de loo de la. Too de loo de la!' The cold was absolutely numbing. The Ethnic Writer wrapped a few of Garuda's giant feathers, thick as fur rugs, around himself and felt as if he were being shuttled back to a time and place primordial.

On the seventh day, they sighted snow-covered mountains and glaciers. Majestic, desolate, vast landscapes, jagged peaks alternating with plains of snow, like melting curd cheese, the sound and fury, the loom of a gigantic wall of ice and then so lonely, a sole crumbling fortress in front of this sheer backdrop of ice-blue snow. The gods are worshipped here, the Ethnic

Writer thought, and he struggled to find his breath. It made him remember all sorts of things: his mother feeding him cubes of ice made with mango-scented water, his father boasting about a hybrid of mango (crossed genetically with coconut) he'd created that was the size of a bowling ball, his grandmother's coffin and how frightening she looked with cotton-swabbed eyes and sewn-shut lips, his first dragon dance, his first kung-fu film, the first time he kissed a girl—her name was Sumathy, with a thick braid of hair swaying down her back and lips that tasted of nutmeg. His memories bore the shape of people he'd loved tinged with twilight, and although they were things that had happened, they felt mythological.

Garuda was tired. He felt it now—the mission felt like pressure on his bladder and it was mounting the closer he flew to soma. His back was heavy with its burdens, his heart pounding with his exertions, but there was no turning back. He glided, soared, flapped, dipped, swerved, emptied his bladder. The air currents buoyed him. In the distance, a pair of black-necked cranes climbed the skies. They were the only other creatures close enough to observe them.

Then, in front of them, the pyramidal shadow of a mountain that rose into the heavens, wreathed in fog and clouds. Without a word, Garuda flew straight towards it. Soma. The Ethnic Writer witnessed but had no words.

They heard it before they saw it, the zinging and whistling of a hail of arrows flying past their heads followed by fireballs that left jet-trails of vapour and gas in their wake. Garuda's beak opened. They turned their heads back to look. It would have been better if they hadn't. What they saw coming at them now at great velocities was an avalanche of hurtling, dizzying meteors, fireballs, a celestial rain of cosmic debris radiating from somewhere to the east of them.

They were in the thick of it, and darkness fell even as the

mass and density of objects were backlit by crimson, silhouettes moving, swirling, spinning. All around them was falling ash. It had suddenly become very hot. Garuda let out shrill cries. The Ethnic Writer hunkered down in terror. The air was thick with the smells of gas and heat and dust. Dante's inferno, and the Ethnic Writer was experiencing it in the prickling of his skin and the pressing down of sulphurous heat. Elephant trumpeted and the strength of his blows spiralled some of these meteors from their parabolic trajectories. Turtle's head disappeared entirely.

Without warning, Garuda started to fly in haphazard directions, and sometimes he tilted so dangerously to one side that the Ethnic Writer, the elephant and the turtle swung by their knuckles in hair-raising ways.

'A present from the gods!' Garuda screeched. 'This is the work of Indra. He's trying to stop us. We must be very near the soma.'

'You failed to mention that we would risk getting incinerated,' the Ethnic Writer whined.

A juddering shook Garuda's body and rattled the teeth of the Ethnic Writer.

'I've been hit!' Garuda said.

The air around them suddenly lit up as if a thousand klieg lights in a stadium had been turned on—and the Ethnic Writer saw tiny figures sitting on top of some of the shooting asteroids, cheering, raising their fists and shaking them.

'Indra's thunder bolt!' Garuda veered swiftly to the right. A hail of arrows followed their flight.

'Those the bad guys, I take it?' the Ethnic Writer pointed at the tiny figures.

'They are the guardians of soma.'

'Aha.'

Garuda plunged and rose, dipped and listed, trying to outdistance the rain of arrows. Where the arrows hit him, feathers were loosened in tufts, floating like dirigibles in the dense air. Of Indra, the Ethnic Writer saw only his shadow looming in the far horizon—his triangular headdress, the lean youthful body, the loincloth and thin legs, mounted on top of an elephant.

They were approaching the Mistral Mountain. Garuda began to flap his wings energetically, rapidly, and the air around them moved in concentric circles. The Ethnic Writer had never seen anything like it. Invisible molecules of air began to resemble translucent rings of waves, cresting outward, spreading, lace-like eddies of air and dust beginning to spin and project, turning, twisting like water going down a sinkhole. Garuda had created a mighty whirlwind of dust, and the air around them was writhing and spiralling, and they were buffeted and churned along with it. Every creature and thing was caught up in this mighty tornado, hurled with centrifugal force, whirling round and round, faster and faster.

The Ethnic Writer felt them dropping. His stomach rose into his throat, the feeling of rappelling down as his body lifted out of its frame. Garuda swayed and canted. They dropped out of the tornado, hurtling towards a giant cantilevered wheel with metal spokes joined in the centre. The metal spokes elongated and retracted. The ends of the spokes were sharp spears. Through the moving spokes, the Ethnic Writer glimpsed two golden cups, top up-ended on bottom, and the rims were jagged. The cups too were shifting up and down, the teeth of the top fitting into the cog-like rim of the bottom with exact precision.

'Holy Mother of God, is that where we're going?' He could see a distant magical glow through the open cracks of the rims as the cups moved apart, which only became stronger the closer they were.

Garuda breathed in deep and lengthened the span of his wings. It was now or never. He had a split second to insert his beak between the metal spokes and the cracks of the cups and steal the glow within. If the spokes or the cups closed over his beak as he was doing so, he and his companions would all be disintegrated into a million smithereens. Sayonara, immortality!

The Ethnic Writer clapped both hands over his eyes, peering through his fingers. At that instant, the elephant and turtle catapulted forward and were swallowed up in Garuda's huge maw, vanishing as if they'd never been. This was Death—you often didn't see it coming. The Ethnic Writer's heart jolted in shock. They had meant something to each other, all of them. He swallowed, wondering what his fate would be.

Garuda's wings were perfectly still. They hovered so close that the Ethnic Writer could see that the walls of the cups were uneven, caulked like plaster. A split second later, and the teeth were upon them, and Garuda's head disappeared from view. The Ethnic Writer looked up—he was dangling right in the centre of this metallic jaw—above, he saw fangs gleaming like blades of a guillotine swinging down, and he felt his heart leap out of its metaphoric cage. Oh, indelible image seared into my brain. Oh death, here it comes. And then, the Ethnic Writer felt their retreat. He opened his eyes. Garuda had done it—his beak was entirely haloed in a luminous glow, as yellow as egg yolk, as phosphorescent as moon jellyfish.

'Yahoo!' the Ethnic Writer couldn't resist. He shrieked with pent-up testosterone and emotion. They were already gliding swiftly away. He turned back towards the wheel and the cups for one last look, and there, arrayed in front of the wheel, were dozens of little figures with ornate headdresses and bracelets around their arms and legs, clad only in loincloths. The gods of soma were watching them depart with their stolen booty, solemn and still. It had been written that this day would come to pass. Many things had been pre-ordained, but some weren't. The Ethnic Writer suddenly understood equivalences.

They flew night and day, over lands, mountains, sea, heading for Garuda's mother. These were mythical lands, ancestral places, and the Ethnic Writer thought he saw similarities with the earth he knew—the taiga, the tundra and the steppes. They evoked feelings of longing and homesickness and nostalgia (even though he'd never seen these places on earth with his own eyes).

They heard music, a lone flute. Playful then sad, haunting then not, lilting then erratic. A ballad of antonyms calling Garuda by his essence. Garuda lifted his beak. His eyes closed for a second. He too remembered his mother telling stories, stroking his hair, grooming his feathers. Stories about her evil twin Kadru. Stories about mortals.

A large cloud drifting by cast a sullen shadow over them. They both glanced up. It was Indra with his thunderbolt, hovering in the airspace on the back of an elephant, looking contrite and accommodating.

'Well, hello. Fancy catching up with you like this.'

Garuda frowned. With the soma transferred to his beak, he really wasn't equipped to speak. Looking at the Ethnic Writer, he gestured towards Indra with his beak.

'Me?' the Ethnic Writer stammered. 'Ehm...what do you...' He cleared his throat for a more authoritative voice. 'What do you want?'

Indra flashed them a toothy grin. 'There's really no point in us being enemies. You have soma. Which is fine. Really. I thought I should tell you, though, that you mustn't let the snakes have it.'

The Ethnic Writer looked at Garuda. Garuda flapped one wing, thinking quickly. He gestured at the Ethnic Writer's notepad and wrote down: *Tell him it's to ransom my mother.*

'It's to ransom his mother.' The Ethnic Writer snuck one hand under his armpit for comfort.

'I understand that,' Indra said, with some impatience. 'All he has to do is deliver the soma to the snakes. They don't have to possess it, know what I mean?'

They didn't really know what that meant. Garuda felt a trick in the offing. He felt the shifting of fates. Indra was king of the gods after all. Kings often knew what they were talking about. Or did they?

'Let's strike a deal,' Indra said. 'What say I give you something as consideration? What do you want?'

Garuda was always hungry. He was also dead nervous about accidentally eating a Brahman. He thought for a bit and selected his next words carefully: *Ask him if I may eat all the snakes.*

The Ethnic Writer smiled. 'May he please eat all the snakes?'

'Sure,' Indra was equally expansive. 'Why not? All-you-can-eat buffet.'

I would also like to study the Vedas, Garuda wrote.

The Ethnic Writer parroted.

Indra's grin widened. 'Done! Now, throw it upon that dharba grass over there!'

They could see the snakes down in the mosh pit below, coil upon coil of writhing black slinkiness, constantly moving. The Ethnic Writer shuddered.

They both saw Indra fly off with this last instruction. Garuda cast out the soma from his beak. It dribbled like a basketball across the valley on to a thatch of grass. Immediately, when the soma came to rest on it, the grass turned a golden yellow. Each blade opened up to reveal a scurrying and bustling of thousands of movements—little people everywhere, Brahmans, gods, celestial beings, baubles of spirit, all inhabiting a briefly transparent realm. The Ethnic Writer blinked in incredulity.

The snakes began to writhe towards the soma as a body. The flow of black lava, cresting with different heads.

'Before you touch the soma, you have to have a purification

bath!' Garuda screeched. The snakes halted. Nothing moved. There could be heard only the rustle of the wind. Distantly, the flute or its echo, could still be heard. Just as miraculously, it worked. The course of this black wave changed. It headed towards the river. Garuda led the way, ensuring no snake slid away from the pack.

The soma was left alone on the grass. The Ethnic Writer couldn't explain why he did what he did next. It was impulse. It was courage, absorbed from Garuda. With a horrific yell, he leapt from Garuda's back. 'Keep going! I'll see you later. Enjoy your snakes!'

He saw the soma. Still resplendent. Still glowing. Then. The Giant Hand coming down from above. Swiftly descending.

'Nooooooo!' The Ethnic Writer had nothing with him to stop Indra stealing back the soma. His heart knocked crazily, his knees buckled, his eyes misted, but his hands threw up all those pages of his notepad, those pages filled with his chicken-scrawly writing, filled with ideas and nubs of ideas and line upon literal line of nonsensical sentences he'd written during their journey north. He'd thought they were finer than anything he'd ever written, and also the least meaningful of anything he'd ever written.

The Hand swept these pages aside. It curled into a Fist and came down and hammered the Ethnic Writer in one mighty blow. His breath left him and he lay there with his eyes open. He imagined he saw Garuda circling back towards him, wings extended, having consumed all the snakes. But the sky was empty, as blank and white as a baby's blanket. He hadn't done enough to warn Garuda.

He watched Indra lift the soma in his hand and ride away, triumphant.

Knowledge came to him of failure and inability. In defeat one finds *atman,* a higher deeper consciousness. The Ethnic

Writer took in a deep breath and it was painful; the sun was directly in his eyes, and his vision dimmed, trailing a dusky halo. He tried to hold his breath in, but that hurt too. Words came to him. *Datta, dayadhvam, damyata.*

Puny mortals metamorphose into pentameters. There is rhythm, and there is sound. But where is meaning? Ha ha.

Verse fragments floated past his consciousness. The Indians believe your father dies and becomes thunder. The Russians believe he takes your childhood with him. The French believe you take his place and become your own father. What father can take the place of Faulkner?

For one moment, as his lungs wheezed, he thought he was dying. But no, he'd merely been thoroughly flattened. Lost to himself, lost to the world. His eyes focused on the white sheets of paper sailing in the sky, fluttering, pages of confetti. Was someone getting married? Was there a plane in the sky? But no, it wasn't paper confetti.

Nothing mattered any more. There'd been only one word that he'd scrawled floating back in front of his dim eyes.

Light.

But did it mean the absence of darkness, or did it mean the absence of weight?

The Heartsick Diaspora

i. Production History/Characters

Our ethnic writers group that used to meet weekly at a Caffè Nero in Bayswater upgraded itself to a Le Pain Quotidien in Notting Hill. Kevan (often mispronounced as Kevin) is our de facto leader because he takes care of all email distributions with a rather dictatorial leadership style, but he has such spiky long lashes, everyone else in the group, who is female, forgives him. He's also an eccentric because he has us writing in strange places e.g. on a bus, while queuing at the post office, and once, at a chippie. To court our ethnically inclined muses, he says. To be at a crossroads, he says. Where flows and places interact. We've written while holding contorted yoga positions, or photographing bicycle racks and empty car parks with cars bisected half in, half out of the frame (hide-and-seek car, as titled). Once, at an art exhibit where the artist had an obsession for tiny animal penises as an investigation into male impotence. None of us could identify which animals were being featured—the photographs were very abstract.

There is Miranda, our 'yogi', with her intermittent mantra-chantings, her downward dogs, her occasional dabbles into tarot card readings, and her immediate jump to alertness whenever anyone mentions their remembered dreams or personal psychological revelations. She's Malaysian Chinese and she's writing a story about an old woman with urinary incontinence, but can't seem to make up her mind whether the old woman is Chinese from the old country—THE MOTHERLAND (Miranda even says this in a booming voice to emphasise)—or whether she ought to be Malaysian Chinese. Makes a difference, she says.

Well, not in Britain, it doesn't, mutters Phoebe (who is Singaporean Chinese, hence 'causeway' rivalry, like Britain and France). Phoebe is the kind of touchy-feely who touches the inside of your wrist and it feels like a poke, the outside of your elbow, and it feels like a jab. She has a four-year-old daughter, and she's writing a story about an Asian mother who raps when she's upset. Little does she know that the old woman's daughter-in-law in Miranda's story is really Phoebe, and the four-year-old girl in the story is Phoebe's precious drama queen, Priscilla (whom we secretly nickname 'Prissy', because she can't stomach a single speck of dirt on her Mary Janes). Phoebe, on a typical day as she peers into your eyes: 'May I ask how your project is going? Are you feeling momentum?' She unloads harsh critique on an ill-written story like a case of stormy weather.

Miranda, bless her heart, has devised a code word for those of us on the receiving end of one of Phoebe's blitzkriegs—MARLIN, as in Hemingway's *The Old Man and the Sea,* when the marlin is devoured by sharks and the old fisherman is sinking into depression. MARLIN is an effective intervention protocol: a hastily gathered band of us converges upon the afflicted with chicken soup, Jewish bagels, or an array of baked goods to restore his/her 'soul'. Miranda has an atavistic faith in the restorative powers of baked goods.

Finally, there's me. Chandra. I tick all the people-on-the-fringe boxes—female who dresses androgynous, ambidextrous, biracial (half Indian, half Malaysian Chinese)—everything about me is ambiguous. My writing is frequently populated by people so quirky and weird that maybe they shouldn't exist. We're all frauds of one kind or another, and our roles are affixed according to the time and place we find ourselves. Miranda and Phoebe think I vacillate between extremes of emotion and personality. Either I'm too militant—*why does everything need to be so political, your Facebook posts are so peppered with denunciations of -isms?*—or I'm too cynical. And I think they're either sickeningly adorable or annoyingly peevish. Still, as one fraud might say to another (apt considering British weather), *you've got too many layers on.*

ii. Act One, Scene One

Was it Tolstoy who said: all stories begin with someone coming to town or someone leaving town? At one of our weekly gatherings, Kevan announces we may have a new cell member. We're a MeetUp group that ended up separating out of a larger cluster, like a reproducing amoeba, unexpectedly bonding due to a readiness to slip in and out of borders. While it was never stated or agreed that we wouldn't include anyone else, we also realised we had good group dynamics, spiced up just enough by the rivalry between Phoebe and Miranda. And to be honest, I think Kevan rather enjoys his 'harem' of Asian women.

The newcomer's name is Wei. Wei looks like a Korean *hallyu* flower boy—double eyelids, long lashes, feminine lips, high cheekbones, six-foot sporting a six-pack. He slings ramen as a line cook at Wagamama and wafts the scent of pork bones and spring onions. He toddles up on a crisp spring morning, the daffodils have just come out in Hyde Park, and I fall in love. Instant, crushing, overpowering jolt of emotion, straight to the solar plexus. Such a clean shot, it actually hurts.

Wei sits down next to me and all my pores open up. Even the hairs on my arms wave their tendril heads.

By way of introduction, Kevan tells Wei that all four of us were glorious once, receiving prizes and accolades for our writing and whatnot. A logroll of our prizes and accolades would include being named Thirty Under Thirty by the prestigious LitFly (one of only two minorities on the list), winning a FOMO (Fiction of Minority Origin) Award, numerous short-listings in numerous 'lucrative' and not-so-lucrative literary prizes started by coffee shops et al., and finally, one of us won the trophy in a gameshow called *Pig in a Poke,* where no pokes were involved and no animals were harmed (that's the whatnot—deuce to Kevan).

Wei throws us all a laddish smile—a little badass, a little conspiratorial, and managing to be megawatt at the same time (how does one even do that, emotionally multitask like that?). Kevan asks us to tell Wei what we're working on. Phoebe lies through her teeth, says she's working on some story setup like David Henry Hwang's play *Yellow Face.* Pretentious git. In her story, an ABC (American-born Chinese) hires a Frenchman to pose as the executive chef of her French restaurant, because in this world of ours, Asian people can't cook French gourmet but they can sure write sci-fi. They can't re-invent American chop suey but they sure can write magical realism. Lie or not, the plot sounds impressive, if she can carry it off.

Miranda opens with an 'amituofo' (greetings from the Buddha? Strange woman!), and laughs, employing all her teeth (molars, even her dangly uvula, quivering like a tiny penis—muse put to good use). Miranda tells the story of an old woman who remembers a particular episode involving Ben Wa balls inserted into her vagina as she rides pillion on a bicycle. Wei's eyes open wide; Phoebe clamps down her teeth.

It's Kevan's turn. None of us knows what Kevan is really working on. We suspect he isn't really writing anything, hasn't been for a while. A Marlin is due. He says, the group is meant to be supportive. We pride ourselves on this. But you also have to learn to withstand pain. Occasionally, in spite of the hail of criticisms, a glimmer of admiration will seep through in someone's remarks, and that's what we live for—that despite all the flaws in our work, sometimes we manage to surprise ourselves.

Wei nods. Like Phoebe, he's also working on a story that incorporates food. His protagonist is a young man who gets haunted by a hungry ghost with a confused identity, so he has to keep feeding it joss paper products that the Chinese burn for their dead.

Oh my god, I won't be able to refrain from planting my chops where they don't belong.

Phoebe's mouth dangles half-open. Then she adjusts the perpetual sunglasses perched on top of her head and pats Wei on the arm. 'You know that Chinese people love proverbs, right? Great minds think alike. Birds of a feather flock together. Three unskilled cobblers are superior to one Zhuge Liang.'

iii. Act One, Scene Two

This particular drizzly London evening, we are at a tiny Mexican eatery in Portman Square, where the owner has a fixation on skulls—skulls adorn every conceivable surface; there is even a pot of tuberose skulls in the centre of the table. As Phoebe relates the plot of her new story, she is annoyingly pulling at and making the little skulls in the pot ping against each other. I begin to feel jealousy, sharp and acrid, worm its way through my innards. I started my story before she did, and I suspect her of 'borrowing'. Her story involves three Singaporean Chinese sisters residing in New York (mine reside in London). The sisters there have a truculent relationship, like mine. The sisters had opened a French nouveau restaurant. My sisters battle over a steamboat, droll compared to high-stylin' gourmet cuisine. It's such a cliché too—Malaysians and Singaporeans obsessed with food; it's practically our national culture to polemicise food.

Phoebe says, with triumph, that if David Henry Hwang's Yellow Face was a white 'Siberian Jew' playing the character of an Asian American, her White Face was a 'Frenchman of peasant stock' masquerading as the executive chef of a French restaurant run by Asians.

Miranda looks lost. But Wei sits up straight, as if someone has zapped him with a divining rod. Kevan does what Kevan does—this particular occasion, he is doodling, drawing spirals and faces with no discernible features but with awesomely styled hair.

Lookie the smirk on Phoebe's face as she takes in Wei's response. I interrupt her flow of verbiage, 'Can we get to what the problem is, Phoebe?'

'Well, I'm stuck.'

Miranda closes her eyes. She often does that during our discussions—for optimal osmosis.

'A New York critic comes to dine and discovers something fishy.'

'So, what's the problem?'

'I don't know what that something fishy could be.'

Wei stands up suddenly. He brings one hand curled into a fist against the upturned palm of his other hand. The gesture makes a *pock* sound. 'I know!' He paces two three steps around our sitting area, then reverses. 'French cuisine is all about the sauces. You could have your Frenchman fuck that up when being asked about how he made the sauce for the duck à l'orange, or something. How could a French gourmet chef not know something so fundamental?'

'Yes! Yes! Yes!' Phoebe bops up and down in her chair. 'That's brilliant, Wei.'

Miranda, despite eyes being closed, makes a small grimace.

'Isn't that a little gimmicky? And trite?' I say.

Wei and Phoebe look at me, and carry on brainstorming. I look at Kevan, whose spirals have now transmogrified into matchstick figures tossed orgiastically together. Not too long back, Kevan and I had a tête-à-tête—he'd said he has trouble making eye contact; he wasn't sure where this overwhelming diffidence suddenly came from, but ethnic diasporic writers sometimes have this crippling self-doubt about the lack of authenticity in their narrative voice (the 'inauthentic native', he calls it). 'If it's all a lie anyway, you might as well make it a big-ass lie.'

'Frauds should stick together,' I'd said.

Kevan smiled. We understand each other. The kind of 'understand' that ended up resulting in a regrettable one-night stand. We work hard to maintain a façade of it-never-happened.

At the end of our gathering, Wei and Phoebe have decided to work on Phoebe's story together and turn it into a theatrical farce. Not that they've ever even written a play. Or have any clue how to write one.

iv. Act One, Scene Three

It's Wei's turn. Wei says he's thinking of using the Chinese coded references 'portioned peach' or 'cut sleeve' to signal his protagonist being gay. Isn't it neat that these are literary allusions: 'Portioned peach' as a reference to Long Yang, a youth so well-loved by one of the Kings during the Chinese Warring States Period (475 to 221 BC), he shared the King's peach.

'Cut sleeve' is a reference to an Emperor of the Han dynasty who would rather scissor off his sleeve than awaken the male concubine sleeping on it.

Phoebe, Miranda and I all look at each other. An unexpected cold front and it's drizzling outside. Miranda is snuggled up in a cape shaped like an enormous sherpa blanket, while Phoebe looks chic in her Burberry trench. Kevan's sweater probably has years of breadcrumbs embedded within—a veritable garden patch.

'I think it's a problem writing about a gay protagonist if you're not gay. Isn't that appropriation?' Phoebe asks.

'More to the point, can short stories have footnotes?' Wei asks.

None of us answers. We blink.

'Well, there's this dictum that anything that takes a reader out of the story is pyrotechnics, more to showcase author than story,' Kevan weighs in.

'Just put all the footnotes in a metastory,' Miranda says, chomping on an apple. We are at Carluccio's and she brings her own fruit, not one to care about restaurant decorum.

Wei is scratching his head. 'What about slang? I'd rather not have a Singlish thesaurus along with the story.'

'Don't use Singlish,' Phoebe says. 'It's pidgin, it makes Western readers laugh at us.'

Miranda nods. 'Wikipedia says it's considered low class. A creole language. It disrespects the Speak Good English campaign the Singaporean government has promulgated.'

'Write what you want, Wei. Don't sweat it. Existential creative anxiety does not lead to the yellow-brick lane, only inertia and crippling self-doubt.'

Wei looks at me gratefully. 'Nice, who said that?'

I shrug. 'Nobody famous. Me, I said that.'

During our break, Wei joins me outside. It's still raining and the awning of the restaurant is dripping, so we huddle and our shoulders nudge each other. 'I didn't know you smoke,' I say. He pushes his hands into the front pockets of his jeans, scrunching up his shoulders. 'I don't. I just wanted to say thank you.'

'You're welcome.'

'You know, I can't make you out.' His look is contemplative.

I flick off the ash into a potted shrub. 'I'm alluring, issit?'

He laughs. 'You wanna grab a drink sometime? Not with the group, I mean…' he breaks off, suddenly embarrassed. How cute. Those innocent eyes of his, those shapely lips. Ooof.

I hear a tap on glass behind me. It's Miranda and Phoebe. Miranda is scowling, and Phoebe is gesturing for us to come back inside. So *kiasu,* afraid I will pull in front of them in this subconscious race for Wei. It's not sexual, per se, because Phoebe is married and Miranda has a bloke. We just can't help ourselves. It's *liddat lor*.

v. Act Two, Scene One

It being unseasonably warm, Kevan has suggested we camp out on the grass in Hyde Park again—enjoy the trill of birds, the gleam of sunshine, the kerfuffle of toddlers and dogs with wagging tails—and see if our muses will favour us today. Miranda has brought a large thermos of hot chocolate to share. She's done it before, and none of us thinks her hot chocolate is any good—it's thick and sludgy, but we don't have the heart to tell her. Phoebe brought a pandan cake. 'You made this?' Miranda is all ready to turn on the fake-surprise.

'No *lah,* I got it from Wardour Street.'

'No wonder, stale.' Which got a moue from Phoebe and a 'Priscilla likes it.'

Wei is late. Yesterday evening, he and I had actually made good on our drinking date and I'd met him at a bar in Ealing, where he lives. It was easy to talk to Wei. We started with our personal history, but it wasn't long before we got into what it feels like to be Malaysian or Singaporean in the UK—you're a subset (Malaysian/Singaporean) of a subset (Chinese) of a subset (Asian)—and on a fair-weather day, the English assume you're a tourist. 'I've been passing through for five years,' Wei laughed. 'In some ways, it's fair. I still don't know where Virginia Waters is, and I don't like British desserts.'

I agreed. 'Every day there are social interactions, minute as each individual episode goes, but cumulatively they begin to absorb into your tissue. Little razors handed to you every day.'

'Yeah, when they joke about the size of the Asian male penis as if you weren't sitting right there.'

'Accuse you of plagiarism for writing too well.'

'Accuse you of stealing a writing class contact sheet because the famous teacher's contact information was on it.'

'Liken your writing to Kazuo Ishiguro just because you're an ethnic person (EP) writing from the perspective of an unreliable narrator.'

'Dating a girl, and her mother keeps confusing your name with the other Asian guy she once dated, even though that other guy was Caribbean Chinese!'

'Cross the street because they'd rather not say hello.'

'The hidden transcript. We act and masquerade, and then we tell the hidden stories amongst ourselves backstage. We laugh aggressively, maniacally. Humour to fend off hurt.'

'We're the heartsick diaspora.'

Wei and I started laughing. For a moment, there was a rhythm, a beat, and that was our hidden transcript. That moment changed into something else when we were paying the bill. The bartender had drawn a little guy with a moustache on the bottom of the bill (representing himself?) and given Wei a wink. I said we should go halfsie; Wei said, the bill or the bartender; I cackled, but then noticed Wei had a little bit of beer foam at the corner of his mouth; he caught the look; the look was exchanged; he leaned over and planted a small kiss on my lips; I said, Miranda and Phoebe thought you were gay, to which he said, that's funny, I thought you were gay, and I said, nope, and he said, me neither, and that was when I reached for him, one hand behind his neck, pulling. We went back to his apartment and it became hot and heavy very fast.

'Right,' Kevan's spiky lashes half-veiled his steady gaze on me, 'shall we begin? I think it's Chandra's turn this week.'

'Skip. I haven't progressed at all with my story.'

Kevan: Why's that?

Miranda: Bit distracted, *lor*.

Phoebe: Is this an inside joke I'm not getting?

Me: I'm not distracted. I've been busy.

Miranda: Uh-huh.

Kevan, still with the veiled assessing eye, 'Okay, fine, I can go first.' His story, he begins haltingly, is a contemporary take on the ancient Buddhist-Hindu myth of Garuda. As Kevan builds up steam, he mounts a soapbox in Speaker's Corner. 'I don't understand why Garuda hasn't been made into a superhero. He's this legendary King of the Birds, and simultaneously the vehicle mount of Vishnu, the airline of Indonesia, and the emblem of Ulan Bator. And that's just off the top of my head. He's so epic he can block out the sun and his flapping can collapse heaven and hell and spin planets out of orbit. In accounts of famous reincarnations, General Yue Fei of the Song Dynasty embodied Garuda's reborn soul as he fought an enigmatic serpent. There are lots of stories that reimagine Greek or Western mythology, but why not Eastern mythology?' The ferocious glare in his eyes pans from one of us to the next. He says, 'I'm trying to achieve an effect of "incongruous parody", what anthropologist Claude Lévi-Strauss called "a Red Indian with a Parker Pen".' In his oratorical flourish, his hand grazes the plate of pandan cake, and a wodge falls over.

We scratch our heads. Kevan frequently loses us this way.

'And?' Miranda asks.

'Well, he's just swallowed a farmer and his tractor, and I'm trying to figure out what he should eat next.'

'Appetites are good,' Phoebe says. 'Appetites are page-turners.'

I'm looking at my watch, wondering whether I should give Wei a call. I'm wondering if he hasn't turned up because it might get socially awkward. He'd stopped me last night from going whole-hog, saying he wasn't ready yet. A tent had set up between our bodies, and he said he wasn't ready. 'Okay,' I'd said, 'let's go slow.'

Miranda snaps her fingers in my face. 'Kevan has been saying something to you for the past minute.'

'Did something good happen?' Kevan says. 'You're smiling like a silly goose.'

His smile, though, is neither silly nor goosey, it's ambiguous and troubling, so I push it away. 'As you all know, I've been writing this story about three Singaporean sisters whose mother visits them in London for the first time. They have reunion steamboat. The story pivots on this, except I'm having the darnedest time trying to figure out what the connection is between the mother's visit and why the reunion turns into a disaster.'

'You want to read a section of it out? Maybe we can help?' Kevan says.

I give him a piercing look. This is against his usual policy. Kevan believes that stories in the process of creation need to maintain pressure—like in a pressure cooker—if you broadcast it too soon, steam escapes, so does momentum and mystery.

'Not really,' I say. 'I think I should let it steep. Oolong makes an appearance in my story.'

Miranda takes up the baton. 'I've progressed from Ben Wa balls to being sat upon in the tube, all good here.'

Phoebe dusts her hands together. 'No oriental objects in mine, thank you very much. I don't care to exoticise my story. It's great, I listen to old-skool rap as I iron. Rap is *sick*.'

Personally, I think she sounds stoopid.

'Why rap?' Miranda says.

'Why not rap? Incongruous parody. What, you think Asian chickas can't rap?'

'What's wrong with you today? Not everything is a hidden judgment of you.'

'What's happened to your three sisters in a French restaurant story?'

Phoebe looks at me pointedly. 'Well, Wei's not here, is he? He's my partner-in-crime.'

'Ladies…' Kevan adds a cautioning tone. And then, Wei is here, arriving with panted breath, in hot leather jacket with a whole lot of suave movement. He drops down on to the picnic rug. Miranda and Phoebe begin to fuss. Hot chocolate? Pandan slice? Free foot tickle? Phoebe jokes. What a tart. I can't take my eyes off him. When he finally meets my gaze, a shiver of feeling passes between us and I have to look away, and that's when I see Kevan catching it all.

At the end of the session, Kevan asks for a word.

We stand away from the group, underneath a tree shedding blossoms. Some land in Kevan's hair.

'S'up, Kevan?' I watch the others pack up the picnic, horsing around with Wei.

'Is something going on between you and Wei?' Kevan seems careful not to betray any expression, but his shoulders look tense, and the question is loaded with the bilge of incipient animus.

'Nothing is going on,' I say, my face turning hot. 'Why do you ask?'

He paws the ground with the tip of his shoe. He shows me the angle of his chin, the characteristic hooded eyes.

'Kevan, what's this about?'

'It's nothing,' he says. 'Not important.'

'Well, I don't think it's any of your business even if there is something between me and Wei.'

A flume of heat rises in Kevan's eyes. 'How can you say that? How can you say that to me?'

Shit. Fuck. It's exactly what I don't want. This excess of feeling. We slept together months ago, once. I thought we had worked it out, clarified like oil and vinegar.

'Ugh…Kevan. No.' Stuffing my hands into my jacket, I see Wei glancing over at us. He waves, like waving a flag.

Kevan's eyes hardening, 'See? I knew it.'

'Don't do this.'

'Don't do what? What did I do?'

I walk away. But there's a boiling, a churning, inside my gut.

vi. Act Two, Scene Two

A week passes and I don't hear from Wei at all. I finally send him a text, or actually, not a text, just a photo of a poster ad for a rescreening of a movie I'd heard was wonderful—*Eat Drink Man Woman*. Emphatically no text. A text would feel like begging. He doesn't reply, and he's turned off his notification so the two little WhatsApp tickmarks don't turn green.

This week, we are meeting at a borrowed theatre stage in Chiswick. It's dark and echoey and smells like cardboard or paper products stored for a long time. Kevan hasn't shown up yet, but he and I haven't spoken since our conversation under the shedding blossoms.

Wei and Miranda and Phoebe saunter in together. There's a familiarity in their body dynamics—the laughter, Miranda holding the door open for everyone, the easy slide in through the entrance one after the other, Phoebe giving Wei her friendly elbow-dig, their trooping down the aisle of seats, commenting on the architectural features and how strange it is to be taking over a theatre. An uncomfortable feeling roosts in my sternum.

Me (while looking at Wei): Did you guys come together?

Phoebe: Yeah, there was a Spanish food festival in Pimlico, so we went. Wei and I were trying to come up with some food inspiration for our play. The last week, he's been over to my house every evening, but I have to stop serving him fried rice and teriyaki chicken.

Me: I would've liked to come but no one thought to invite me.

Miranda: Don't look at me, I wasn't invited either. I ran into them at the entrance.

Me: You guys spending so much time together, doesn't your *husband* mind?

Phoebe: I thought I mentioned, we're separated.

Miranda: Where's Kevan?

Me: Separated? Miranda, did you know about this?

Miranda: Maybe we should start without Kevan. I have to leave promptly today.

Me: Wei, did you get the text I sent you?

Wei (speaking quickly): Uhm…Phoebe and I have been working on our play. Phoebe and I concocted this entire menu centred around salt. Okay, not very French. French nouveau. The point is…

Kevan has come into the theatre silently.

Me: Miranda, how's your story going?

Wei: Did you just cut me off, Chandra?

Kevan: Let's get in a circle on the stage.

(awkward silence descends) We all take a seat in a circle, Wei to my right, Miranda to my left, Phoebe to her left, then Kevan.

Me: You know what, I'm just going to come out with it. Phoebe, I feel hijacked by this news of yours. How could you not tell us you got separated?

Phoebe: I don't see that I need to tell the group everything in my personal life.

Miranda: I bought peaches from the farmer's market for us to share. Have a look at these awesome peaches. Perfectly rounded and luscious.

Phoebe (under her breath): Not peaches, again.

Me: What I want to know is, Wei, what the story is with you?

Wei: My story? The teenage boy and the ghost are friends. The story is about friendship. I'm really tired of the conventional love story, aren't you?

Me: Don't you know the Alice Munro philosophy for a good story? The erotic moment as narrative pivot! That's what makes a good story! (far off, the sounds of Chinese cymbals—a dong dong chiang! becoming louder)

Kevan: Miranda, yes, I would like a peach. Fiction is all about being at the crossroads holding a peach.

Phoebe: Chandra just wants all the spotlight on her. As usual.

Me: You *siow cha bor* you, you're a little backstabber, you know… (a dong dong chiang, dong dong chiang, dong dong chiang dong chiang dong chiang)

Phoebe: Name-calling, slut-shaming, people-blaming/All these games we BAMEs playin'.

Miranda: Why don't we all partake of peach? Or a muffin. Would you like a chocolate-chip muffin?

Kevan: Suddenly, it occurs to me writers have this in

common: we all labour under the anxiety of influence, but the ethnic writer crumbles. He has no one to emulate, so he emulates his father.

Miranda: MARLIN! Let's call a Marlin.

Wei is not looking at me. Kevan is. Phoebe is looking at Wei. Miranda is looking at Kevan. We're all not allowed to look at the person to our right. It's a bloomin' Law School Admission Test (LSAT) question, which I once took.

So who is Wei looking at?

vii. Act Three

Today, we are meeting at Camden Lock. Three weeks since the theatre fiasco, which we don't talk about, like the passive-aggressive EPs we are. Wei has been MIA, even though Kevan keeps calling him.

Kevan makes us traipse down to view the Robbo wall (we obligingly gawk like crows with open beaks), as he waxes knowingly about the famous graffiti war between King Robbo and Banksy. Then we walk all the way back to Camden market and rock up at a rather posh eatery, where you can order hummus and falafel at a tenner a pop. Miranda brings out a Tupperware of Chinese sesame balls filled with red bean paste. 'Put that thing away!' Kevan hisses. Miranda refuses. We all sheepishly troop out again, with Phoebe mock-bowing to the contemptuous staff.

We end up settling on a small patch of grass overlooking the grim sludge of the canal, just so we can eat the sesame balls. Behind us is the wall of a local school, and we can hear the scrabblings and shouts and chatter of little voices out in the playground during break. In front of us is a houseboat, anchored by the back garden of a house, profuse with flowers and hedges. The day promises to be all lovely sunshine and crisp spring weather. Midges cloud around the water bank. Some mutual eyeballing with a couple of elderly residents out for a walk. Some shooing of pigeons attracted to our food supply.

The sesame balls are heaven. As I bite into one, the rich bean paste has a clayey sweetness that fills my mouth. Suddenly, a memory of home—sitting at a hawker's centre early in the morning with my grandmother, the ceiling fan above whirring and creating a ripple across the scrim of kopi kosong in my cup, my grandmother who is racist to my face and calls me hybrid monkey, but who loves me so unconditionally she once threw herself in front of a moving trolley full of mandarin oranges when I was six, and then joked, despite her bruises, that it was raining 'gold'. Without warning or any sense of where it came from, I had the uncomfortable feeling that my days with our group are numbered. Slippage. Slipping between borders, it's what EPs like us do.

But for the time being, there's a sense of expansive comfort. Maybe it's the sesame balls. Maybe it's the resident on the anchored houseboat opposite, come out to water her hanging plants. She sees us and waves her watering can. An incongruous couple walks past us—man in colourful Caribbean clothing with dreadlocks, woman in a generic parka dragging a little girl walking a toy dog as if it were real. What a hodgepodge people are, what willy wonkas, what bricoleur and collage we hide within ourselves, identities super-imposed upon one another like composite negatives. And we sometimes choose to surround ourselves with bars.

This would have been an epiphany of sorts if Kevan hadn't opened his mouth. 'We need to take a decision,' he says, 'no more hanky-panky within our group.'

'What do you mean, hanky-panky?' Phoebe says.

'Or sexual intrigue.' Kevan eyes me accusingly.

'Is that why Wei says he left?'

Chinese Almanac

My father lives by the Chinese Almanac (通勝)—it tells fortunes. Like when might be a good day to marry your lover or move house or landscape a garden.

Me, I have no truck with that kind of hocus-pocus. Keep it simple. Two rules: you don't turn down food; you stay the fuck out of your parents' love life. Born in the year of the horse, I'm pretty good at running.

My sister, Tina, calls to say that Mom's best friend, Mrs Poon, has died. She died last week. 'One minute she was crunching salted peanuts, next thing, her face fell smack on the mahjong table between the Five Bamboos and the South Wind. Mom wept that Mrs Poon didn't pay attention to the signs from the Almanac. She had hot ears and twitching eyelids the entire day she died. You know what they call that? Tragedy about to strike.'

I mumble, 'I thought it meant someone was cursing you behind your back.'

Tina ignores me. Reminds me to pick up the turkey from Delmonico's.

The news comes as a shock. Mrs. Poon, if I'm guessing correctly, was all of fifty-six, only two years older than Mom. She, her husband, Gerald, and two other Chinese couples formed the set our parents hung out with in Morristown, New Jersey—hitting the jai alai on Saturdays and mahjong on Sundays. Uncle Gerald was the first to 'pop off', as Tina describes it, setting off a tsunami of chain reactions, like a fifty-episode Chinese historical drama. They'd all immigrated from the Mainland at one point or another, except for Mrs Poon, who was Singaporean Chinese just like Mom. Was also the reason Mrs Poon and Mom were tight buddies, since their Chinese quotient or pedigree was more questionable than the others.

'PS,' Tina says, 'Dad's been having hot ears every night. Consulting his Almanac and keening. Last night, Mom chased him around the house wielding her vibrator yelling why they no longer have sex.'

Though I'm even less tuned in to my Chinese roots than Tina, who makes Mom look good in this respect, I know she's making this shit up. The Almanac may be useful to consult regarding where to place the *bagua* or water feature to stimulate mountains of wealth, or inauspicious days to dig a grave or fell trees, but is dead silent about when to have relations with a bereaved wife.

You know this year's turkey is going to be a boondoggle when you arrive at your home doorstep and find your mother dressed in Lycra and flirting with the UPS delivery guy. The clip on his lapel says: *Hernan*. Mom has got her hair up with a scrunchie, and she's pasted on false lashes that look like furry caterpillars. Her leotard is fuchsia pink; her thighs look like hot-water bottles.

Hernan claps me on the back. '*Hermano*. This the intern doctor from the city? Looks like you should doctor yourself, eh?' He gives my thick-cut midriff a mock punch. 'Too many kung pao chickens right here,' he sniggers.

I give Hernan my best jaundiced eye. To Mom, I say, 'I found you a ten-pounder, like you requested.' I swing the trussed-up turkey in the Delmonico bag, barely missing Hernan. Tina appears, looking like a twin upgraded 2.0 version of Mom, but in pigtails.

'Dad's in the garden shed, hiding,' she whispers.

Mom snaps her heels around, lets the screen door shut with a bang.

Dad is hunkered in the gloom next to the pitchfork still clumped with soil, cleaning his garden shears.

'爸, you ok?' I ask.

He speaks in Mandarin. 'Your mother offers the UPS bad dude Red Bull and chocolate chip cookies. The guy has a [crawdad] tattoo on his arm.'

I hope I've understood him correctly. 'UPS' and 'Red Bull' were in English; crawdad because I saw it on Hernan's arm. This is how we've always communicated—in two languages that don't have a common root, and I fill in between the brackets with my imagination for words I don't understand. We're like SpongeBob and Patrick, except I'm the version of SpongeBob who's more honest about the fact that Patrick is usually clueless as well as brainless, and I humour him. Tina likes to say, 'I've seen you both talk. You talk plenty. You argue just fine.'

'You've pulled up all the weeds but left the roots, Dad.'

'Sex, sex, sex! That woman's like a horny rabbit.' 兔子, the Chinese words for rabbit, I actually understand. A hapless uncle—or was it Uncle Gerald?—had once told me it was also slang for being gay.

I help Dad bag the mulch and weed cuttings in black trash bags. Cleaning up is what I do best with him. And it's not that we don't talk, but that we don't ever say anything important. 'You should talk to her, maybe?'

Dad blows one nostril with a fingertip, leaving a dark

smudge, so now he looks like a sad clown. 'You can't trust a woman who [beats her eggs with a rotary egg beater]. What's wrong with [a good old-fashioned fork]?' He flicks his fingers. Soil flies everywhere. 'Did you know, before your Uncle Gerald died, he asked me to find a way for him to [have virtual sex with a transsexual]?'

'Well, good for him.'

Dad frowns. 'Married for twenty-seven golden years, and he wants to have [virtual sex with a transsexual].'

'He should be so lucky.'

'What's the matter with you? I'm telling you,' Dad raises his voice, 'PEOPLE AREN'T WHAT THEY SEEM. You spend your whole life with someone—YOUR WHOLE LIFE—and lo, she wakes up one day and it's not the same person you went to bed with the night before.' He suddenly switches to English. 'Tell me, Pooch, why that happen?'

'Dad, don't call me Pooch.'

Dad's shoulders sag. He says, '叶公好龙.'

'I don't know what that means.' I've never seen him so full of non-sequiturs before.

'Lord Ye, you know? He say he love dragon, but really he fear dragon.'

So, the turkey's been stuffed with pork egg foo young, and Tina has invited a Japanese student from her church. When we sit down to dinner, Dad's the only person missing. I volunteer to get him from the shed.

Mom picks up her chopsticks, the only person I know who eats Thanksgiving turkey with two sticks. 'Tatsuro?' she lowers her voice when she addresses Tina's friend. 'You look like a dark meat kinda guy.' Tina turns the radio on.

Dad walks in the door with Mom's cocker spaniel, Popeye, who looks as though he's flung himself into a hedge, peppered as he is with grass cuttings. 'The neighbours are talking about you and that UPS bad dude with the [manboobs], Eileen.'

The grandfather clock ticks in the hallway. Popeye barks at the word UPS.

Mom clicks her chopsticks. 'You don't want to end up like Gerald, having weird libido and dying at sixty.'

Tina rolls her eyes.

Dad rubs his pate, frustrated, answering Mom in Mandarin, 'What are you doing, Eileen? That's not for common consumption. Stop [throwing tantrums] like a big baby. What will Tina's friend think?'

撒娇. Now, those are actually two characters I know. Dad used it often enough when I was growing up, when he wanted to say, 'man up'. When I looked up *sā jiāo*, the online dictionary said: *To act in a coquettish manner. Or to act like a brat.* Both translations seem to apply equally in this instance. And I don't know that Dad really cares what Tatsuro thinks of us; 'face', here, is a shaming device to regain control of a situation, and a totally inadequate one at that.

'When you die, it's finito,' Mom declares to Tatsuro. 'Death waits for no one. Or rather, it waits and pounces on you. I'm no sitting duck.'

Tatsuro spears a piece of turkey gingerly, puts it in his mouth and chews.

Then it all goes pear-shaped. Dad refuses to eat the egg foo young, and Mom refuses to serve him any turkey. Dad slaps his hands on the table, up-ending the platter of egg foo young, which slips off the table and crashes on the floor. He yells, '莫名其妙' (ridiculous) and exits stage left.

Tina starts quoting Matthew 8:14, 'When Jesus came into Peter's house, he saw Peter's mother lying in bed with a fever.' But who is Jesus here? Who is Peter? Who, in fact, is being betrayed?

Tatsuro eyeballs all of us. Popeye starts lapping up the goo on the floor. Mom begins to cry. We hear about *The Tibetan Book of the Dead* on her side-table. We hear about Hernan's 'nice manners'. 'Offers are still coming my way, you know?' Mom sobs. She wants us on her side. 'Did you know Mrs Poon died all sexed-up? Is that any way to go?'

From the door to the back yard, we hear Dad: 'So get dildo, may God will save the queen.' In English!

When I was little, Dad tried to tutor me in Mandarin. At least learn some character. He meant the letters, of course, but the Chinese often mix up their singular and plural. There's a beauty to character, can you see? He would try to teach me Chinese calligraphy—that bastion of high-class Chinese breeding, see how the word for fire (火) in Mandarin looks like a man running and waving his arms, and water (水) looks like a flowing stream? To me, they looked exactly the same, and I used to mix them up, until Dad would run his fingers through his hair till it stood on end, exasperated but trying not to yell, holding it all in. That was what I understood Chinese character building was: holding things in, damming them up. Until one day, you literally have a meltdown. In psychology, having a meltdown is an emotional eruption, when you can no longer control or hide overwhelming unpleasant feelings. It's cathartic. Therapeutic. There is no equivalent in Chinese—a nuclear reactor can have a meltdown, the financial markets can have a meltdown, but a person collapses, tumbles down, completely falls apart (崩溃). This is not good for a Chinese person.

Theirs is the kind of marriage built of sacrifice and mutual façades. It's all about appearances. What I know of the details of their history and courtship is skimpy. With the help of some relatives in Singapore, Dad had actually escaped (good at running away even then) during the Cultural Revolution, and was working at a Chinese printing press in Singapore. A mutual friend introduced my father to my mother in the late '70s at a swimming club party. Mom said she thought Dad looked like a skeleton in swim trunks, while Dad thought Mom looked as glamorous—in her one-piece, with her hair tied up in a bandana—as a Shanghai movie star. Or Sophia Loren. How those two categorical entities are conflated in Dad's mind is baffling. After marriage, they soon learned they didn't have much in common: she liked the urban night life of Geylang and Bugis, buzzing as it was then with transvestites and transsexuals, while he preferred his Chinese arts—painting *huāniǎo* (birds and flowers), calligraphy, sculpting bonsai, and meditating in temples and botanical gardens. They immigrated to America shortly afterwards. The Golden Mountain offered a better life. Tina was born in Morristown, sliding out like the force of nature—a veritable squall—she would be.

Likewise, I keep my sex life secret from my parents—this frequenting of gay bars in the Lower West Side and chasing Gatsbys everywhere—to save them 'face'. There's an exchange rate: the act of telling them is to reveal my inner shame, which bizarrely gets plastered on them, thence environmentally eroding the face they wear as ballast against the world. There's a hierarchy of sins: being gay is not as heinous as being unfilial. I can do whatever I want, so long as the world they inhabit has no idea who I am or what I do. It would 崩溃 their façade.

Dad tries to bury his sadness in garden implements. When he cries, he cries along with the snip of secateurs. He says he misses Mrs Poon's black sesame cookies. Tina asks Tatsuro if he would like to visit again. He gives an emphatic nod. We're as exciting as the circus to him. A not-banal Asian American family, come again? I go back to New York City with twitchy eyelids and a headache.

Two weeks later, Dad arrives at my apartment in Midtown Manhattan. He brings a small suitcase. 'I'm coming to stay for a while, Pooch. I can sleep on the couch.'

But of course, he doesn't sleep on the couch.

The two of us have Chinese at Fock Sem the first night, and Dad asks for extra fortune cookies, dissatisfied with each one he cracks open.

'Dad, I thought you're a Chinese Almanac kinda guy.'

He looks me dead in the eye. Says in Mandarin, 'It's good for some things, not so good for other things.' No kidding. He reads off another fortune: 'You don't have a claim to any place in this world, but each has a claim on you. Story of my life,' Dad huffs. He stares at me stealing the zodiac paper placemats from Fock Sem and zipping them up in my windbreaker. 'The dog is loyal and trustworthy, but not too smart.'

'I'm a horse, Dad. What fortune did the cookie give you?'

He shows me another one. *Meh,* the cookie says. The back of it is the character 没—*to not have/be,* although perhaps I've gotten it wrong.

'What's this say?'

Dad looks at me. 'You don't know? I must have taught you this same character a million times.'

'Don't start.'

'I don't understand why your Chinese is so horrible. We even had Gerald come tutor you in Chinese when you were little.'

The Chinese believe that all humans have a male and female side—yin and yang. This must be what facing your mortality does to you: your dad becomes yin and a nag, while your mom grows a pair and gets frisky.

For a whole week, we eat at Fock Sem every night. Dad greets my suggestion of Western food with mournful eyes. While I'm on call or doing rounds at the hospital, Dad wanders around New York City by himself. I have no idea how he fills the time. A degree in Mathematics, and he ended up working in a Chinese supermarket after immigrating here; there was never any need to venture beyond the confines of the familiar, or learn English properly. I worry about him out and about, whether a policeman on a horse will arrest him, whether he'll get mugged or pickpocketed, whether he's lonely or sitting on a park bench somewhere throwing bread crumbs at pigeons.

I come back to my apartment and find him doing the washing, stomping on his wet clothes in the bathtub the way *I Love Lucy* stomped grapes to make wine. He hangs them from the radiator, where they drip, transforming the bathroom tiles into a hazard of soapy puddles.

'Dad, there are laundry machines in the basement.'

'I tried,' he says, dejectedly. 'I couldn't figure it out, Pooch.'

'Don't call me Pooch.' I'm left with trying to figure out whether Dad just can't make out the instructions because they're in English or because he's never had to do his own laundry before. I have a party invitation coming up this weekend; it's not the kind of party my father should see me going to. I could get dressed at Matt's, but then I would have to explain why I've never mentioned him to my parents. Either way, thinking about it, getting dressed at home or getting dressed at Matt's, there's uncomfortable explaining to do.

Dad asks if I would like to have Korean instead of Chinese. His tone seems to suggest he's crazy to even think about it. 'The ladies at Seoul and Cozy in Korea Town are something. They gave me all this free food in little dishes. Free dim sum!' Too much stimulation has him as excited as a bumblebee.

I can't sleep. I watch my father watch TV in the dark without sound. I want to talk to him in our cross-intentioned languages, but I don't know how. How do I say, 'It's time for you go home' in Chinese without sounding like I'm throwing my old dad out of my apartment, like I'm that second rung on the hierarchy of sin, right beneath being traitorous to one's country—unfilial?

Tina calls. 'Dad having a good time at yours? Livin' *la vida loca*?'

'He's conquering brave new worlds.' From the corner of my eye, I can see Dad's back straighten, his face turning slightly towards me, listening.

Tina snorts. 'Mom says to tell you she does not want Dad to come home. She's happy to send over some tinned Milo and condensed milk and his Chinese horsehair brushes.' From the way she's slurring her words, I know she is massaging her face with a roller.

'Tina, you have to talk to Mom for me. Dad's a mess. He needs to be surrounded by his orchids and Venus flytraps.'

She snorts again. 'Talk to her yourself. Why am I the go-between?'

So much for Christian charity. Dad's shoulders slump.

Dad tells me the shoe-shine guy at Grand Central Terminal and him both play Chinese chess. They're like best buds now.

Sigh.

The neighbours knock on my door to ask if 'kind Dennis' wouldn't mind walking their dogs again.

The hotdog vendor on Seventh and Thirty-fourth is from Chilpancingo, and Dad knows his whole life story. It's a Marxist enclave and the guy thinks that's where terrorists are being bred, Dad declares.

He flirts with the Korean *ajumma* at the drycleaners. She calls him '*chagiya*' (sweetheart). But he's so rusty he tells her he likes her 'bobble chin'. I watch this interaction with a portion of incredulity, a portion of amusement, a portion of ineffable catch-in-my-throat.

My apartment superintendent claps me on the back and tells me my dad gives the best romantic relationship advice. 'He's better than Dear Abby!' That's my dad: all preach, no practice.

Every day is a new headline.

I cave and call my mother. She listens to me hem and haw. Then she says, 'Thirty-odd years of being married to each other, and do you know, Pooch, your dad and I have never taken a holiday together? We don't even go back to Singapore on the same flight. He always has to fly a few days later or on a different airline. Lufthansa! What kind of marriage is that?'

'Mrs Poon was Dad's friend, too.'

'So why am I doing all the grieving?'

She hangs up.

Tina likes to say that not knowing about our parents' marriage issues is a blessing in disguise. We can maintain our collective façade, play 'Happy Family'. Who knew that an abnormal sexual appetite would end up shaking things up like this, starting a reckoning of sorts?

Saturday rolls around and Tina does not answer her phone. When she finally does, she's in Poughkeepsie on a church retreat. She tells me Mom has bought herself a package tour to see the Northern Lights and ride a snowmobile in Lapland.

Alone.

'What? She hates snow.'

It feels like the beginning of the end, except that it's anti-climactic, because she's actually abandoned Popeye, stuck him in a dog kennel, which she's never done before. Popeye will end up biting some other dog and we'll get slapped with a lawsuit.

When I tell Dad, he looks at me as if I've just spoken to him in Bulgarian.

'Crazy lady, what I tell you?' Dad wants to know if I feel

like watching a movie together. A couple of movies sound interesting—Batman's playing and afterwards we can go have dobbokki together, he pronounces it 'dog-bogey'.

'Are you serious?'

Dad shrugs. 'Cannot jump on plane and bring her back. 生米煮成熟饭!'

It feels like I ought to be able to sally forth with some Chinese proverb to counter Dad's, something that would deactivate a bomb—what was that saying about not using a hatchet to remove a fly from the forehead of a loved one?

'I can't watch a movie with you. I've got plans.' Even saying this gives me anxiety.

He looks a little miffed. 'What sort of plans?'

It's impossible to answer this question.

When I come out of the shower, Dad is on the other side of my closed bedroom door. 'Listen Pooch, what about after you come back? These places open late.'

I throw open my wardrobe door, trying to think up a reply. It's then I see them: his row of Oxford shirts hanging neatly in my closet, his tasteless geometric-patterned sweaters, also hung up and drooping at the shoulders. They have this look about them: able-bodied and suggestive. I have a vision of Mom careening down a slope on skis with her scarf sailing behind her, Tina falling over in front of the tabernacle, vociferating in tongues, having a Pentecostal fit. I think about Dad and his Almanac. What does the year hold in store for dogs and horses? Does it say: a good day for encoffining, or residence relocation? Is it an auspicious day to come out to your father while he's snacking on sunflower seeds and dropping shells all over your suede couch? Would the opposite of straight love be curly or crooked? What is another slang for gay in Mandarin—brokeback shorts?

Big dramas push away small dramas, let that be a Chinese proverb.

Dad stares when I come out of my room. He stares at the eye makeup, the gold lamé shirt with front ruffle detail, the pink trousers, the long turquoise boucle overcoat I pull on. He clears his throat. 'You look like your Uncle Gerald, Pooch.'

'Gerald is not my uncle. And stop calling me Pooch.'

Dad stuffs his hands into the pockets of his gym pants. 'I remember once you came out wearing one of Tina's dresses during your Mom's Amway party. It didn't look good, I lied.'

This moment is one I've imagined umpteen times in my head, and inexplicably, the Mandarin trips out, just when I thought the correct words wouldn't come, 'Dad, I have something I need to say to you.'

His gaze darts about. Dad does not look at me. He makes an effort bending down; his nylon trousers make a rustling sound. He picks up his Chinese Almanac, which has fallen to the floor. The sum of his gestures is a nervousness; the filaments of knowledge thread through me, docking in all the places where blockage has occurred.

I won't need our cross-intentioned language for what I'm about to convey. Something tells me Dad's known about Gerald all along, that he pities Mrs Poon, and that he knows subconsciously about me, too—those words Dad supplied that I didn't understand, so scared I blocked them out with my imagination—curly love that is also a [divided peach] (分桃) about to [shorten its sleeve] (断袖).

Still, as I'm about to hoist myself up the hierarchy of sins here and watch my father's face crumple, a different expression of his slides across my frame of reference: his face composed with long-suffering patience as he watches me hold the calligraphy brush, guiding my hand with just a thumb nudge; his beaming face as he presents me with my first set of stethoscopes upon graduation, telling all and sundry about his doctor-son, even the canvas-wrapped kayak beached on Chelsea Pier (Dad, that's not a hobo!); his look of determination as we trawled multiple fabric stores in the fashion district looking for cotton sacking for an art project because I insisted my pinto bean baby had to be Chinese, and the closest we got to was ochre. That's how my father tells me he loves me, without ever using the words.

Never say anything important with words. Chinese fortune cookie.

Always believe a Chinese fortune cookie.

Florida Rednecks Love Moo Goo Gai Pan

THE SUMMER OF 1996, waitressing in Tampa, a Vietnamese boy tried to take me on a date to Busch Gardens, and a lecherous cook pinched my thighs and wanted to buy me a car.

That summer too, my father wrote, in formal stodgy Chinese, from Malaysia, that: *Crucial funds may have to be diverted* from my college education towards my mother's illness. *College may have to be aborted.* Translation: I may have to go home in dishonour, not finishing what I set out to do.

Flat out broke, I shacked up on a friend's couch while she and her boyfriend canoodled in a canvas tent in the living room, which was devoid of any other furniture. I'd walk in the door and find the tent jostling all its corners, as if it had captured two prize-pugilists. When Lu Pin and I had dinner, she'd deliberately angle her cheek so I could see the red, welting bite marks on her neck. I hope we're not making too much noise, she smirked.

I got a job passing out pizza coupons, but I couldn't hack the miles of walking in the baking Florida sun. My sneakers were too tight, a hand-me-down from a co-ed in college, and my soles burned from pounding the asphalt. The Hillsborough County neighbourhoods all looked the same to me: sprawling single-family homes camped out around circular gravelled drives overlooking a golf course.

I stole a baseball cap from a tourist vendor stand. The cap had hand-stitched oranges and the words 'Sunshine State' in bright yellow. I'd walk these neighbourhoods, soaked with sweat, and alternately chant, 'No more funds', 'No more sun' to the tune of some Beach Boys' tune stuck in my head.

Desperate, I chucked in the pizza-coupon job and got myself two waitressing jobs—weekdays at Tok-Cha's and weekends at Hunan Garden. What I loved about Tok-Cha's were the bamboo lanterns along the floor-to-ceiling windows; it was a high-class establishment, even though the clientele was plain redneck. Tok-Cha herself was Korean, though her last name was Martinez; she chain-smoked huddled on top of a stack of old *Yellow Pages* in an arched nook. The cook wore coke-bottle glasses and his back curved like an arthropod. We all ate dinner together every night. He'd look at me over the egg-drop soup, his glasses all foggy. What you like? Beef pepper sauce? General Tso's chicken? You say, I make. And Tok-Cha would smirk. Waitressing had its dishonours. Dishonour was no big deal, but sometimes it left a taste of cinders. The cook pinched my hams, like they were drumsticks, and he gritted his teeth. Kinda plump, aren't you? Under his breath, Ee...i...ya..., as if he couldn't stand it any longer. The pinches hurt.

Compared with Tok-Cha's, Hunan Garden was dim and schmaltzy. Someone had stolen a broken police siren and attached it to a hat stand next to myriad old postcards featuring Chinese scenery—Cheng Du, Guilin, Wuxi, Xinjiang. The tables were crowded together; on weekends, groups of customers had to share tables like refugees. It was run by a Mainland Chinese couple, but the lone waiter was Vietnamese. My first day there, I broke two teacups. To pay for the damage, the Chinese couple garnered my tips. As I got ready to leave that night, the Vietnamese waiter, Lonh, offered to show me how to stack dishes along my arm, like some circus act. I thought I saw pity in his eyes; it made me want to challenge him to a game of hawking lugers, just to show him a girl can do these things.

Lonh offered to drive me home at night. I told him I'd rather take the bus.

Florida rednecks were desperate for someone, anyone, to tell them what to do. Customers cracked open their fortune cookies at Tok-Cha's, desperately trying to glean personal-life directives from those slivers of papers tucked in dough. They'd show them to me: *If you don't enter a tiger's lair, you can't catch any cubs,* or *Play the lute to an ox*. They'd shake my arm, What does that mean, huh? Is that some sort of Confucian teaching?

Truth had a wildness, like a foraging animal. Tok-Cha took me aside, and I watched her over-painted red lips move. You must treat customers nice, Cake (my name is Khek Lin, damn it), you must treat them nice or they complain. Put on some makeup, your face too much like moon, Cake. When Señor Martinez called her to take her out Friday nights, I would watch Tok-Cha paint her lips, carefully outlining the contours with a pencil, filling in the fleshier folds with crimson. The Florida rednecks kept sneaking glances down my blouse. They'd whistle between their teeth, call me Girlie, crook their finger and I'd have to go pick up their leftover dishes and lean in to listen to their dirty talk and CB-radio lingo.

I wrote home: *Please do what you must to save Mother*. But the envelope wouldn't stick from too much spit.

The cook kept asking me if I liked Miatas or Hyundais. I never walked past him if I could help it.

At Hunan Garden, Lonh tried to give me take-outs every night. They were customer leftovers. Moo goo gai pan and pork egg foo young were Florida redneck favourites. I accepted them gratefully and Lonh was getting hopeful. He was so earnest that his round, dark eyes gleamed and tugged; when he proposed Busch Gardens, his lower lip trembled.

When would we have the time to go? I said. Who had time for fun, I thought, but couldn't say.

July 4th, how about July 4th?

I calculated. It was a Saturday. You sure we don't have to work?

Are we open July 4th? he shouted out to the kitchen.

No. The woman proprietress shoved her head through the swinging doors. Go have fun.

Okay, I said. Okay. Though I had misgivings.

The evening of July 3rd, after closing up at Tok-Cha's, I handed her the cash register, cleaned up the kitchen counters. The night's takings were over a thousand dollars. I looked outside; the cook was smoking with dirty fingers. Inside, Tok-Cha was busy painting her lips. It was Friday night. I looked at the drawer full of money again and my mouth went dry.

The cook came in while I was getting my bag. You need a ride? he said. I shook my head. He stood casually in the doorway. I tried to slide past. His hand shot out. Barely a second—a grope and a squeeze. But the imprint on my breast scalded me red-hot all the way home.

I cried hot salty tears of humiliation that dampened my earlobes. I cursed Florida, yelled out to no one in particular (Lu Pin and her loping boyfriend had gone away to Orlando for the long weekend) in that living room devoid of any furniture, that Florida was one gigantic spewing fraudulent fortune cookie. *Bǎi gǎn jiāo jí* (a hundred feelings are welling up inside me), I shouted. *You can go anywhere you want if you look serious and carry a clipboard. Find release from your cares, HAVE A GOOD TIME!*

I thought of Mother. What came to me, like a puff of powder from a shaken compact, was how she sang during one Chinese New Year—her hands dancing along. She'd stood by the wok in her red jacket, stewing e-fu noodles, and she had on red lipstick. All this before she got sick. And then, it was as if she materialised beside me. As if she took hold of my jaw and pulled open my mouth—there! She smiled, pleased. Your crooked teeth are all there, still the daughter I recognise. Will you give me some advice? I begged. But all she seemed to say were more fortune-cookie platitudes. *A fall into the pit, a gain in your wit. Pride is bottomless.* Later, I couldn't stand the darkness any more and went out and bought a light bulb for the lamp fixture. After I bought it, I realised I had no way of reaching up high enough to change it.

As I neared my friend's house, I saw a red Camaro parked out front. Lonh was sitting on the hood, twirling something in his hand. When he saw me, he leapt up. He held out his hand to display a red rose with petals made of some synthetic fabric, complete with fake pearlescent drops, fakery that was so genuine it hurt. I couldn't touch it. Lonh looked wounded.

I told him the living room had no light. I told him about my predicament. He had a clever idea. He got the black trashcan from around the house and dragged it in. While I held it steady, he clambered up and fixed the bulb. Voila, all of a sudden, there was light.

I couldn't help it, I was so grateful I looked deep into Lonh's eyes and allowed him to kiss me. Before we knew it, he was trying to get me into my friend's tent, which bore a fusty smell that suddenly made me retch. I told Lonh I'd see him tomorrow and we'd go to the Busch Gardens, but he left looking discontented.

The next day, Lonh showed up again in his red Camaro but I let him knock and knock. I pretended not to be home. My heart thumped with a wild banging the longer he knocked; I felt like a fraud. How could I have made him a promise if I had every intention of breaking it?

I never actually gave Busch Gardens any serious thought. The idea of walking down the Disney-esque esplanades with him—eating salted pretzels, or fine-spun cotton candy—seemed completely unreal, as if we were a movie playing in my head.

The knocking finally stopped, but I didn't go and look if he'd left. Through the closed door, he shouted, AMERICA IS FULL OF OPPORTUNITY! Why won't you let me in? Half an hour later, the knocking started again. Lonh knocked for hours that day. But I didn't let him in.

Back at work at Hunan Garden, Lonh's eyes tracked me reproachfully, but not once did he ask me, Where were you?

I told the Chinese couple I quit. They paid me, but didn't even bother to ask why. Chinese waitresses were a dime a dozen. I couldn't face Lonh. I didn't even say goodbye.

I received another letter from Father. Mother was rallying. The treatments were working. *May be you don't have to come home. If you're able to find a way to pay for the rest of what you owe the college after your scholarship, maybe you won't have to come home.*

Two days later, Tok-Cha left the cook and me alone to close up. He came up to me and said, You want to go for a drive later? See my new Miata? He pointed a finger at the parking lot where the Miata must be, but all I noticed was the dirt encrusting his fingernail, rimmed with black. I grew afraid when I saw his eyes, sneaking glances full of a furtive delight. I told him I was busy closing up and quickly counted up the night's takings. He rested his arms on the counter, very close, leaned over and his glasses slipped down his nose. We're from the same village, he said. You and I have the same Chinese surname, we're relatives, Khek Lin.

The only person able to pronounce my name properly in this damn country and his shirt was ecru and streaked with oil stains from the wok. He reeked of stale pan-fries and something else, sweaty and heavy.

So what? I said.

Don't you trust me? I'm a generous man, willing to help someone from my own village. If you like my Miata, I'll buy you one. But first, you have to come for a drive with me.

If you touch me again, I'm going to call the police, I said.

He laughed. He wasn't afraid of the police.

I have a boyfriend. He'll beat you up if I tell him to. It took a lot of mental steadying for me to say it in one breath—I pictured Lonh sitting on his red Camaro to calm myself—then looked the cook in the eye, and made every word count.

He backed off. Walked out the door without saying anything else, his shirttails flapping. I breathed deeply for the respite and found myself staring at the pile of cash in the register. I could easily skim off five hundred dollars, no way for Tok-Cha to find me, not knowing where I was shacked up. The greasy greenbacks seemed to be floating on the tabletop, the face of George Washington fading into a patchwork pattern.

I peeled off two twenty-dollar bills, stuffed them in my bra. I also threw one of the customer receipts into the trash can. All night, I dreamt of sirens and the police coming. They would arrive at the doorstep of my roommate's house and refuse to come in because the light wasn't working. The next day, I replaced the money in the roll of bills. Tok-Cha asked why the intake exceeded the customer receipts. With a start, I realised she was none too bright. Why did I ever listen to any of her insipid advice about men?

That night, I took pencil to pad. Like soldiers, each thing I wrote paraded past, marching, triumphant. Like a horde of multitudes.

Bǎi gǎn jiāo jí, I wrote until dawn arrived, pink-hued and dewy, and I took the pieces of paper with my writing on and stuffed them in my bra where they scratched me for two days. Then I burned them in the backyard of Tok-Cha's restaurant. The only person who witnessed this was the cook. He didn't say a word, but watched me behind lenses flickering with the reflection of my burning words. Only when the lit pieces of paper singed my fingers did I finally let go.

One week later, at Tok-Cha's, Lonh showed up. He sat at a table, making me wait on him. All he ordered was a Chinese ice tea. I fumed, setting it down with a heavy thud. He twiddled the fake rose in the vase, he fingered its pearlescent drops.

What is it you want? I said.

Why didn't you tell me you quit?

I don't owe you anything.

Lonh looked at his ice tea as if he were about to cry. Can you bring me a menu?

Please go. Please. Get out.

Civility, I'd like to order some civility, he said.

Tok-Cha jerked her head out from her alcove. The cook was rolling chicken in breadcrumbs. I covered my eyes with both my hands. Nothing like that on the menu, I said. Moo goo gai pan. Try some moo goo gai pan. Try some America.

I never saw Lonh again. He threw a ten-dollar tip on the table, three times the price of his ice tea.

I looked at the money. Honour, shame, compassion, sacrifice. People lost little pieces of themselves all the time in America. No fortune cookie to spell that out.

I looked at the ten-dollar bill for a long time.

Then, I pocketed it.

Friends of the Kookaburra

'It's Irene Fenner. I'm in London!' The familiar voice on the other end of the line throws Sansan into a state of disorientation. The pencil she's been holding to mark up the underwriting agreement makes a squiggly line on the page. Through the floor-length, plate-glass window of her Canary Wharf office, Sansan sees two sodden crisp packets, bereft of their contents, float on the breeze. She can even identify the brand of one of them: Wotsits.

Irene Fenner's image toggles into mind—the last vision Sansan has of her is graduation at their prestigious elite New England liberal arts college. 1998. Irene, dressed in a skin-tight, fuchsia, leopard-print dress, a big pink bow-ribbon acting as hairband. Was she trying to look like Britney Spears or Madonna? Sansan had wondered. Probably Madonna, what with her toting her African boyfriend on her arm like that, like some kind of dark prize. How the parents had stared and tsked. Irene even made a V with two fingers, put it to her lips, and poked her tongue through. A gust of wind lifted a male parent's hat off and revealed a balding pate even more obscene than Irene's irreverent gesture. Kwame, his name was, the African boyfriend. How his eyes had glowed with spiteful glee, as if he were taking the piss. Which he probably was. It was a prestigious elite New England liberal arts college; even the rows of chairs set before the stage were white. Irene's offside joke: he Tarzan, she Jane. And Sansan had caught Kwame's smirk. Kwame had given her a wink also, which Irene didn't see.

'Wow. How did you find me?' Sansan says. Twelve years since graduation from a prestigious elite New England liberal arts college and not a single correspondence between them. Now, Irene has somehow tracked her down through the alumni network in London. Quite simply, ghastly. As Sansan has learned to say, mimicking the Brits in a faux British accent.

'I have my ways. Heard you got divorced?'

Sansan recoils. Trust Irene with her bullseye style. At least that hasn't changed.

'What brings you to London?'

'I'm here for a pharmaceutical conference. Was hoping to catch up with you after all these years. Maybe we could meet for lunch somewhere and you can tell me all about life after divorce.'

'Darling, I'm over that. There's nothing to update.' She hopes she doesn't sound defensive.

'Back in the saddle then?' A hint of amusement in Irene's voice. Or is it a sneer?

'Depends what you mean by saddle,' Sansan laughs, uneasy. The alumni gossip-mill has its uses—Sansan has heard that Irene was 'left at the altar'. A guy she'd been engaged to for a few years skipped out on her days before the wedding. Apparently real life can be a TV sitcom too.

'Oh, come on. If you are, you are. No shame in hungering for a man. So, would you like to get together for dinner or something?'

Sansan bristles at the word 'hungering'. Impertinent trollop! Her gaze lands on a photo of herself and her ex-husband, Dewar. Out on a sailboat off Nantucket, although it's obvious in the photo they are both seriously out of their element. Dewar looks as if he's quite literally clinging to the mast or rigging, whatever those parts of boats are called, trying not to be blown away by stiff winds. Sansan grits her teeth; her face has a frozen macaque-being-menaced quality to it.

Irene chatters in her ear about what she's already experienced in two days in London. It occurs then to Sansan that she holds many past remnants of her life close, even though she has no use for them.

'Yes, that sounds splendid,' Sansan says. 'Let's meet up.'

At the prestigious elite New England liberal arts college, Sansan and Irene were—what did they call it?—thick as thieves: in freshman year, Irene recorded Sansan's lectures for her if she missed classes, and vice versa. They worked in soup kitchens together, fed Cambodian refugees, taught brown-eyed children English as a foreign language. Even their menstruation cycles synchronised. The nights spent camping out in Sansan's bedroom cramming for exams. They were both Economics majors, but loved English literature and hated American Politics. That winter, Irene auditioned for the role of Kate in *Taming of the Shrew*—Irene declaiming in front of the mirrors in the women's toilets, *Fie, fie! unknit that threat'ning unkind brow,* and then letting out a loud, wet parp. How they both had rolled about laughing, fit to burst. Other memories now intervene: during her sophomore year, when Sansan desperately needed money, Irene put in a call to her father's law office in Arlington, Virginia. Got her a job as an intern. Irene buying Sansan a winter puffer jacket (from Bloomingdales!), offering her hand-me-downs: denim shirts and sweaters with pictures of globular fruits stitched in sequins. The *essence* of Irene, Sansan had thought then, was a capacity for great kindness.

Chemistry lab partners together. Chickening out of dissecting female guinea pigs in an exercise to examine their reproductive systems by carving up raw chicken liver to look like ovaries. Eating dinner together six days out of seven, at the one dining hall that actually served brown rice and allowed you to steam the salad bar broccoli with soya sauce in the microwave. These are great memories. Sansan was so proud then that an American girl was her best friend. Sophomore year, they saw each other almost every day, and when they didn't, they talked on the phone. Endless three or four-hour conversations when Sansan told Irene all about her childhood growing up in a city that belched cement smoke in Malaysia. With Irene, Sansan's ethnicity ceased to matter; Irene embraced culture as if it were Gaia. Spending Thanksgiving and Christmas with Irene's family in Virginia. Also the first time Sansan saw a turkey the size of a small pig, with an abdominal cavity big enough to fit several hundred Oscar Mayer hotdogs. Even today, Sansan believes this is infinitely better as stuffing material than sage and pignoli and breadcrumbs and whatnot.

Junior year, Irene began to hang out with another Caucasian girl, Sandra, who'd renamed herself Xanadu. Xanadu: a roisterous rabble-rouser and party type; loose, long black hair; wore caftans made from vibrant African fabrics; a nasally voice that grew throaty when she talked to boys; eyes that sized you up quick and dirty. In Xanadu's footsteps, Irene too became popular. Both of them running their smart mouths off, sharing spliffs while doing ballet splits. Irene's wild talk, throwing around buzzwords like 'sectarian politics', 'cultural hegemony', 'power dialectic' and 'post-modern veneer'. When Irene introduced Sansan to Xanadu, Xanadu's scornful eyes limned Sansan's visage, then cut away. Sansan, with her thick unruly braid, her fruit sweaters, her coverall jeans, probably looked like top-drawer peasant stock, too 'authentically native' even for those in search of authentic natives.

One day, Irene upped and moved to Xanadu's dorm without telling Sansan. Sansan discovered it only when she knocked on Irene's door and found a new tenant there, who threw Sansan a smile that glinted with braces and glasses. But devastated as she was, Sansan couldn't bring herself to ask why. Why shouldn't Irene move whenever she pleased? Was the intimacy Sansan felt a 'white gape of her mind', not as reciprocated as she thought? How had her feelings become so disproportionate to Irene's small act of peevishness?

The enormity of her hurt. It'd taken months to heal, for the closeness to fizzle out. Several soft toys destroyed. Sansan marvels at the grubbiness of her own feelings. How immature. Was it an adolescent crush she had because Irene was her first white friend? Oh, god, those pangs of hurt at the salad bar remembering the broccoli. Having her period, gazing mournfully at her sanitary pad, wondering if Irene was having hers. At graduation, Sansan tried to escape when Irene asked for a picture together—one of all three of them—Sansan, Irene and Kwame—arms interlinked like sausages.

In her senior year at said prestigious elite New England liberal arts college, Sansan's mind exploded. She became one of the editors for *Madness This*. Experimented with political poetry. Wrote prose full of raging reality jabs, not unlike the gritty lyrics of Public Enemy, and her subjects ranged from academic arguments about racism to the misogyny of frat culture. Quoted at will Paul Gilroy or Cornel West. Read Gertrude Stein and Hélène Cixous and Roland Barthes. Took to heart the transgressive art of Cindy Sherman and Barbara Kruger. She published a long poem (which read more like a diatribe, except for clever spacing) about what it felt like to be Asian American, although she wasn't American, and suddenly lots of Caucasian boys called her and asked for dates. And she did go out with one. His name was Jeff. Apparently, at this prestigious elite New England liberal arts college, male students liked poetry that had Asian women talking about sucking dick, but with riotous anger. Overnight, her appearance changed too. From money earned at her part-time jobs at the library and cafeteria, she got herself a sharp, spiky cut, an old leather jacket and tie-dyed T-shirts, learned to smoke cigarettes and hung out with cool trans people.

Just before graduation, she received a book in her mailbox. It was Chinua Achebe's *Things Fall Apart*, and in the inner leaf, Kwame had inscribed: *Surely some revelation is at hand; Surely the Second Coming is at hand. Now I know that twenty centuries of stony sleep were vexed to nightmare by a rocking cradle.* Still one of the most beautiful things Sansan had read.

She'd run into Kwame the same evening she received the gift, at the Campus Centre. He was checking out pool cues and a rack of balls from the receptionist. They ended up in the café, talking long into the night—the kind of deep, intense, philosophical combative discussion salted with sexual undertones that landed them smushed together behind the campus bicycle rack, underneath the overhang of a building, teeth gnashing and crunching against lips. Kwame wanted to go to Sansan's room, and Sansan desperately wanted that too, but some raft of honour intervened, *she couldn't betray Irene even if Irene betrayed her,* and she eventually fobbed him off. She remembered so clearly walking back to her dorm, slammed by the thought that she'd assumed the words in the flyleaf of the book were Kwame's when, in fact, he confessed that they belonged to W. B. Yeats. How dishonourable, Sansan thought, how dishonourable not to give credit where credit was due, to pretend he was the genius behind the words. Kwame and Irene were a perfect match for each other.

Ipanema, where Sansan agrees to meet Irene, is a trendy, Cuban-Chinese restaurant just opposite Covent Garden station. Even the food has trendy names, like Moo Chow 'That Other White Meat', or Wonton Snappers with Black-eyed Peas Arroz. Sansan arrives early and seats herself at the bar looking out, half to people watch and half to spot Irene before Irene spots her.

Before long, Irene emerges, swinging her handbag by its strap. My god, Irene has let herself go. She's put on weight. The fiery-red trouser suit she's wearing can't quite disguise the roll of her midriff. Sporting a wavy-layered haircut that makes her look middle-aged, and so vastly different from the hip, Cleopatra kohl-eyed look in college. As she approaches the window, she sees Sansan and waves. A sharp feeling inexplicably invades; a feeling akin to hurt, and Sansan is surprised at herself.

'Hey, you.' Irene gives a big hearty smile. Throws out her arms.

'Wow, here you are.' Sansan embraces Irene, gives her a double air-kiss.

'You look great. Nice pashmina.' Irene's chin points to the pale pink shawl around Sansan's shoulders. Her eyes travel to the chandelier earrings that swing slightly when Sansan shakes her head. 'Gorgeous earrings,' Irene says. 'You're looking a tad pasty, but a week in Marbella will fix your tan.' She laughs at her own joke. 'Let's sit down and eat. I'm ravenous.'

Sansan bites her lip. Pasty? How dare she assume such intimacy?

As Irene studies the cocktail menu, her own eyes discretely roam Irene's face, noting the fleshier areas, the heavy layer of foundation Irene is using, her thickly bunched lashes clumped with mascara. Despite the make-up camouflage, Sansan notices some puce-coloured marks along Irene's jawline. These are new.

Irene orders a pisco sour. Sansan sticks to prosecco, her drink of choice.

'What do you do with your free time?' Irene's eyes dart about the restaurant as if she is looking for someone.

'I don't have much of it, truth be told. I've taken up cooking lessons. And I have an aunt here, who lives close to Wembley.' At Irene's puzzled look, Sansan explains, 'Wembley is Little India.'

'That's wonderful. And what do you do to meet men?'

Sansan laughs uncomfortably. She doesn't. Other than corporate functions, where she meets the occasional back-office type slogging away in a financial house, or the young Asian men her aunt foists on her through her network of agony aunts (mostly Indian, as if having married one once predisposed her always to like only Indians), Sansan doesn't meet anybody. Time is cantering sideways away from her. Occasionally, she might strike up a conversation with fellow travellers on the tube or bus, but these are awkward and never really amount to anything. Although that was how she'd met Stephen. Nothing is ever going to happen between them, but they've become friends in a desperate, clinging way—stridently attending exhibitions and theatre and art galas and comedy stand-ups, and debating them with each other like pseudo-intellectuals. Recently, Sansan has found herself wondering if she could, in fact, date Stephen, but it has the aftertaste of a cop-out.

'New York is a bizarre wasteland where men are concerned,' Irene declares.

'Oh?'

'A toxic cesspool, incestuous barbecue pit, Dante's Second Circle.'

'Surely you exaggerate.'

'Every guy out there is unavailable in some way: gay, married, psycho, asshole, molester, dweeb. Sometimes, they come in these complicated combos where you can't even suss out which aspect bothers you more.'

Sansan's eyelid twitches.

'Yeah, it's totally bleak. I should move to London.'

Sansan hesitates. 'Oh, you wouldn't like it here. It's even bleaker here, that whole stiff-upper-lip sort of thing. You'd have to practically stalk a British man before he'd go out with you.'

Irene pauses, weighing Sansan's words for truth. 'So, do you have a boyfriend here?'

Sansan has no idea what possesses her to lie, but it trips out with the smoothness of lichen. 'Yes. His name is Stephen.'

'*Alamak*! I want to meet him.'

Irene's exclamation of surprise is a throwback to college days, when Sansan, fresh from Malaysia, used to '*alamak*' anything she'd heard or seen that made her gurgle with delight. Irene would mimic Sansan for laughs. Irene's spontaneous evocation now causes Sansan some nausea. A tingle settles along her neck and jaw as if she's taken a sip of Irene's pisco sour.

By the end of dinner though, the jarring mismatch-of-cogs feeling decreases. Irene talks about what the aftermath of being abandoned at the altar was like. She'd gone through a bout of depression. Was put on a cocktail of meds, including Prozac. The medication made her sweat excessively—a major source of embarrassment. She'd take off her jacket at work and her co-workers would stare at the large wet spots underneath her armpits, so large that the stains covered her breasts. 'I looked as if I was lactating,' Irene laughs, 'and I'd put on so much weight I wouldn't be surprised if half the office thought I was pregnant. Shotgun wedding, and even that failed.' She chuckles with false mirth. Her eyes scan Sansan's face for residual historic fellowship.

Such an intimate revelation. Such profound public humiliation. The surge of pity is hard to stymie. Sansan volunteers her marriage history with Dewar, how Dewar hadn't wanted kids but had seen fit to omit any mention of this during the entire time they were dating and later married. When she asked why, he'd said that mixed-race kids were 'piteous', and also, given his traumatic childhood, he didn't think he'd make a good father.

Irene's eyes become large and round and full of sympathy. She leans closer, and Sansan gets a waft of her perfume. 'It's so interesting how you've become someone different entirely. I feel like I hardly know you. For one thing, you sound so different.'

'Really?' Sansan says.

'Yeah, the accent. So British. Or is that faux-British?'

Sansan blinks. Once again, Irene's bullseye style.

'I've missed you,' Irene is saying. 'I've really missed our friendship.'

Sansan smiles a little uncertainly. Irene's pause, though, makes it seem as if she's waiting for a response. 'Me too,' Sansan says, feeling insincere. After the words are out, and she sees Irene's eyes soften, she realises it's strangely true. But is it Irene she misses, or the promise that Irene represents? The thought smudges her heart, but with what: bittersweet nostalgia, or hollow yearning?

Stephen loves the conspiracy aspect of it. 'So, do I get to lip lock with you in front of her?'

Corn-fed, tall, lanky, fair-haired Midwesterner. Out here with an IT consultancy gig for private schools in London. Slightly effete, favours bright coloured V-neck sweaters draped over expensive twill cotton shirts. Loves nature walks and bird-watching. Avid blogger, firm environmental advocate. Seeking MOTOS with GSOH for LTR. Would such a dating profile of Stephen secure any offers? Instead, Stephen is constantly approached by gay men at museums and bars, which he aggregates as proud moments of conquest. Sansan is fond of him because he is quirky. And he has the ability to make her laugh.

'Listen, stop with the wisecracks. She's an old friend. She wants to meet you. So can you pretend, just for one evening?'

'You know I'd do anything for you.'

In that tone, he's definitely teasing her.

But then, her seriousness slips out of its own volition. 'It's weird to have an old friend you haven't kept in touch with visit like this. It's like I've found something I lost.'

Irene is really excited about going to Wembley with Sansan, agreeing with Sansan's wry comment that they're both cultural tourists and ravagers of a sort. They exit the station at Alperton to balmy, heady sunshine and open blue skies on a summer afternoon, no trace of a cloud anywhere in gloomy old London. Wembley is almost as exotic to Sansan as it is to Irene: Sansan comes and goes from her aunt's house, without visiting Wembley once, even though she's been in London five years.

Irene exclaims over everything—the piquant and spicy aromas of lamb kebabs, fried onion bhajias and vegetable pakoras; the streets teeming with women kicking their heels in vibrant saris, the men touting Alphonso mangoes with stentorian cries. She jots down everything in a little spiral notebook, taking photos of everything.

'Oh, I'm going to blog about this on my website. I own one called *The Friends of the Kookaburra*—it's a collective travelogue where members are free to blog about obscure places, myths and legends and discoveries. I haven't told you about it, have I? It's wildly successful.'

The pavement is so crowded they constantly have to jostle elbows to make their way forward. Irene talks about her website nonstop—all the sponsors and advertisers clamouring to advertise. It has taken off beyond her wildest imagination.

She now has eight hundred and fifty-four bloggers contributing essays, travel anecdotes, travel photos on her site. She's thinking of starting a food travelogue section to further boost its growth. 'This Wembley thing will be perfect to kick it off.'

Seeing Irene so effervescent about Wembley, Sansan feels credited with a generosity she's not sure she possesses. Feels good to give Irene something. In college, Sansan had simultaneously felt grateful and like a charity case. Was Sansan's ethnicity never a factor for Irene? She wonders if, perhaps, it was Irene's rapacity, her 'hunger', her knack and instinct to triumph over what she perceived as a biological weakness, that launched their friendship. Ergo, would Irene instinctively choose a fat or ugly girl for a friend because it gives her a competitive advantage? Though, similarly, didn't being seen with Irene also confer on Sansan a certain power by association?

Sansan gets her eyebrows threaded while Irene watches with fascination. The salon owner pulls taut a lime-green thread and with rapid, deft hand movements uses the thread to pluck and shape Sansan's eyebrows.

'Ow, how can you sit there leafing through a magazine when she's ripping out your eyebrows?' Irene exclaims.

'Want to give it a go?' Sansan chuckles.

Irene declares she doesn't believe in waxing. She lets it all 'grow itself out'. Sansan is genuinely amused. She finds Irene's fascination touching.

Then Irene says, 'It's nothing compared to getting your heart ripped out.'

Sansan sobers. Irene looks at her, expectant, and Sansan inwardly sighs, feeling an inchoate surrender, as she volunteers, 'Nothing like getting divorced.' And for a moment, a thread of mutual feeling shivers between them. Like in the old days.

Afterwards, they stop for bhel puri at a stand next-door and sit outside, people watching together.

'Thank you for sharing this with me,' Irene says. 'You might find this sad, but so far, it's been the highlight of my trip.'

Sansan pats Irene's wrist. 'You're very welcome.'

Irene swallows. 'You know, I don't know if I told you. After I went off Prozac, I was so lonely and down all the time. I even thought about just ending my life. It was then I started *Friends of the Kookaburra*. People blogged from all over the world, and all of a sudden, I had all these *friends*.' Irene casts her eyes down in mock abashedness. 'I've just been offered a lot of money to sell it. A media outfit has expressed deep interest.'

'That's great! How much money?' Sansan says.

'Well, you see, I was hoping you could give me some financial advice about all this. Being a transactions lawyer for a bank.'

Sansan's face creases with pleasure. 'Sure. I'm happy to take a look at the proposal.'

'You should join as a member.'

Sansan shakes her head. 'I don't really do social media. I can barely hang on to one identity, let alone manufacture several avatars.'

'Oh, come on! It isn't social media. It's got a chatroom.' Irene's sudden vehemence startles Sansan.

'I don't think I will join,' Sansan says. 'Putting all sorts of private information on the web could be a lure for identity theft.'

Irene says nothing. The mood has changed in an instant—for the rest of their shopping spree, Irene sinks into an unenthused patter tempered with froideur, much at odds with her earlier liveliness.

Irene's mercurial change of mood bewilders Sansan. Feeling guilty, she insists on buying Irene drinks while they wait for Stephen at Molto Bene. They order their champagnes in fancy fluted glasses, and after two each, Irene's mood has lightened considerably.

To further semaphore her goodwill, Sansan links her arm through Irene's and says wouldn't it be wonderful if Irene were to move to London. It could be like college. She says this even as she wonders about her own insincerity—what is she hoping to recover here?

Stephen interrupts this tableau vivant by walking up and cracking a joke about how sapphic friendships are such a tease. They both shrill with laughter.

'So, how long have you two been going out?' Irene says.

'A couple of years.' Stephen winks and hooks an arm around Sansan.

Much to Sansan's surprise, Stephen and Irene hit it off. Irene exclaims over the primrose-yellow V-neck Stephen has on, and Stephen listens to Irene's mouse droppings of wisdom like apocrypha.

At some point, with a whole bottle emptied, the waiters are frowning and Sansan finally orders food for all of them—linguine alle vongole for Irene (apparently still her favourite), spaghetti amatriciana for Stephen, and swordfish with capers for herself. This sets off Stephen and Irene's slipstreaming about pasta, noodles, pancetta, truffles, bottarga, Italian sauces of all kinds. Even though it's Sansan who took the Italian cookery class, Stephen talks about it as if he did. They move on to wild foods, comparing notes about the most exotic things they've eaten. Stephen claims to have eaten dingo in Australia, and Irene tells a childhood story, which Sansan suspects is fabricated, about how she used to nibble on magnetised iron filings. Stephen loves the story.

The talk swirls around her—Stephen and Irene are on to travel now. *Friends of the Kookaburra* comes up again and Sansan barely lifts her eyebrow in surprise when it turns out Stephen is one of the eight hundred and fifty-four members.

'You're *IF300206*?' Stephen exclaims.

'Yeah!'

'I'm ES9988!'

'Oh my god, the one with the Nietzsche quote? I totally thought you were an arrogant prick. One of those quasi-intellectuals too big for their britches.'

'Must not anyone who wants to move the crowd be an actor who impersonates himself?' Stephen intones, joined halfway by Irene.

Disgusted, Sansan excuses herself to go to the bathroom. When she comes back, she's just in time to see Irene retrieving her tongue from the whorls of Stephen's ear.

What she has just glimpsed is so sudden and quick it might've been a mirage. Sansan does what she did those many years ago when Irene moved dorms—exactly nothing. Pretending she hasn't seen anything, even though Stephen's eyes are foggy and Irene's haven't acknowledged Sansan for a good long while.

After dinner, they move on to a bar on Greek Street. With the rounds of drinks, the conversation between Stephen and Irene grows increasingly flirtatious. Irene's body language, too, has changed—the sour desperation that wafted from her has become a confident, snarky drive, with the two of them leaning in to each other, making snide comments about the other bar patrons. Sansan goes to get the next round of drinks. This time there's no mistaking what she's seeing when she returns. Stephen's hand is rustling beneath Irene's skirt.

'What are you doing, Stephen?' Sansan's throat feels clogged with tears, hot and acrid and salty.

Stephen has the saving grace to look embarrassed and guilty while quickly retrieving his hand. Irene, however, turns her face full on Sansan, her eyes glazed with mad laughter. 'But Stephen told me you aren't actually dating. It's a bluff.'

A tumult of inexpressible accusations roil inside Sansan. 'You're the sort of person who doesn't think this is wrong, that's precisely the trouble!'

'But what exactly have I done that's so reprehensible?'

Sansan has no answer for this, only a choked cry in her heart. Only an enormous welt of pain.

Irene's face, on the other hand, smooths out, the puce-coloured stains on her jaw darkening. Her spiky haircut seems to crest. A thought descends: Irene is preening, not unlike a kookaburra with crimped eyelashes.

Sansan finds herself eschewing public transportation, walking in the light drizzle almost all the way to Tower Bridge, unwilling to go home just yet. Through a shine of tears, she watches the black eddies of the Thames, the heavy clouds hanging like theatre curtains, a floating restaurant anchored near the Embankment still ablaze with lights and crowded with diners. London, so beautiful, so remote. A passing black cab, then another. The cabbies inside looking at her—their faces reflected off sodium streetlights have a pale sheen. Glinting wet pavements. The loneliness feels like a stranglehold, and Sansan, with an inaudible gasp, hails a black cab home to her Canary Wharf condo.

Opening a bottle of Pinot, the anger rises in cloudy steams. She could have slept with Kwame. Why didn't she? Is it possible she loved Irene more than Irene herself understood, more than Irene loved her—is that what Sansan is finding so hurtful? Her mind rages with counter-arguments. Naïve to think ethnicity isn't, has never been, a factor: Irene might embrace foreign cultures like Gaia, but she accumulates friends with skin tones the way Stephen considers his potential conquests as notches on his belt. Irene is once again using a man to assert her cultural superiority over Sansan. Thrice betrayed—twice by Irene and once by her mate Stephen. And yet, she has no entitlements to Irene, nor to Stephen. No entitlements that can stand up to logic, only the pedantic demands of a raging heart.

She cracks open another bottle of wine and switches on her computer. She googles for Irene's website and begins to read the posts on it. They are full of people animated by walkabouts all over the world and rare bird sightings. A raw innocence pervades—as if in the world of serene bird-watching there is no trace of avarice or betrayals. No whiff of contretemps, no sullying of equilibriums.

It's been a long time since she has written anything. The words don't come easily. But as she plods on, her feelings acquire a kind of emotional logic. She writes a long, torturous account of her flirtation with Kwame and signs it, *Your college friend.* Then feeling as if she's given herself away, she codes it in purple prose about the forest of friendship, the wings of love spanned with floes of ice, the fiendish trickery of a kookaburra bird. *Did you know it's also called a laughing jackass?* She quotes from an obscure Ecuadorian poet about the emotional spaces for breakage and mourning; metaphors of gentian flowering within the crevices of ruins, and the beating heart of the Cordilleras, and how vast and limiting these spaces are at the same time, because even as the heart is filled with the overflow of anguish, its atriums have begun their narrowing.

She chooses not to source the poet. By this small thievery, she has the odd intuition that a moral equilibrium is restored.

Over the next few days, Stephen tries to reach her, but Sansan lets his messages slip into voicemail. She hears from Irene just as Irene is about to leave for Heathrow. 'Listen, Sansan, I just wanted to say goodbye. If you're ever in New York and you feel like it, give me a call, okay?' A pause of static on the phone, and then Irene's quieter mumble, 'I hope we're still friends.'

The message sounds genuine, and Sansan is left wondering at her own overreaction. For all their formative years spent together at a prestigious elite New England liberal arts college, and for all that they had believed that love and friendship and morality exist on a spectrum, theirs have been shown up against each other by these microcosmic frictions in the values of friendship. Over the next few days, Sansan avidly checks *The Friends of the Kookaburra* to see if Irene has responded to the new anonymous blogger.

There were lots of goodwill messages from other bloggers, telling her what a lovely poem she'd written. But no message from IF300206. Sansan even knows instinctively what those numbers mean. Thirty years old, Irene's birthday February 6th.

Then, several days after Irene has returned to New York, she messages Sansan through the blog's website: *I know who wrote this. Would the responsible party like to own up?*

During the next several weeks, there are new messages from Irene—Irene becoming less certain that the anonymous blogger is Sansan—*Is that you?—Why are you hiding?—Who is this? Name yourself.* Then abruptly becoming bland and random and anonymous herself. She writes about a rare sighting of magpies out on Long Island. She likens a speed-dating experience to bird mating. Amusing but droll.

Sansan never writes on the blog again. Their friendship is finally broken, as it ought to have been ages ago. It has just taken her longer to expend all her emotional currency where Irene is concerned. Like her marriage with Dewar, perhaps their closeness didn't stem from actual understanding or pure camaraderie, but rather a mimesis of it. A longing for it that did not always translate into the actual thing.

The cradle moon outside her window can be glimpsed through a dense bank of clouds. The nature of things is always partially obscured this way. She goes to bed and mounts her bolster pillow, something Dewar taught her is called a Dutch Wife; she sometimes goes to bed and unwittingly, accidentally, thinks of him. Dewar's words now come back to her—he'd once told her she was lonely because her friendship contained too much heat, that she was too sultry in her affections. Her heart fights his words still, *how could it be?* Outside, the emerging moon is furry in its edges and looks to be made of melting curd cheese.

The Chinese Nanny

SU CHIN HAD BEEN WORKING as a nanny for two weeks, even though she had no experience. However, she was a native Mandarin speaker and the agency took her on after a cursory interview and CRB check, because it was all the rage just now: British parents wanted their children to be exposed to Mandarin from a young age, even though these parents had no links to China, had never been there. The head of the agency, who hired Su Chin, had taken a shine to her, but Su Chin was taken aback when the woman said, 'I've hired lots of Zimbabweans and Nigerians,' and then lowered her voice, 'just between you and me, they've got a bit of attitude, haven't they?' Su Chin decided not to say anything about being from Malaysia, and not really from China.

The English woman Su Chin started working for had a four-year-old little girl. Gwenny, short for Gwendoline. Gwenny had hair so blonde it was almost white; on the first day of work, Su Chin couldn't resist touching those curls. She'd touched Gwenny's hair as Gwenny was wrapped up in her game of cookery and no one else was looking. She'd touched the girl's hair, let its silkiness graze her fingers, and the feeling was one Su Chin felt hard put to identify. Not envy exactly, more like greed.

Gwenny did not take to Su Chin immediately. In fact, on her first day, Gwenny stood hiding behind a door while one insuperable blue eye gazed at Su Chin from between door hinges. No amount of coaxing would draw her out. Su Chin was conscious of her own voice. 'Is this your dolly? She's so pretty. What's her name?' She was conscious of her own intonation and accent, conscious of her need to sound *unforeign*, if not exactly English, even as Gwenny's mother, Fiona, watched this interaction without saying a word, assessing Su Chin's suitability and experience. Su Chin's English was fluent—in fact, she considered herself *almost native* since she was third-generation Malaysian Chinese—but it still surprised her when submerged assumptions and attitudes leaked out once people heard her accent. It made her envious of the university students who were Chinese like herself, but who had grown up in Britain. Sometimes, she had less in common with them than with someone from Zimbabwe or Nigeria.

Fiona ran a real estate investment consultancy in Holland Park, and increasingly, many of her clients were from Mainland China. Hence, her interest in her daughter learning Mandarin, she explained to Su Chin, although the logic didn't exactly compute; it seemed to Su Chin she ought to teach Fiona instead. 'Be a dear, come out and play with the Chinese nanny, sweetie.' And then to Su Chin, in a brook-no-argument tone, 'We can't have you speaking to her in English, now can we? You mustn't be tentative with children.' It was on Su Chin's lips to quip—*yes ma'am*—as Fiona swung her crocodile leather tote and turned smartly on her heels. Patent leather, one-inch heels with a buckle, Su Chin noted and pressed her lips together. 'Go on then,' Fiona urged, issuing a last sally before heading out the front door, 'don't be shy with Gwenny. She loves teatime.'

But Gwenny just gazed at her. There was no expression in those eyes. They were twin glass balls. Perfectly swirling blue-glass eyes. Dollies' eyes. Su Chin did not blame the child for not trusting her. Some foreigner had just infiltrated your home and been saddled with the responsibility of being your minder, and instructed to jabber at you in a foreign language you'd never encountered before. Not everyone could be Alice in Wonderland. By the end of her first day, Su Chin had resorted to half-English, half-Chinese; every sentence in English was translated into Chinese, and vice versa. The girl only responded to the English. Su Chin repeated the nouns for 'cup', 'spoon', 'tea' in Chinese, tried getting Gwenny to say them, but Gwenny simply ignored those bits. By the end of the week, Su Chin was exhausted from the daily eight-hour simultaneous translations. Once at Starbucks, she caught herself making a translation to the barista, who snorted in laughter. But Fiona was right. Gwenny did love playing teatime. She also loved pretending to be asleep, and would giggle when Su Chin took one of the dolls and rubbed the doll's nose against Gwenny's, saying, 'Wake up' in Mandarin. Gwenny would whisper, 'I'm dead, come back later.' And her lips would twitch at the corners.

About a month in, there was a breakthrough. Su Chin had taken Gwenny to the museum. On the way home, at a pelican crossing, the walking-man sign had started flashing, and Gwenny had panicked and started to turn backwards. Su Chin pulled her hand, inadvertently yelling in Chinese, 'Let's hurry.'

Later, Gwenny had asked her, 'What's that mean, guy dum?'

'It's not guy dum,' Su Chin explained. 'It's *kuài diǎn*. That means "hurry".'

Gwenny's brow waggled. 'It sounds funny.'

'It probably does sound funny to you. Not to me, though. It makes perfect sense to me, just like the word 'hurry' makes perfect sense to you.'

Gwenny thought about this. 'I don't like it when you speak in that funny language. You sound angry.'

Su Chin was surprised. 'Do I?'

Gwenny nodded. 'Quite angry. I hope you're not angry with me. I'm only four.'

Su Chin laughed. Why was it that so many little girls these days demonstrated such precocity? They often made you feel that they had the upper hand.

Su Chin went home, puzzling about what Gwenny said. In the end, she wondered if it was because Mandarin was spoken in tones. The 'up and down' tones might have triggered Gwenny's sensitivity. It gave her an idea for how to break the language barrier.

'This language I'm speaking—Mandarin—has four tones. You know what's so magical about it?'

Gwenny shook her head.

Privately, Su Chin wondered whether it was better if a complicated thing was equated with 'magic' when being pushed on to children. It was one way to get them to take something *on faith*. Magic and fantasy had become a kind of religion, she felt.

Her parents had never kept it a secret—they wanted another child, but there were attempts, then miscarriages, then bleakness. There was never any attempt to describe where all the babies had gone. They stated facts—'The baby died in my tummy', 'The cord strangled him'—and she had to take the fact, that there would be no baby, *on faith*. Once, Su Chin got a doll for her birthday from an aunt who'd visited Holland, and the doll was porcelain with primrose yellow braids, dressed in a starched gingham frock with a white, lacy apron. Su Chin's mother had snatched it away and placed it on the top shelf of a glass-panelled wardrobe. She didn't get to play with it once, not even during special occasions, and there the doll stayed, until years later, it became moth-eaten and stained with age. Which was the bigger crime: to squander away your child's childhood, or to let her revisit her own too late in life?

To Gwenny, Su Chin said, 'It's a secret, all right? You can't tell it to anyone. It's the secret to learning Mandarin.'

Gwenny watched her solemnly.

Su Chin leaned down and whispered, 'You don't speak Mandarin. You can't speak it. No one does.'

Gwenny furrowed her brow. The way she frequently did when she was trying to digest a big nugget of information, or perhaps take something on faith.

'You have to sing it. Like this. *Mā má mǎ mà.*' Su Chin rendered the 'ma's in the correct four tones.

Gwenny giggled. 'Sing it again.'

Su Chin did, and they were off. Of course, Gwenny didn't limit herself to four tones. They wandered up and down the scale. But then Su Chin explained that the four 'ma's all meant something different. Mother, hemp, horse, scold.

'Mother hemp horse scold.' Gwenny was running around yelling that at the top of her lungs when Fiona came home.

Fiona had the same way of furrowing her brow. The furrow made a little dip towards the bridge of her nose, like a horizontal curly bracket. 'What's that she's saying?'

Her daughter galloped by. 'Mother, hemp, horse, scold.'

Fiona tried to catch her by the sleeve. 'You've got to stop that racket, Gwenny. My head will pop off in a minute if you don't.' She turned to Su Chin. 'I thought you were supposed to teach her Chinese.'

'She's had a big day,' Su Chin said. She explained about the four tones and the way she'd managed to get Gwenny to latch on, but she could tell Fiona was only half listening, with her, 'Well, that's good' and 'Isn't that interesting'.

'Right,' Fiona said. 'What will it be for supper? Sausages or pasta?'

Gwenny wrinkled her nose. 'I'd like an omelette.'

Fiona frowned. 'Omelettes are for breakfast, Gwenny.'

'Su Chin gives it to me for lunch.'

Fiona looked at Su Chin. 'What *have* you been feeding her?' she said, and Su Chin caught the verbal undercarriage, the things one didn't say to someone of a different race.

Gwenny only made it worse by adding, 'Su Chin puts little green things in it. And shrimp. I love those.'

'Shrimp?' Fiona's tone had more than surprise in it.

'And *she* eats it with rice!' Gwenny sang.

'Right,' Fiona squared her shoulders. 'Isn't that interesting.'

Su Chin pursed her lips. 'It's something we used to make at home. It's healthy, got all your basic food groups, protein, veg, starch.'

Fiona looked unconvinced. 'I'd rather she didn't eat an omelette for lunch every day. It might confuse her at brunch on weekends.'

'Of course,' Su Chin said. She didn't say, 'But I've seen you give her a cupcake for dinner. Wouldn't she confuse that?'

'You can make pasta, can't you?' Again, that tone, just on the side of arch.

'I thought it might be nice for Gwenny to try Chinese food,' Su Chin said. 'A bit of cultural exposure. Part of the package.'

The side of Fiona's mouth curled up. 'That's all very nice, and you'll have to forgive me for being slow, but how is an omelette Chinese food?'

A surge of emotion overwhelmed Su Chin, the top note was a kind of fury that couldn't be breached, a swarm of words like wasps which could not be articulated. 'I'm very happy to make her whatever you'd like me to make,' Su Chin managed.

Fiona set her mouth grimly and said nothing. She walked away, and later Su Chin heard what sounded like whimpers. She made Gwenny pasta, gave her a bath and put her to bed. When she called out to Fiona that she was leaving, Fiona emerged. Her eyes were red-tinged, and her face was pallid.

Su Chin realised, with a shock, that Fiona had been crying. Couldn't have been over the little unpleasantness just now, surely? Su Chin felt baffled and uneasy; there was more to Fiona than met the eye.

Over the course of two months, Su Chin and Gwenny bonded. It amazed Su Chin to witness how a child's mind worked. The 'playing dead' gave Su Chin pause—she didn't understand the fascination with 'being dead' and wasn't sure if it was something she should be worried about. Fiona's husband had died of colon cancer when Gwenny was only six months old, and Gwenny didn't remember him at all. This was a fact that Fiona mentioned one evening when she'd been a little snippy with Su Chin after coming home from work. 'This single mothering isn't as easy as it looks. You wouldn't know anything about death, being as young as you,' Fiona had said. It was on the tip of Su Chin's tongue to say Fiona was wrong, but Su Chin hesitated: it would change the employer/employee dynamic, the cultural Western/Asian dynamic, and without those frameworks, would they know how to relate?

But it was different with children. The minute Gwenny accepted that Su Chin was going to be part of her life, she repeated Chinese words automatically when Su Chin said them. She was happy to have her intonation corrected. She'd just started learning phonetics in reception year at her school, but she took the learning of Chinese pinyin in her stride. Su Chin was amazed at Gwenny's progress. She'd already learned to nod 'yes' or 'no' to simple questions in Mandarin, such as 'Are you tired?' and 'Would you like a snack?' Su Chin smiled to herself when she caught Gwenny teaching her dolls how to say certain things in Mandarin while playing teatime. A child's mind was borderless, but for how long?

Fiona was not exactly difficult to deal with. However, she seemed to carry a load with her on a daily basis. She was a beautiful woman, but she often looked haggard in the mornings, before she 'put her face on', as she phrased it. There didn't seem to be a man around. Or rather, there seemed to be a couple. Su Chin couldn't make out the situation. The biggest problem Su Chin had with Fiona was over how Fiona was underpaying her. If Su Chin worked a quarter or part of an hour over, Fiona wouldn't round out the hour. When Fiona went out on evenings with her male friend, Su Chin would babysit. Fiona sometimes came home past the time the Underground ran, and would cajole Su Chin to stay the night, without paying her extra. Su Chin understood this was to save on cab fare, since she lived all the way out in Peckham, and she didn't mind, really, bunking in with Gwenny, who simply shouted with excitement and wanted to have midnight fairy feasts. But she did wonder if Fiona wouldn't be quite so blithe about asking this favour if she wasn't so agreeable—that 'Asians-hate-confrontation' demeanour most of her compatriots adopted. One more thing: Su Chin wished that Fiona would at least call if she was going to stay out past the time the carriage turned back into a pumpkin. It would be nice to know whether to expect to go home, even though the bed she slept in at Fiona's had much the nicer sheets and the bathroom was so clean and modern. Su Chin sighed. She'd taken to putting an extra change of clothing and underthings in her voluminous carryall.

Late one evening, well past midnight, Su Chin couldn't sleep. She sat next to Gwenny for a while, because Gwenny's little snores amused her. She tried watching the telly. She made herself some chamomile tea. Then, as she passed Fiona's room on her way back to Gwenny's, she couldn't resist. She went in and walked around, marvelling at the crimson-red quilt and the white shag-pile carpet. She opened the tops of all the perfume bottles and took a sniff. She leafed through all the women's magazines. She peered at the strands of pearls and costume jewellery hanging on an iron tree, then she opened the wardrobe and looked at the shoes, all neatly lined up on shallow shelves, arranged by colour and type. A deep covetousness overtook her as she gazed at the pairs and pairs of gleaming patent-leather heels, the brogues, the furred boots, the court shoes, the peep-toes, the slingbacks, the stilettos, the wedges. The brand names reading like the authors of literary classics. A fortune in shoes.

Su Chin took down a pair of Louboutins. The buckles were three letters, spelling *SEX* in shimmering crystals. She put them on. They were a little large for her. Still, she took a look at her legs in the mirror. For maximum viewing advantage, she took off her baggy black trousers and walked around in her knickers with the shoes on. *Wa sei,* she thought. Get a load of my gams. She heard the key in the front door lock, and in a panic fled the room. As soon as she reached Gwenny's room, she hid the shoes in her carryall.

She did have ample opportunity to return the shoes the next day after Fiona had left.

But she didn't.

She took them home instead, and waited to see what would happen. Every day she was sure Fiona would catch her out. She didn't feel afraid, strangely, it was more like walking on eggshells, waiting for something to happen. Su Chin found herself willing to chance it because in her calculations, even if Fiona accused her, she'd have a hard time proving it. Su Chin found this side of herself unfathomable. She'd never even thought she could be so underhanded and criminal-minded, but wasn't Fiona's appropriation of her time and services a kind of theft also? Why did the former receive the heavy-duty sanction of society's moral approbation, but not the latter?

Fiona weighed on Su Chin's mind every day, as she took Gwenny to the park and they serenaded the ducks with

Mandarin nursery rhymes. Su Chin waited, and wondered if, perversely, she wanted something to happen.

Exactly nothing happened. Su Chin never wore the shoes, because they didn't fit, but the thought of having them was an odd thing. It was like carrying mother-and-daughter with her, even at home. Her watchfulness of Fiona must have triggered new sensibilities, however. One evening, Su Chin found Fiona lingering in the kitchen as she made Gwenny dinner. Fiona was in a chatty mood. She poured herself a glass of white wine and offered to pour Su Chin one. Su Chin shook her head. Stealing shoes and drinking on the job. She couldn't allow herself to sink to such levels of depravity yet. The conversation drifted from Gwenny's day to Fiona's feelings of guilt, of neglecting Gwenny because of the demands on her time and the travails of running a business. Fiona revealed that she used to work in a big bank, and people in finance were an acquisitive lot, hence all her shoes and bags. Su Chin felt a sudden pang of dread. She gave Fiona a close look: did Fiona notice her missing shoes, was this why she was bringing it up? But Fiona didn't look as if she meant anything by it. She barely looked suspicious.

The bond between Gwenny and Su Chin grew. There seemed to be nothing Gwenny loved more than flowers. She said the funniest things. People looked like flowers to her, with their tall bodies and waggling heads. Su Chin had laughed. 'Aren't flowers more like people, not the other way around?' Gwenny had shaken her head solemnly. 'No, flowers have faces. I like the faces,' Gwenny said. Su Chin was struck by the enormity of what Gwenny was saying, something the child seemed beyond capability of understanding herself. Wasn't that true? All the mystery in people and flowers were in their faces. She'd heard that people in the West thought Asian faces implacable, austere, blank, mask-like. Put another Asian girl next to Su Chin and

Caucasians would often get them mixed-up. Did such things happen to people with silken, blonde hair? Why was it that people never said that Western faces were implacable, austere, blank, mask-like? Did minority races put on masks because they wanted to hide their real thoughts?

Most of the time now, it was Su Chin who took Gwenny to her activities: her school, as well as her ballet, art and music classes. Fiona prevailed on Su Chin to come on Saturdays. Pay would be at an hourly rate as overtime compensation, but it had yet to materialise, meaning Su Chin found herself inadvertently paid more but not at the rate she was promised. Su Chin came early on Saturday mornings so Fiona could have a lie-in, and as she said, 'get all the household chores done', although this last was a joke because Su Chin now did all the laundry for them and made dinner as well, all also at no extra pay. How ironic that the woman who complained about her cooking was now prepared to eat Chinese omelette (shrimp included) for dinner. Su Chin did not like the blatant advantages Fiona was taking, but she'd also come to see there was a vulnerability in her, a kind of thirstiness mirrored by the gallons of water she drank in the morning as she mooched about, flicking pages of the magazines she bought then getting to her 'beauty regimen'. Fiona wasn't as well off as she pretended to be, nor was her business as enjoyable and prosperous as she made it seem. Her insecurities often made her distant with her own child.

One Saturday afternoon, Su Chin was getting ready to take Gwenny to a birthday party out in Chiswick when Fiona said she'd come along.

'Really?' Su Chin was surprised. She knew how much Fiona hated children's birthday parties. *All that screaming and usually there's nothing for the adults. Not a single drop of refreshment.*

They rode in the taxi in a buoyant mood. The sun, which had been hiding behind a bank of clouds, had finally come out and the pavements were teeming with people in shorts and sunglasses and straw hats, pushing strollers with big, plump babies. Fiona was extra chatty, but it was the kind of drivel Su Chin's mind had difficulty getting a purchase on. Gwenny was just ecstatic to have her mother along and kept pulling at Fiona's sleeve to attract her attention, which irritated Fiona. Gwenny was sitting prim and proper in the cab, dressed in her most beautiful summer dress. For some reason, she'd gone off pink and now yellow was her favourite colour. Su Chin gazed at her and felt a pang of love for this beautiful child. So they started playing 'I Spy' which Gwenny loved. Amazingly, Gwenny could do parts of it in Mandarin now. She'd say, 'I spy *huà*!' as they passed a flower stand with its riotous profusion of flowers. But she could also say now, '*Hěn duō hěn duō huà*.' A lot, a lot of flowers. It just filled Su Chin with pride close to bursting to hear Gwenny in Mandarin.

The taxi driver had obviously appreciated Fiona's long limbs, encased in stripy shorts and cork wedges, as Fiona climbed in. He began weighing into the conversation and soon Fiona and he were engaged in a sort of friendly exchange with suggestive overtones, so much so that he almost ran over a cyclist at a traffic light. The cyclist swore at the cabbie, the cabbie swore back, and Fiona thought it all hilarious.

The party was already in full swing when they arrived. It was in a dim cavernous church hall, and the entertainer was a clown whose act was about balancing. He balanced on stilts, on balls, on seesaws, then on a unicycle while spinning a plate on top of a pole teetering on his nose or forehead. The children—all boys and girls, aged about five—were gathered around him, already hooting with laughter, which was amplified by the acoustics of the hall into a crescendo that made Fiona rub her forehead.

Su Chin had noticed this before: Fiona had a kind of aura when she moved, and her looks drew people to her, so before long she'd talked to several mothers, quite a few dads, and Su Chin ended up in a corner, as she always did, by herself. No one spoke to her.

It was during the meal that it happened. Forever after, this scene was seared into Su Chin's memory. The children were all seated at a long party table, decorated with some kind of sporty theme—bouncy balls in blue, red and white—and Su Chin was busy helping to serve the sausages and cheese cubes at one end of the table. There was a commotion at the other end. She looked up to see a child being lifted up. It took her a split second before she realised that the child was Gwenny. Something was very wrong with the way she'd flung her head back. Su Chin rushed over. What she saw chilled her. Gwenny's face was blue. Spatters of red around her mouth from something she'd eaten. Her eyeballs were rolling. She was suffocating. It didn't seem possible, but no one knew what to do. The dad who had grabbed Gwenny was shaking her violently, and this seemed wrong, completely wrong. Fiona was distraught and kept shouting, 'Someone do something.' The rest of what happened became a dreamscape, where one thing after another happened in a rapid sequence that could not be interfered with.

The ambulance arrived.

The church hall went silent. Or did it seem so because Su Chin could literally not hear anything else but the medical jargon, do nothing else but watch the bustle of the two paramedics around Gwenny? One immediately administered a series of strong blows on Gwenny's back, then switched to placing pressure on her abdomen. It must not have worked because he then lay Gwenny down flat, opened her mouth, and again placed both his hands on her sternum, thrusting, and finally dislodging what looked like a big gob of mushy strawberries. He proceeded to administer CPR. For twenty minutes, they pumped up and down on Gwenny's little chest, breathing into her little lungs.

When they strapped Gwenny's body on to the stretcher and loaded it in the ambulance, Fiona climbed in as well. Su Chin watched the ambulance careen off; Fiona's bent head in profile still visible through the square lit window of the vehicle. Su Chin had all but been forgotten in the commotion. Looking around, it was only then that she registered that the other mums had gone, taking their kids home to spare them, leaving only the dads who all stood around helplessly. Was it like this for her mother—this sense of awfulness that spread to all your extremities? Did ambulances arrive in the night during all those episodes when her mother felt as if she were dangling from a precipice and Su Chin was too little so she slept through them all?

Gwenny died. The days that followed were unconscionably endured. Inconsolably endured. There was the funeral. There was Fiona to tend to. There was a mechanicality that was called for. Su Chin, in a befogged fashion, went through each event as if she were riding a bicycle. Somewhere in her psyche, she'd already been trained for this and she cycled on, because what else was to be done? She thought about her mother most during this time, how her mother had come home from the hospital in a billowing cotton dress, a bump on her tummy as if she was still pregnant. The wads of sanitary napkins, stained with red, in the bin. Her mother would eat raw chillies until her lips looked as if they were bleeding. Su Chin had cycled through all those periods of the inevitability of carnage—a learned emotive response from her mother, leaden and weightless at the same time, with the same indescribable roil of terror. She was Cinderella who didn't make the carriage before midnight. Rapunzel who cut her own hair in penitent Greek tragedy. Thumbelina suffocating between two slices of bread with someone pressing down very hard.

There was one moment—a post-mortem moment—that made Su Chin gasp with unbelievable pain every time she remembered. She'd followed the ambulance to the hospital, waiting in the hall to hear news, watching Fiona from a distance. Then that moment in the hospital when the staff had finally given up. A doctor and nurse came to sit with Fiona, whose eyes didn't seem to have blinked once since it happened. There were tear tracks down her face, her makeup was ruined, and snot stains were visible on her shirtfront. Su Chin had asked for a minute alone with Gwenny, to say goodbye, but all she'd wanted to do was to shake the girl, as the dad had done, and yell at her to stop pretending. Stop pretending to be dead, the wail in Su Chin's heart began, and then the drag of disbelief. This can't be happening. This can't be happening to Gwenny. What a stupid thing to think. A cacophony of voices in her head, all speaking at once, all saying something different, in Mandarin and English.

In her nightmares, Su Chin dreamt different scenarios. She'd been near Gwenny and stopped her from stuffing her mouth with strawberries. She was at the hospital, they pronounced her dead, and then Gwenny woke up and giggled, 'I'm not dead.' Worse, and this Su Chin would wake up from in a clammy sweat, she dreamt the same thing happened but she hadn't recognised the child. The child that woke up and hissed, 'I'm not dead,' had indecipherable features—black hair and black eyes.

There was an inquest. The head of the agency was interrogated. Her modus operandi was to go on the offensive when told to hire child minders with a minimum of CPR skills. A slap on the wrist, as the media hoopla worded it, but no crime. No one was punished with legal sanctions, but there was plenty of blame. It was in everyone's face, Su Chin realised as she sat in the courtroom looking at the wall of faces on flower-stalk necks, nodding or shaking their heads, that she would pay for the rest of her life for what had happened. Was this rough justice? Hadn't she been a two-faced, thieving, unqualified wretch in Fiona's house? Who said that the punishment ought to be proportionate to the crime? Here was the rub: what separated normal life from a treadmill of punitive self-recrimination was a solitary event. We were all just one event away from the tragedy of loss.

Fiona suffered the most of all. She lost so much weight she looked skeletal. Her face had frozen into a waxy, fleshless mask. Her eyes were stone, her nose a cliff, her face rock-hard, her chin the jutting overhang of survival and keeping up appearances. Who said that only Asians had masks?

Su Chin went to collect some of her things from Fiona's house. At the front door, she was greeted by Fiona's sister, who had come to stay. The house seemed full of women; she could hear two of Fiona's best friends in the living room, chatting. In Su Chin's bag were the Louboutins. She could no longer hold on to them. They'd been as heavy as rocks in her bag, but she couldn't throw them away, no matter how hard she tried. Su Chin asked to see Fiona.

'She's not well, she's just having a lie-in,' Fiona's sister said. 'Perhaps you could come back tomorrow.'

'I've got something I need to return,' Su Chin said.

'Well, all right, you can give it to me and I'll see she gets it,' Fiona's sister said.

Su Chin shook her head, and the tears came of their own accord. Alarmed, Fiona's sister clucked, 'Oh dear. Oh, you poor thing. It's been so difficult, it really has been. For all of us. Of course, you must be heartbroken. Oh, you poor thing.'

At the noise, the friends came out into the hallway. One of them volunteered to get Fiona. Fiona came downstairs in a tank top, wearing the bottom half of her silk pyjamas. Her nipples were erect and showing. Her shoulders looked incredibly white and bony, and the veins in her arms showed bluish-purple under the dangling pendant light in the hallway.

Fiona looked at Su Chin. Her hand reached out and grasped Su Chin's. 'Please don't go blaming yourself.' But there was a flatness in the tone that made Su Chin cry harder.

She extricated her hand and took out the Louboutins from her carryall. 'I stole these from your closet. I shouldn't have. Go ahead and charge me if you want.'

Fiona looked at the shoes in Su Chin's hand. She looked at Su Chin's face, uncomprehending. 'What do you mean?' she said.

Her sister let out a small gasp.

'I'm sorry. I couldn't resist. I was greedy.'

'But that's monstrous,' Fiona said. 'Do you actually mean to tell me that you've been stealing from me? What else have you stolen?'

'Oh, my goodness me,' her sister said.

'Nothing else. Only these. I'm terribly sorry. I know it's wrong.'

'But, why? Did we not treat you well? Did we not welcome you as one of the family?' And here, Fiona began to weep. 'Why? I don't understand. Gwenny loved you like a *sister*.'

Su Chin dropped to her knees. She herself hadn't known that she'd fall back into the ritual of begging forgiveness that she'd been taught when growing up. An elaborate gesture one performed before an ancestral tablet or at a grave side, a spectacle of culture, but it felt right. Su Chin lowered her temple to the floor in the deepest of bows. She stood up, put her hands together, and again kowtowed, resting her palms on the floor beside her forehead. Again and again she did it. 'Forgive me. Please forgive me.'

One of Fiona's friends gasped. The other put both her hands to her mouth. Fiona, after the initial stunned reaction, moved to lift Su Chin by the arms. 'Please, that's not necessary. It's just a pair of shoes.' Su Chin refused to get up from her kneeling position.

Fiona's sister took charge. 'This won't do. My dear, please get up from the floor.'

Su Chin shook her head.

Fiona let go of Su Chin's arm. 'I'm not going to go to the police. It's…it's ridiculous to be upset about this, considering all that's happened.'

Fiona's sister said, 'Do get up from the floor. We'll have a cup of tea and sort this out.'

'We will *not* have a cup of tea,' Fiona said.

Her voice had changed. Su Chin looked up.

Fiona's sister put a hand on her sibling's arm. 'Don't you see? It's not about the shoes.'

A series of emotions flickered across Fiona's face, a click of understanding, a flit of compassion, a momentary plea for solidarity—this wasn't a moment like all the other moments—but then, Fiona's gaze hardened. What did it matter? It seemed to say. Gwenny was gone. And Su Chin was just the Chinese nanny.

The parting came with a sense of profound unreality for Su Chin, as if none of it had really happened. This was fakery—pretend living—the real deal had passed unnoticed by all of them, like the glimpse of a wall, or a field of flowers, their heads weaving in the wind.

Love, Nude

ALL WEEK TECK HIN has been tossing about in his mind how to ask this of Yee Lan: *will you pose for me*? He wants to draw her. Paint her. A silhouette of her. Front. Back. Yee Lan as a representation. Yee Lan as a multitude. He wants to manipulate medium. Oil on canvas. Chinese ink on rice paper. Gouache cut-outs, like Chinese New Year paper cut-outs. East blended with West but with a transgressive element.

But nude. Totally, baldly nude.

Yee Lan is Aunty Boon Leng's sixteen-year-old daughter—as seemingly fragile as rice paper itself, her hair a straight fall of oleaginous black, her expression as serene and graceful as the Goddess Kuan Yin. Which is why Teck Hin, who is studying at the Nan Fang Fine Arts Academy, wants to draw her.

The year has just turned 1961 and this is his breakout year. With all the political turbulence and the sense of a nation rising, Teck Hin's iconoclastic art mentor at Nan Fang, himself a firm believer in the 'art for social change' school of thought, wants him to follow on the heels of the latest social realist painters, like Chua Mia Tee. Chua made a splash with *National Language Class* two years ago—a socially engaged piece of art that took on the political issue of whether Malay should be the national language, if Singapore were to merge with Malaya now that they're both independent of Britain. But Teck Hin is drawn towards the traditionalists. The Nanyang Style masters like Cheong Soo Pieng and Chen Chong Swee. Both are Chinese émigré artists to Singapore. Two of the several Chinese artists who sought refuge in the British Straits Settlements at the outbreak of World War II. Nanyang, literally meaning the South Seas, is an old Chinese trading denomination; thus Nanyang Style is more a place of mind than an aesthetic style; a subject matter and thematic preoccupation that encompasses a wide range of media and practices. Teck Hin was inspired when he read about Cheong Soo Pieng's trip to Bali along with three of his artistic peers in 1952, from which Cheong produced a number of paintings of Balinese women—topless, exotic, but never completely nude.

He wonders if the female nude is forever a site of contestation. From Goya to Courbet, Matisse to Modigliani, the nude women they painted transgress and break boundaries, whether with their candid, challenging gazes or their bushy armpit hair, their outrageous sexuality or their mysterious impenetrability. He wants to produce a female nude that escapes boundaries in the Nanyang Style: has it ever been done? Do women bathe wrapped in sarongs in the Malayan rivers any more? In the privacy of their own bathrooms, do they bathe in hibiscus-scented water? From the profound influence of Western aesthetic sensibilities (especially Schiele), he finds himself migrating east: looking at Japanese shunga (erotic art) for illumination (although carnal acts and oversized genitalia don't really appeal to him): what he is seeking is something old, something new, political yet pure.

However, there's a logistical problem and it's two-fold. Yee Lan will probably be hesitant, if not refuse him outright—he can already see the blush creeping up her neck and face. He knows he's utilising the fact that she has feelings for him, has had them since primary school, which will make it difficult for her to refuse. Add to that the fact that she now attends a Catholic girls' school in Toa Payoh. Yee Lan has a weak heart, metaphorically and literally: in Primary Five, she'd collapsed due to arrhythmia when he was taking her to buy cut guava at a roadside stand. Luckily, there was a hospital two blocks away, and Teck Hin had hauled her on to his back and rushed her to Emergency. In return, Yee Lan told him solemnly that as a good Catholic, she would pray for him for the rest of her life.

The other part of the problem is Yee Lan's mother. Aunty Boon Leng believes in Teck Hin's talent, while nobody in his family does. *Oh, he's going to be famous artist someday, is it not? Look, so gifted. Can draw those attap houses and kampongs and mangrove swamps like nobody's business.* Aunty Boon Leng constantly remarks on the gratitude she feels because he saved Yee Lan's life, to the point of cloyingness. Though not a real aunt, but a friend of his mother's, Aunty Boon Leng dotes on him. *You like my own son, noble and so cool* leh*?* Asking Yee Lan to pose nude will dispel this magnified image of realism she has of him.

The urge to draw Yee Lan comes upon him heedlessly; he finds himself stealing glances at her soft, plump arms when she wears a short-sleeved cotton blouse, or at her pale thighs when she wears shorts. He examines her toes minutely, the way the little toe curves inward, and curves more than the others. He memorises her face, her almond-shaped eyes, her smooth cheek line, the one tiny brown freckle right underneath her left eye in an otherwise unblemished face. Yee Lan blushes like a fiery bride when she catches him looking at her so intently. Acting coquettish, batting her eyelashes, smoothing her skirt, crossing and uncrossing her ankles, a virgin ingénue. Her mannerisms are so incongruous with her posture and mode of dress that she appears all the more adorable to him, like an impish sister. She is so enticing that it makes him tingle from wanting to draw her.

Sitting on the grass at her house after breakfast one Saturday morning, he begins in stealth. Broad pencil strokes to capture the outline of her in a white blouse and demure parachute skirt, her hair neatly plaited on both sides, playing with Dunia, her Scottish terrier, who means the *world* to her. He leaves her face a blank oval; he will fill that in last. Dunia he captures with all the dexterity he can muster, its limpid eyes, its furry face, its tiny protruding tongue.

'What are you doing?' she asks.

Teck Hin does not reply, intent on drawing.

'Are you drawing me?'

'Why would I draw you?'

'Don't you want to draw me?'

A question so pointed can hardly be avoided. Indeed, it's the perfect moment to broach the question, yet Teck Hin finds himself overtaken by a perverse impulse. 'Are you worthy to be drawn? Modigliani's nudes are astounding.'

'Oh, I wouldn't ever show my body. That's disgraceful.' But in the act of rearranging her skirt, Yee Lan pulls the hem higher, revealing her rounded, peachy knees.

Teck Hin smiles to himself. They spend another hour in the shade of the garden's large banyan, and then it is too hot to sit outside.

Teck Hin draws Yee Lan surreptitiously, ubiquitously, multitudinously. Soon enough, he's produced multiple sketches of her. A myriad of charcoal outlines. Yee Lan on a bench underneath a bucolic Nanyang-style coconut tree, tilting her face up to the sun. Yee Lan peering from behind a Chinese fan (imagined). Yee Lan at the piano, her back ramrod straight, her fingers captured forever in sprightly action. Yee Lan cupping her hands at a water fountain, the water drops so scintillating an effulgent reflection of her face can be seen. Yee Lan with Dunia, in various guises and activities. From these sketches, he tries to paint her at the school studio. In watercolour. In acrylic. In oils. But for whatever reason, the paintings fail to satisfy. They seem to lack an intrinsic essence of Yee Lan. He tries to imagine her without clothes on. Tries to draw an outline of this, but again, fails.

But what if? If he can't draw Yee Lan nude, could he perhaps superimpose her face on another nude? Would that be dishonest? Didn't artists in collectives substitute one naked body for another, so that the final nude you saw was not one person but actually a composite of perfect limbs and anatomical magnificence? It's a thought.

Aunty Boon Leng considers herself his godmother because she single-handedly persuaded his mother, a High Court Judge, to allow Teck Hin to switch from Law to Art. The two families are so close they could be related, living as they do next door to each other. The mothers go swimming together; the fathers used to play cricket and boules with British colonial service administrators. Teck Hin spent his entire childhood going in and out of Aunty Boon Leng's house whenever he wanted. Even now, he sometimes spends more time at her house than his own, because Aunty Boon Leng cooks like a dream, while his mother is never home. Secretly, he knows Aunty Boon Leng cherishes the thought that one day Teck Hin might marry Yee Lan, even though Yee Lan's bad heart makes her defective in other people's eyes, certainly in the eyes of his parents. Teck Hin feels duplicitous, this betrayal on the part of his mother. *Why should you be saddled with looking after her? You have a promising career in front of you.* There are a number of illusions his mother still harbours, for example, his art obsession is just a phase. Eventually, he will come to his senses, go back to Law, maybe even matriculate from a university in England, find himself a proper sustaining career. Aunty Boon Leng speaks up for him. *Eh, don't* kacau *him, he's going to be the Singaporean Picasso what.*

Yee Lan discovers the stash of secret drawings. Not entirely secret, because Teck Hin hopes for her to find them. He leaves the sketch pad lying on top of his satchel, excusing himself to go downstairs to bring up a glass of milk and some biscuits for them both.

When he enters the bedroom, Yee Lan's eyes are round with wonder. He pretends to be embarrassed, putting the tray down hurriedly, snatching the drawing pad away. She snatches it back. Gazing at the sketches, she has the look of someone encountering a mystery. It reminds Teck Hin of the painting by Gérôme, of Pygmalion and Galatea. Truly, Yee Lan has never looked as glowingly beautiful and delicate as she does now. The mirror effect is not lost on Teck Hin: we do not know ourselves until we see ourselves reflected in the eyes of our beloved.

'I didn't know you felt this way.' A film of moisture now dances and flickers in her eyes. The emotions surging within her are making her chest rise and fall in rapid succession, her cheeks subsumed with rosiness. He feels a quickening, it is now or never. But wait, is she, is she thinking that…

He says, 'I want to…'

She looks up. Oh, that tilt of chin and elongation of neck. Teck Hin moves swiftly to sit beside her. He covers her hand with his. *What if?* His face draws close, his lips even closer, his breath feathering the epidermis of her upper lip. Yee Lan's breathing goes into overdrive, her nostrils flaring slightly, her lips parting, her eyes darting to his and then looking down. Yes, she has misunderstood. For a second, Teck Hin is struck by the

Damocles' sword of what he's doing. Is this the artist playing God, the master puppeteer? If he kisses her, Yee Lan will say yes to anything. And then what? Is he really willing to fabricate reality in order to get what he wants? But isn't that what art is: fabricated reality? Two-dimensional illusions that attempt to impart another reality—of substance and depth, light and colour—when, in fact, all you are playing with is just surface?

Isn't he leading her on? Confusion flares in him, making him pull back. The spell breaks. Yee Lan flushes violently and bows her head. As if in shame. As if he'd gone ahead and asked her to strip.

But the deception has begun, despite his inner conflict. Yee Lan has asked her mother for a drawing tutor, and her mother claps her hands and says, who else could she trust but Teck Hin? On the pretext of teaching her how to paint, Teck Hin is allowed to go up to Yee Lan's bedroom. She deploys the full arsenal of female biological behaviour at her disposal, short of an actual love confession. Her eyes full of hope and expectation. Her tentative touches of his wrist and knee. Her giggles. Her batting eyelashes. Love aeroplanes flutter in through his window in the mornings; pressed dried flowers and tins of Quik chocolate milk left on top of his satchel when he takes bathroom breaks during their afternoon tutorial sessions together.

The change is not lost on Aunty Boon Leng either. If she wasn't already enamoured of him before, now she practically showers gold dust in the wake of his footsteps.

He feels rotten and undeserving. He's not sure that what he feels for Yee Lan amounts to love. He does know she does not make his heart beat faster. An instinctual nagging feeling tells him that he needs to maintain a certain detachment. The need is aesthetic: the need to capture something as elusive as her beauty and purity. The same feeling that explodes in him when he sees a magnificent sunrise, hears a chorus of birds trilling on the branches of trees, sing-songing, serenading each other in the language of bird-love. A sense of being. A purity in the merging of the eye and soul, and the transfer of a vision on to paper. With respect to the Nanyang-style masters, he's thinking: not *what* is represented, but *how* it is represented. There's a German word for this will towards immanence: *kunstwollen*. Riegl's word for man's desire to express his relationship with the perceptible appearance of things. In short, Teck Hin's own interpretation and rendering of beauty. The movement of his hands on canvas, his rough gestural strokes with the brush in the Southern calligraphic style of *xieyi*. No one else's gaze, his own.

Yee Lan wilts under the weight of her own daily expectations, the waiting, the second-guessing of when Teck Hin will make a move. This pains him: seeing those eyes full of limpid hope and desire turning into self-doubt, taking on an expression of desperate longing, searching his face for a glimpse of reciprocal feeling. Throwing little fits of pique. He tosses about in bed, losing sleep, unwilling to disabuse her of the notion that he likes her, yet unable to move forward to ask her to pose for him.

Inevitably, the sword drops. Yee Lan corners him when he arrives one afternoon, satchel slung across his chest, leaning his bicycle against the wall. 'Mother isn't home,' she begins, already flustered.

Teck Hin pauses in the middle of unbuckling his helmet. 'Oh?'

'Come in quickly. We don't have much time.'

'To do what?'

But Yee Lan has already gone indoors to her bedroom.

When he enters, he sees that she is standing behind a screen. The screen is made of Chinese mulberry paper and the silhouette of her figure is visible. His heart begins thudding when he sees what Yee Lan's shadow is doing. First, the skirt. Then the unbuttoning of her blouse. Her bra, sliding off. Her panties being dropped. Teck Hin starts to tremble. 'What are you doing?'

'Wasn't this what you wanted?' she asks.

'Yes, but...'

'I saw your sketches of those nudes in your sketchpad. Isn't that what every artist wants? To draw naked women?'

A laugh, derisive and at the same time weakening, escapes him. Her innocence. Her attempt to please him. He puts a trembling hand against his neck. 'Are you sure?' he says.

In answer, she comes out from behind the screen and takes his breath away.

He does draw Yee Lan nude. He draws her nude in many different poses, front and back, lying on a couch, playing with Dunia, looking coquettish, barely draped in linen. He draws her shunga style—wrapped in a kimono with one exposed breast. Then Nanyang Style—carrying a basket of local fruits on her head. He draws her academic-salon style, in bold modernist strokes. Even renders her in dreamy surrealist flight. He draws her as a series of lines, abstracted. Then with fragmented anatomy. He draws her with his moods and temperament, sometimes playful, sometimes romantic, sometimes in melancholic diffidence, sometimes in tarnished anger.

Such liberties have a price. When Yee Lan finally becomes audacious enough to tilt her chin up, he plants that chaste peck on her lips that she so desires. If she were ever to demand that he marry her, he would make the sacrifice. She's given up her modesty by having her nakedness on show, after all. Teck Hin draws her until he begins to understand himself, and in understanding himself, he sees Yee Lan's body as only he can, her physicality, her paradoxical demureness, her joy at being kissed, her spill-over sexuality, and also her ability to repress, her willingness to blind herself to certain truths. The act of seeing and capturing an essence of Yee Lan in different media transforms him; he feels himself tunnelling back in time towards a state of un-being, a prelapsarian state of unknowing. The more he unpicks Yee Lan, the more he himself is coming undone. In reverting to the *xieyi* style of Chinese ink painting that he has been trained in, Teck Hin feels the inner psychic rumblings of nostalgia—its Greek transliteration, *nostos*: the myth of the heroic return. A journey has come full circle, and yet, he has arrived at a place different from when and where he set out. A search that yields beauty in many forms, but it's the kind of beauty that you might just as easily miss, obscure and elusive, but also a beauty that is all-encompassing, with an illimitable largesse.

The painting he submits for his end-of-year folio is a nude of Yee Lan. A full-frontal nude on rice paper, drawing mutually from the 'spirit of the beings' and the spontaneity of the lines that characterise the *xieyi* style. Yet his nude is no Chinese painting, even with the flowing limbs and sloping shoulders resembling the topography of a mountain. Far from it. With her pomegranate-sized breasts and shaggy pubis, she is vulgar and yet eminently desirable. With an unmarked oval for a face enframed by a square (could be a crate, could be a form of prison), and with her hands bearing up the weight of the frame, she is every orientalised woman that has ever been desired, and she is faceless, subject to many interpretations: conceived and yet she does not exist, unknowable and unrecognisable.

It causes an uproar at school. His advisor is scandalised. The examination board refuses to allow it to be shown at the year-end exhibition. Too syncretic, says one instructor. The female nude is glorious, not discombobulated. Too idiosyncratic

Mapping Three Lives Through a Red Rooster Chamber Pot

Min Fong, samsui woman, 1938

Blood in her urine, blood in her faeces. For the last month, there's been blood whenever she pees in the chamber pot. Look at the red rooster featured on the pot, mocking her with its beady eye. Stupid cock. The chamber pot was part of her wedding dowry in China, along with the washbasin with the red rooster design, her *zǐsūn tǒng* 子孙桶. Her husband on their wedding day looking so fine in his livery, bringing the sedan chair, accompanied by the popping sounds of firecrackers and drums. Turns out he's a dolt, a ne'er do well, good only for lolling around with the pipe, sunk into a stupor. And now, Min Fong, out of filial duty, has to remit money every month to support him and his mother. With effort, she lets the stream run, grunting a little. Po Jie snores in her corner while Ah Lan bats at invisible mosquitoes as her mouth moves like a ruminant. Rustlings and giggles issuing from between the wooden slats—that *si-futt-hahn* Chin Leng at it again, canoodling with Mun Heng the clog maker, whose wife has run off, leaving him three daughters to foster out. Isn't one of them working as a *ma jie,* a nursemaid for a British colonial household? Lucky girl, last time she came to visit her pa, she had belly fat poking through the frog buttons of her *samfoo*. Belly fat, imagine! Or maybe not belly fat, maybe she's in that way, and Min Fong imagines one of those mixed-race babies, all curly brown hair and florid red skin, and would it even get to take on the father's last name? Chin Po walla-walla-something, those tongue-twister names, think about that.

Not so much blood this time, a relief, but she knows something is very wrong. She's been getting fatigued as the day wanes; once, her knee gave out as she was carrying her two pails of cement, slung across her shoulders with a bamboo pole. The pails up-ended, wet cement oozing out. Lucky she's on good terms with the *kepala* and he came running with a scraper. Maybe Dr Fan down the hall can give her just a pinch of this or that powder, stirred into a cup of hot water. Costs about ten cents—a day's meal. Her share of the rent is due, tomorrow in fact, just a *pok-gai* situation—two dollars a month she pays for a four hundred-square-foot room shared by four, living on top of each other like cockroaches. She's due to send money home as well. What to do? She's just gotten hired for this Bukit Timah job—by hanging around Tofu Street day after day, where the head honcho does all her hiring—it won't do her any good to skip work, she'll get replaced in the blink of an eye. Many samsui women around, just as hardy, just as stoic. Kind Mrs Cheng, from a few rooms down, says to just catch a dead rat, cook over burning charcoal, make into liquid and drink. Quite a few scoundrels of the rodent variety walking bold as brass across her hanging larder, she says, can catch one for you. Oh, don't listen to her, Po Jie says, Mrs Cheng is so *san ba*, like it or not the drink will kill you, country bumpkin that she is.

Po Jie is her dearest friend. Po Jie it was who sent word through her family network that women could get jobs in the colony of Singapore. Pay the *tsui haak* thirty yuan and it would be seven days' journey by boat—eating, lurching about, vomiting, shitting on a big boat, first to Hong Kong, then onward to Johnson's Pier. Po Jie it was who found Min Fong her first job on Eu Tong Sen Road. How time flies—back when she got married, she never thought she could do this kind of hard labour, working on a construction site carrying buckets and buckets of cement and bricks, clambering up and down rickety scaffolding better than a long-tailed monkey. Walking two hours to these sites just to spare the thirty cents tram fare. A samsui woman doesn't think about danger or accidents, she worries only about rainy days because work stops and she won't get paid. Last month also no work, long days sitting on her chamber pot—upturned it doubles as a stool—gazing down from her *papan*-shutter window at the inner courtyard where the landlord has his apprentices scurrying around, trimming roots, peeling bulbs, skinning snakes, or setting horns of mountain goat and penises of deer out on round, rattan trays to dry. Landlord Lu is like a multi-coloured wolf, god knows what he imbibes from his own medicinal store—that *sik long*—seven offspring, warbling or various degrees of bawling, the wife shouting curses in Hokkien, which no one understands in this Cantonese-ridden shophouse. Well, at least it's entertaining. *Ach,* maybe if she passes, Po Jie would see fit to send her ashes home, or burn her some hell-money, seeing as how they've shared a room for five years. Or at least Po Jie might think of her when she prays for her adopted daughter at Kwan Im Thong.

Thinking about Po Jie's adopted daughter makes Min Fong's heart itch like a mosquito bite—you don't want the burden, and yet it worries away at you. She gets approached often enough by families with too many daughters, it being assumed that like the *ma jies,* samsui women have also taken a vow of celibacy and have money to spare. Min Fong pushes the chamber pot back under the table—to be emptied first thing in the morning before the night-soil man comes—and gets back on to her bamboo floor mat.

Four of them sharing a room, if Tai Mui hadn't left, it would've been five of them. Still, not as bad as the six coolies down the hall, two in the top bunk, two in the bottom, two on the floor. A dull pain in her bowels, Min Fong tries to ignore it, but lies awake, her head on her porcelain pillow staring up at a gecko slowly creeping across the ceiling, marking its territory. A daughter would empty her chamber pot for her; a daughter would massage her abdomen with White Flower Oil, fan her slowly until her cold sweat disappears.

As darkness gives way to the wash of blue-grey dawn, she sees Chin Leng silently skulking back into the room. Maybe it's the smug smile on her face, or maybe it's because Min Fong couldn't get to sleep and the day is bound to be a rotten-egg day, or maybe because there ought to be a modicum of face-saving decorum in this sardines-packed-in-a-tin-can they call a room, but Min Fong, with sudden ire, says what's been sitting in her heart for a while now, 'You really shouldn't carry on like that.'

Chin Leng stops in her tracks. A surprised look on her face, but not overly perturbed. 'Carry on like what?'

'The man is married. Just because no one says anything does not mean it's right.'

'Oh, don't be such a *kay poh,* what business is it of yours?'

'I'm just saying, people talk. A woman who is too non-fussy brings everyone's morale down.'

Chin Leng doesn't speak. The issue has never been raised before, it's clear to see. That it's raised so directly is really *diu-min*—a major loss of face. Min Fong, older than Chin Leng by a good half-decade, has the right to chastise; Chin Leng is obliged to listen, these are the unwritten codes of 'face'—but Min Fong can make out the series of emotions skirling Chin

Leng's features, even in the dim light, objections swelling upon the tongue and then quelled. The moment balloons out; it's clear Chin Leng has heard her, Min Fong can read the frustration in the clenching of her upper arms as Chin Leng settles down in her spot on the raised trestle bed next to Ah Lan. The silence extends, takes on a bristling quality.

Finally, Chin Leng says, 'I'll try to be quieter, Sister Min, but if you don't like what you see, you shouldn't look.'

A week passes, and the pain in her bowels becomes naggy; she keeps feeling the need to defecate, but when she goes, no dice. She has no appetite and consequently, has had to miss a couple of days' work. Swallowing her misgivings, Min Fong asks Dr Fan for a consultation. He asks her to lay her wrist on top of the small pillow on his desk, and as his two fingers take her pulse, Min Fong looks him over. His glasses are foggy, in need of cleaning. His shirt collar is too big, making his corrugated neck folds look like sugarcane stuck in a planter. A thin, bare moustache sits in the space between his upper lip and nostrils, not quite belonging there. In fact, everything about the room, at once his clinic and also his bedroom, looks out of place. From their fellow residents, Min Fong has heard that Dr Fan comes from an illustrious, scholarly family in China that collected scholar's rocks and Ming Dynasty porcelain. What a come down, the more malicious of them say, having to eat stinky tofu just like the stupid and illiterate among us.

Mrs Cheng is cooking in the communal kitchen at the back of the shophouse. Oh, the fragrant smells, the woman is a genius with the wok—she can make anchovies and peanuts taste like an emperor's meal. Dr Fan clears his throat. 'How long have you had this...ah...problem?'

Min Fong shakes her head. 'I can't remember, quite a few months already. Is it something I ate?' Was it the gecko droppings accidentally fallen into the rice-gruel, which she ate anyway because she couldn't bear to waste?

Dr Fan adjusts his glasses. 'Besides the blood in your stool and abdominal pain, anything else?'

'I feel tired a lot,' Min Fong says.

Dr Fan makes her lie down on the charpoy in the room, rolls up the edge of her tunic, rests a hand on her abdomen. His hand feels papery dry, yet steady. He taps her abdomen with two fingers of the other hand, his ear cocked. Finally, he tells her to get up and sit down.

He offers her a cup of hot tea. Min Fong isn't one to refuse beverages of any kind when offered. As she sips—*wah,* Dr Fan serves such fancy tea—he tells her she has an intestinal problem—leaky pipe, and it's not likely to go away. In fact, the pain will get much worse in the next few months.

'What happens then?' Min Fong asks. Her lip is stinging from the hot tea and the room feels overly stuffy.

Dr Fan looks anywhere but at her, his glance shifting to the shaving mirror to her left, then sliding right to the shelf full of his medicinal powders. 'Do you have relatives back in China? Perhaps you want to see them?'

'To ask them for help, you mean?'

Dr Fan finally looks her dead in the eye. 'No. To go home.'

It isn't that Min Fong chooses to disbelieve. It's just that she's only turned twenty-seven by the Chinese zodiac. Once upon a time, Min Fong remembers walking down a cowpat-littered path beside the river that meanders through the sleepy village she grew up in, a place not just oceans away, but a time long past, and her memories feel sifted and hazy, bits of them drifting past like leaves on a river. That day, she'd set aside the pretty flower-embroidered shoes she was wearing, before heading down to the riverbank to pee behind a tree. She came back to find them gone, and a village matron bustling down the path, dangling a cloth-covered basket on her arm. Min Fong had run after her, accused her of stealing the shoes. The matron had chastised her for disrespect towards her elders, but in the end, Min Fong had been right. When she yanked the cloth from the basket, there her dainty shoes were, a vibrant red with hand-sewn pink peony flowers. Stealing was such a big crime in her mind then, but look now how she steals drops of White Flower Oil from Mrs Cheng for her sore shoulder blades and her abdominal pain. Mrs Cheng is getting suspicious, demanding to know if the coolies next door have been sneaking into her room to nick drops of her oil. Thinking about Dr Fan's words, Min Fong feels a certain outrage, even shame: who has ever heard of women like her, women with red headscarves, women strong enough to lug bricks and mortar eight hours a day, falling ill? She consults with Lu *Daifu* downstairs, choosing to reveal only that she has difficulty with her crapper, and he packs for her a mixture of dried herbs wrapped in fuchsia-coloured rice paper, ties it with raffia. It uses up a day's pay. She asks Chin Leng to request the letter writer in Sago Street to write, on her behalf, to her mother-in-law to say that she won't be sending money this month because of unexpected expenses.

'There's no need to broadcast to all and sundry,' Min Fong's tone is a little airy, but the atmosphere between her and Chin Leng is still a trifle brusque. 'It's nobody's business but my own.'

Chin Leng smirks, but simply holds out her hand for the money to pay the letter writer.

However, quick as the turn of a body, the word is out. Po Jie comes and asks her if anything is wrong. What unexpected expenses? Mrs Cheng also pokes her head in with concern: I hear you went to see Dr Fan. Is anything the matter?

Min Fong turns upon Chin Leng with fury, 'Was it you?'

Chin Leng sits in her corner, insouciantly darning her torn

samfoo trousers while sucking on a sour plum. She shrugs. 'Don't look at me. Your silly secrets don't matter a horse fart to me.' But adds, under her breath, 'I guess you'll need more White Flower Oil now, the way you're moaning and groaning in your sleep.'

Mrs Cheng looks dumbly on, before catching Chin Leng's sly meaningful glance, and then her mouth drops open. Po Jie looks nonplussed, while Mrs Cheng looks slightly horrified. It's nothing compared to what Min Fong feels at having her little theft revealed this way.

As the months pass, Min Fong's health weakens. It has become impossible to work. A smell emanates from her bowels; her roommates say nothing but avoid staying in the room if they can. The shophouse inhabitants also avoid Min Fong. As if she has nits. Suddenly, everyone has become stupidly religious, diligently sticking their incense sticks in the prayer urns for the Sky God and Kitchen God shrines at the proper times. In her heart, Min Fong doesn't blame them. She'd probably be no different if another shophouse resident was similarly afflicted. Po Jie cares for her, continuously, without complaint, procuring her food and medicine. But Min Fong knows: sooner or later, in order not to pollute the shophouse—death is such a contaminating thing—she's destined for one of the death houses in Sago Lane. She's been keeping up a grand charade of how she's not ill, but in fact making preparations to sail home to visit her no-good husband and dependent mother-in-law. Po Jie asks if she may 'borrow' the chamber pot and washbasin during the time she's away, and Min Fong, with a heart that suddenly feels pricked, knows what she's asking. 'Of course, you can borrow it. You can borrow it for as long as you want.'

During a rare burst of energy one day, Min Fong gets up and cleans the wash basin and the chamber pot in the back shower stall, scrubbing so thoroughly the white enamel paint within pans back the quivery glimmer of her own reflection. A few weeks ago, with a similar jolt of startling strength, she'd actually walked to the letter writer in Sago Street to have a letter written to her husband. A final letter, though she didn't let herself speak those words. On the way there, however, she was winded and couldn't continue. It occurred to her then, she had no inkling what to say. Sorry, you emperor-tortoise egg, you have to pay your own debts now and feed your own mouth? Oh, how to say such a thing!

In front of her sat a coffin shop, bad luck on any day to pass by one, and here she was, planting herself right in front of its five-foot way. The shophouse door front had been folded back, and a lad was sitting on a sawhorse inside being taught by his master how to plane a chunk of wood with an axe, while a girl, no older than eleven or twelve, swept up the fallen wood shavings. There were many things Min Fong would've liked to do—the thought arrived as gently as spooling thread—and it's this, this bending over and cherishing a young one. What kind of feeling would that have been?

Katharine, bookkeeper, 1969

The couple interested in buying Mr Lu's shophouse in Bukit Pasoh look as resplendent and minted as new money. As Katharine leads Xiao Mei around the house, she hears her kitty heels tap-tapping behind. Dressed in a tight, flowery cheongsam, Xiao Mei is beautiful and delicate, but her tone, in commenting to her husband on the dilapidated state of the shophouse, is peevish: *Eh*, very dark *leh* in the inner courtyard, tiles all broken, I bet when it rains, it leaks all over the place, and can you smell the trapped odour of decades of cramped communal cooking? She inspects the lighter patches on the wall and the burnt marks on the ceiling, marks left by the de-installed shrines of the Sky God and Kitchen God, marks of incense burning. Tsks.

The husband, Daniel, is a serious, smartly dressed office type; his facial contours are strangely flat, with wide nostrils and even wider lips, full and thick. In his crisp, white shirt, navy blue trousers, ducktail-gelled hair, he doesn't say much in response, but every once in a while, he trades conspiratorial looks with Katharine, and despite being older, more mature, and infinitely less attractive than the wife, Katharine feels flattered, caught within the net of that secretive gaze. Disturbed even.

They are the fifth young couple to look at the shophouse. Strange, most prefer the Housing Development Board flats, a scheme promulgated by the government that's been wildly successful; HDB flats are brand-new and ghost-free. Xiao Mei is making disparaging comments about old Taoist superstitions. Katharine doesn't reply. The Kitchen God protects the hearth and family. The Sky God is the Chinese equivalent of Zeus, responsible for proportioning yin and yang, creating the order of the cosmos and the four seasons, putting all the dots and sparkles and spangles in the sky, offend this God and you're probably going to be reincarnated as a dung beetle, what does this girl know? But, then again, these are heady times, look now, Singapore is independent and the ground underneath their feet seems constantly shifting, what with the rapid demolition of the old and the massive construction of the new. Who can blame the young people for casting off all manner of shackles and superstitious beliefs?

The wife wanders on ahead, banging open the front window shutters. The husband hovers nearby, his presence causing the hairs on Katharine's forearms and the back of her neck to stand alert, a sort of electric anticipation. If only she dares tilt her head towards him, return his forceful gaze. They're actually in the room where Katharine grew up from age eight to sixteen. Out of nervousness, she hears herself telling the husband about growing up in a family of six daughters. Being 'fostered out' is neither here nor there; she was lucky. While Po Jie had 'adopted' her, it was essentially an arrangement of upkeep—taking the burden of an extra mouth to feed away from her parents, but without Po Jie insisting that she come and live with her to serve as servant. But all that changed when she was eight and one of Po Jie's roommates succumbed to a mysterious disease, leaving a room vacancy. Katharine remembers vividly the day she arrived to stay, carrying a bundle of two changes of clothing and the book of Chinese characters she was learning on her own. She'd been taken to a funeral that day, a day she never forgot. The coffin sat in a death house, and a washbasin with a rooster design had sat on a stool in front of a portrait of the deceased, who was a young-looking samsui woman with a stern expression, as if ever ready to cudgel you around the ears if you sassed her. Inside the washbasin was a cup, complete with toothbrush, toothpaste and a towel. Katharine remembered thinking, what the heck is this, are you supposed to wash your face and brush your teeth before you kowtow to the dead?

Daniel, the husband, laughs. She realises she's talking like a fool. In fact, Katharine half-subscribes to all the Chinese rituals and rites, but maybe it's because she wants to seem agreeable; she's trying to sell a shophouse here. Showing the shophouse is a favour to Mr Lu, her boss. She keeps books for Mr Lu's import-export business—from a Chinese medicinal shop, he'd since branched off into *kelapa sawit* (palm oil) and Sarawak pepper, taking advantage of Singapore's port and regional-hub capabilities.

Daniel smiles at her. 'I also don't go in much for these old Chinese superstitions. My mother still observes all the rituals, so *lou-tou* and old-fashioned, but then, can't blame her, she immigrated as coolie labour from China.'

'So did mine,' Katharine says, thinking of Po Jie who has been more of a mother to her than her own.

'That's how it is, isn't it? You just follow like a blind bat. Very primitive.'

'The Chinese are superior.' The wife has suddenly snuck up behind them, how had they missed those annoying tip-tapping kitty heels? 'Industrious, thrifty, hardworking, enterprising. That's how we made it here.'

Katharine and the husband both say nothing. He looks sheepish, as if caught out, while Katharine feels deflated by the smug racial pride. Oh, what would this couple think if she told them she'd once gone out with a Malay man? She was half-crazed with love. Now, she's a disappointment to her parents, taking a vow of celibacy like a *ma jie* of old, turning into a *lou-gu-poh* (spinster).

The young couple says they'll call her if they want another viewing. With some regret, Katharine watches the husband open the door of his Austin Minor for his wife. He gives Katharine a last look and a small wave. Likely she'll never hear from them again.

Her bodily response to him, though, had her all shook-up. Still some life in the old *lou-gu-poh* body after all. She heads towards Smith Street, where she's due to run a historical tour for a group of Taiwanese tourists. She volunteers at the Tung On Wui Kun, one of the clan associations in Chinatown to which she claims lineage. Because of her versatility in both English and Mandarin, Katharine is pressed to do the walking tours every Saturday. European tourists have commented that she seems very knowledgeable, her English excellent; they loved her stories about how Chinatown got its name of *Niú Chē Shuǐ*, the opium dens, the death houses that recently inhabited Sago Lane.

A group of seven middle-aged women are waiting, thoroughly equipped with sun and heat protection: newly bought *nipah* fans, sunhats and sunglasses, and sleeves to protect the arms. Katharine greets the group in Mandarin. Right away, one of the tourists, a woman wearing a lovely dress with a full skirt and tortoiseshell glasses, comments that it's peculiar to have a Chinatown in Singapore when Singapore is already so Chinese; isn't the entire city a veritable Chinatown? No Chinatown in Hong Kong or in Taiwan, only places like San Francisco or Toronto, where the Chinese *piāo lái piāo qù*, where identity sloshes about, as if afloat on a boat.

Slightly taken aback, Katharine explains how Chinatown in Singapore is a function of colonial history, how Sir Stamford Raffles, that astonishing, enterprising upper-class statesman and scholar, had cleverly segmented Singapore along ethnic lines with the Jackson urban planning scheme, forming *kampongs* for the Malays, the Indians and the Chinese, in pursuit of 'communal harmony', a Confucian value!

She's led the tour group down Smith Street now, and in front of them is the former famed Chinese opera theatre, Lai Chun Yuen. Quickly changing topic, she mentions that, in its heyday, it staged Cantonese operas twice a day. The Taiwanese tourists are all agog. But the woman who had made the Chinatown comment seems dissatisfied. She stands slightly apart from the group, fanning herself slowly, an air of mystery about her. As a history hobbyist, Katharine wonders if her spiel has become too pre-packaged, too convenient. What other stories does the façade of Lai Chun Yuen hide? Her mind casts back to what Xiao Mei had said about the industriousness of Chinese immigrants; it's not that she disagrees, it's just that her viewpoint feels like one of those movies-on-wheels of old—a peepshow of Mickey Mouse cartoon, partial and disjointed. Chinese coolie labour had no choice in their 'adopted' home—don't work, you don't eat. How many other stories about Chinatown, indeed about Malaya as a British colony, and Singapore and Malaysia as newly developing nations comprised of large percentages of migrant labour, are just as real, just as full of sacrifice and hardship and sheer toil, but remain buried and lost in time?

After the tour, Katharine is exhausted. She catches the bus to Bukit Merah, to visit Po Jie, for whom she cooks dinner three times a week. Po Jie, who still does construction work, even though she must be close to sixty by now. When Katharine urges her to think about retirement, Po Jie laughs. 'What, retire to an old folks' home? I don't want.'

On the bus, she finds a seat next to a window. The entire day feels like a grafted skin of perturbation and disquiet. She finally allows her mind to go where it's wanted to go since the shophouse. Hayqal. Their love affair that had ended so abruptly, so unceremoniously, leaving her wounded and desolate for months. Ten years have passed; yet she remembers their first date so vividly. They'd gone to see P. Ramlee's *Madu Tiga* at the Cathay, clutching each other in a giggle fit when the three wives of a cheating husband lounged together at the beach and said, in sweetly saccharine tones, that they'd scoop each other's eyeballs out. Afterwards, Hayqal had taken Katharine to have satays on Beach Road, then they put-putted home on his moped. At the wrought iron gate, he'd grasped hold of her hand, boldly intertwined their fingers, and led her to the night shadows of some overly-luxuriant *nipah* palms. He wasn't much taller than her, and as he leaned in close, he hesitated, as if unsure, as if he were aware of all the leapfrogging of boundaries with this one minuscule gesture. 'May I?' he whispered. Such a gentleman, how could she refuse? Katharine moved her mouth just infinitesimally closer. His thumb and fingers encircled her chin to tilt her lips up; his mouth opened and took hers.

Her parents had put their foot down. What was the point of all that money she earned, helping Dr Lu in the shophouse by being his assistant, pounding roots and herbs with mortar and pestle, doing his accounting and washing up, if she were to end up being a Malay housewife? Didn't she know, after a year or two, he'd tire of her and get himself another? They can have four, you know. Katharine had felt like retorting: the Chinese have multiple concubines, what about that? Then her mother's weary countenance even as she said, What good is it to have such a nimble brain, good with remembering numbers and facts, and all that schooling she had, a diploma in accounting some more, if all she did with it was marry beneath her status? What did she say he did for a living? Making outdoor furniture? What, not even furniture for inside? What a terrible loss of face!

Was that all they cared about? Their *min zi*? Whether they lost face or not? Katharine had shouted. Her mother had shouted back, 'We don't want you to spend your life being looked down upon. What parent wants that for her child?'

She defied them by continuing to date Hayqal, even as she felt a knot of shame inside at her lack of filial piety, bringing her family honour down, and yes, her inability to curb her unruly heart. Each date though was also a triumph of self-definition, of self-reclamation—biryani in Serangoon Road, kway teow at the outdoor eating stalls on Albert Street, nasi rawan at Bussorah Street—each date was an affirmation that the real matters more than the surface markers of identity, a belief that there's an inner smoulder of the inexorable and illimitable and indescribable that only the two of them could experience in the other. They made love in his furniture shop, no more than a shack really, in Punggol. To Katharine, he was so sexy—she loved his throat and shoulders, the skin there as soft as a baby's bottom. He was so gentle with her, sucking at her as if she was pure honey, calling her his honeybee. His fingers, they knew how to work a body, to coax, to smooth, to shape, to spring, to release.

Po Jie had intervened at her parents' request. Katharine might have gone on defying her parents, but how could she disobey Po Jie, her 'adoptive' mother, the one who had ransomed her life? What she owes Po Jie is not just filial duty, but also a debt of honour, to be repaid till death. Po Jie forced a *seung-tai* on her—introduced her to the tailor's son from the shophouse next door. Out of deference, even as her heart stormed and raged, she went with him to see a Hong Kong romantic melodrama at the Capitol—*Love With An Alien,* starring the incandescent Yu Ming. Throughout the film, all Katharine wanted to do was hurl dried sotong and kacang puteh at the *ngong lou,* who laughed whenever a melodramatic line was delivered. Afterwards, Katharine vomited by the side of the road, into a *longkang.* The sheer difference in her reaction did not elude her. The tailor's son jeered, 'Did you want to see a Malay film or something?' It was a slap in the face, for sure.

When Hayqal unceremoniously ended the affair—one day, he simply failed to turn up for an assignation, and also oddly, didn't answer any of her subsequent letters—Katharine swore she could give him up as easily as he gave her up. Her own mother rubbed salt into an open gaping wound: I told you so, I told you he would dump you soon as he catches sight of another pretty skirt. Only Po Jie was there for her. Cooking for her, feeding her, nourishing her. Chubby frog's legs in ginger sauce. Steamed lotus-wrapped sticky rice, rich with dates and salted egg. Homemade zha jiang mian Po Jie had learned to make—these really Chinese dishes, as if to remind her she's a true-blue Chinese. Katharine felt like the Kitchen Goddess, her lips being sealed with sticky grease so she wouldn't cry. But at least Po Jie cared, even if her methods were inept. Katharine had her movies. At Rex or Cathay or Majestic, she could watch *The Adventures of*

Pinocchio or *The Real McCoy* or *Sumpah Orang Minyak*. Scream her lungs out at the frightful oily man and feel some relief.

At the front door of Po Jie's HDB flat, she takes out her key for the metal accordion gate, but before she can unlock it, Po Jie is at the door.

'You're home!' Katharine exclaims with surprise.

'The back is doing me in today,' Po Jie sighs.

Katharine feels such familiarity here. Her home away from home. All of Po Jie's most prized possessions, her sparse Chinese antiques—a circular rosewood table with an embedded slab of marble and ornately carved wooden stools, the Sky God and Kitchen God shrines, which Po Jie had relocated here when Mr Lu moved his family to a two-storey bungalow in Katong. Nothing thrown out. The Chinese chamber pot with a red rooster design, chock-full with old rubber slippers. Up until a few years ago, Po Jie had used it to stash her savings underneath the rough working shoes she'd hewn out of car tires. In the Bukit Pasoh shophouse, Katharine had kept a goldfish in it, her sole childhood entertainment, watching it finning around. Its paint is flaking off now, revealing bald patches of rusty metal. All these cultural objects as proxies to salvage the past, to cement a sense of heritage and belonging, to act as receptacles, as the Taiwanese tourist had charged, to give form to liquid identity.

In Po Jie's kitchen, a wrapped newspaper bundle lies on the counter. The fishy smell of newsprint emanates as Katharine unwraps it. Inside is a Cantonese *lap ngap*. Jiminy Cricket, a flattened waxed duck. She yells out to Po Jie, 'Ma, what's with the duck?'

Po Jie answers, 'Do something with it, will you? Old Mr Chow gave it to me.'

But certain Cantonese traditional delicacies flummox Katharine—this is one of them. She throws it back into its wrapper, sticks it in the fridge. In the end, she makes steamed egg with mushrooms, stir-fried dow miao, and Po Jie's favourite, peanuts and anchovies stir-fried in fragrant sesame oil.

Po Jie eyes the dishes on the table. 'I thought you'd make something fancy with the duck?'

'It'll keep, it's waxed,' Katharine says.

As they eat, Katharine says, apropos of nothing, 'I guess I'm not as Chinese as all that. I don't much care for Chinese sausages either, I guess I never told you.'

Po Jie scoops rice into her mouth vigorously with her chopsticks, holding her bowl close to her chin. 'You're more a kangkung and belachan person, I know. Rendang, nasi kandar, that's more up your alley. Rojak food.'

Katharine pauses. 'That's what you say. I suddenly remembered that boy today.'

All these chewing noises Po Jie makes. Why must Po Jie always live as if life is only about eating, sleeping and shitting?

Absent-mindedly, Po Jie says, 'Didn't take much to scare him, I thought he'd hold out. That *dam-siu-gwai*.' Coward.

Katharine's chopsticks halt at midpoint to her mouth. White rice cascading like pellets of snow. A slow drip of knowledge, an intuitive understanding bleeding into tissue. 'You spoke to Hayqal? When would you have spoken to Hayqal?'

Po Jie's turn now to become motionless. Her eyes becoming furtive, evading. Katharine realises, with a lurch, that in a momentary lack of vigilance, Po Jie had divulged something she meant to take to the grave. Po Jie rolls her rice in her mouth, preventing herself from speaking. She smacks her lips, then picks up a large tuft of dow miao to put in her mouth. She chews. Katharine understands that this will be all that's ever said. Her heart spins like a barrel, the words *sem tong* in Cantonese slip into her mind like the muted refrain of a Chinese ballad. Cantonese expressions for emotions are so melodramatic, nothing like their pale reflections in another language—*sakit hati* or heart pain, *jatuh maruah* or loss of face. She looks at all the objects on the table, steam from the rice preventing her from seeing them properly, the chipped Chinese crockery and slightly corroded tin mugs, these traces of lived, hobbled lives.

Heidi, documentary filmmaker, 1996

The five samsui women Heidi has gathered together in the shophouse on this torpid afternoon look as frisky, as *lóng mǎ jīng shén* (vigorous horse and dragon spirited), as nursing home inhabitants watching a Malay oldie they don't comprehend on the telly. Two are dozing with mouths open; two are chatting, although given the lengthy pauses between give-and-exchange, it sounds more like a random soliloquy than a conversation. Only one appears alert, her eyes tracking Heidi and Ben, Heidi's cameraman. Her name is Po Jie—Sister Po—her passport name is Chen Po Chun. Not many of these pioneering women still alive, and of the ones Heidi contacted, only these five are fit to travel. For funds to be disbursed the documentary's mandate is 'authenticity', thus Part Two of the documentary will be a trip to China—the return HOME—because it will be a tearjerker of reunions, and when tears flow, people believe it's true. But here's Problem No. 1: not all of them are enthused about going HOME. One is worried about what or who she'll find, while another says she's not sure the old house hasn't been torn down, she seems to remember a letter telling her so, but her memory being what it is, maybe it was the outhouse that has been dismantled. Problem No. 2: not all are from the area of Sanshui, and the budget is too tight to film separate village trips. A bit of a Potemkin Village issue, that, Ben remarks. Heidi shoots him a doleful look.

It's twenty-two degrees, but feels twenty-eight; a storm is brewing and the sky looks swollen and bunged-up. Through the open window the juddering of a pneumatic road drill interjects.

Ben pokes his head out the window. He reports, 'It looks like they're breaking up cement. Do you want to have a chat with these blokes, p'raps, considering you're local?'

Heidi takes a peek. Two Indian migrant labourers in yellow hard hats and neon vests are juggling the drilling. No, she doesn't want to have a chat with them. 'I don't speak Tamil, you ninny.' She feels irritation out of proportion to Ben's surface misreading of language syncretism in Singapore. It's more a cogs-mismatch feeling, like they're missing the bigger picture altogether.

The ceiling fan whirs slowly, beating the soporific air with lazy paddles. On afternoons like these, Heidi wishes she was back in the UK. Having just relocated home, this idea brings ambivalent, mixed feelings, even an anxiety of sorts: ironic, given that in London, she thought of HOME often and waxed nostalgic about ham jim baeng, salted pancakes, and yau-ja-gui, fried dough sticks. Or maybe it's ice kachang and banana fritters she dreamt more about.

The idea for Part One of the documentary is to film the samsui women in their home environment. As Heidi was interviewing them and hearing their life stories, she realised that the story she wants to tell isn't about how feminist and epochal these women are, even though the very idea of women construction workers helping to build a nation's infrastructure in 1960s and 1970s Singapore is pretty bad-ass, nor is it about their pioneer spirit—their resilience, industriousness, thriftiness and diligence, harnessed as part of a heritage industry of memory-making and a nation-building narrative bent on inculcating desirable values—but rather, Heidi wants to tell a story simply about the individual lives of these women. Stories that aren't singular, stories that show that they are flesh and blood, 3D. The good, the bad, the ugly. Stories without an agenda. Is that even possible? If stories of these women are allowed just to be stories of a lived life, would it return ownership and agency to them? Would they thank Heidi for unflattening them, portraying their individual stories, neither condemning nor extolling them? Or would Heidi herself be considered exploitative? How important is it for the auteur to interrogate her own motives?

Problem No. 3. This gathering feels off. The ladies do not actually know one another. None of them wants to travel to China on her own. Heidi is hoping that this gathering will enable them to befriend each other and become more comfortable with the idea of travelling as a group. Plus, yield some nice footage.

Yesterday, at Po Jie's flat in Bukit Merah, even the props had looked all wrong. Ben had walked around the flat and collected some items. Placed them on, or in the vicinity of, the circular rosewood dining table and stools, while Po Jie and her unmarried daughter, Katharine, chattered away, not minding him. A Chinese-style, fleur-design thermos. A celadon teapot and teacups set. A pair of endearing bamboo mother-child chairs.

'Ben,' Heidi said, 'samsui women are supposed to have taken a vow of celibacy.' From the corner of her eye, she could see Katharine glancing out the window. A stiff set to her shoulders, possibly from the noise aggravation outside.

Ben shrugged. 'Just snazzing things up. These are from the house.' Nevertheless, he took away the mother-child chairs, came back with a chamber pot with a red rooster design. Plonked it next to a Chinese silkscreen.

'Ben, that's for peeing in.'

He stood still. Looked around. Grabbed a potted shrub and plopped it in. 'There now.'

Heidi gave up. Ben loves goofing around. He tried durian when they first arrived and the taste was so vile to him he spat the mouthful into someone's handy glass of Coca-Cola.

She'd thought Po Jie and Katharine were chatting, but their raised voices finally registered. Not understanding Cantonese, Heidi observed Katharine rising from her chair. Po Jie didn't look up as Katharine took her mug of tea, ready to quit the room. To Heidi, Katharine seemed standoffish and cold, although impressively—Po Jie had told Heidi proudly—Katharine spoke English, Malay, Mandarin and at least two other Chinese dialects, Hokkien and Cantonese.

Heidi approached Katharine with an enquiring eyebrow lift. 'Everything okay?'

Katharine didn't look at Heidi. The tension in the angle of her neck was now palpable. 'She wants me to accompany her on the China trip. I have work obligations. I can't simply take a week off.'

Heidi was surprised. 'Po Jie told me you're retired? You used to be a bookkeeper?'

The change in Katharine's face was astonishing: from a frozen visage, her eyes were now flashing with fury. 'I run historical tours for a Chinatown clan association. I take my duties very seriously. I don't just play play.'

Heidi was taken aback. Katharine was insinuating that her documentary was 'play play'. Coming from left field, Heidi wasn't sure what she'd said or done to offend Katharine, but not wishing to antagonise her further, she gave her most winsome smile. 'Please don't worry, we can discuss this nearer the date. You might change your mind as you see how the film develops. I think your mother would enjoy your company on the trip.'

'She just wants me there to play nursemaid. And I won't be changing my mind.'

Abruptly, Katharine turned and walked to the kitchen. Heidi and Ben traded looks.

All that now seems smoothed over as Heidi watches Katharine open a Tupperware box of peeled clementine segments for her mother and the other samsui women. Ben is filming this, his eyes fixed to the camera viewfinder. She knows the shot: two generations sharing a convivial moment around food, food as metonymic reference for nourishment, kinship and heritage continuity, and it's happening unscripted. Sometimes there is an uncanny mind meld between them. Heidi met Ben at NYU Film School. Right from the beginning, their instant attraction for each other was off-the-charts, but she was a shy foreign student and he was one of those charmers who only needed to open his mouth for his nondescript North London accent to trip out and women in New York dropped at his feet like flies. So, they played cat and mouse through an entire semester. Then, one evening, as she entered a lecture hall, he was there, sitting two rows from the front. He looked up and straight at her. There was no avoiding saying hello, and the sudden expectant look on his face made her take a seat next to him. As they waited for the lecture to begin, the entire side of her body close to his felt as though it was burning. Finally, she snuck a look over and saw he too was rigid with tension. Without meaning to, she said, 'Are we going to have trouble concentrating?' The dawning of understanding on his face was a sight to behold; she never forgot it. Ben looked at her. He grinned, 'Looks like it.' When they left the lecture hall, he grabbed her hand.

As if sensing what she's thinking, even with his back to her, Ben is making gestures at her, his hands—his paws she calls them, with their fat, pink fingers—twisting behind his back. What the heck is the nutter up to now? Peering, Heidi watches as Ben contorts his hands, then slowly she sees it. Hand shadow puppets: first two raised fingers, middle and index finger, two lopsided ears—ah, a rabbit—next a dog, a butterfly, and what is that...a moose? Heidi bursts out laughing. Ben turns and gives her an air smooch.

Their troubles continue. Turns out one of the samsui women has Crohn's disease. 'What's Crohn's disease?' Ben asks. They look it up. Ruptured intestinal walls. Blood in the faeces. Yikes.

To distract themselves from the multiple roadblocks they've encountered for the documentary, Heidi and Ben take a weekend jaunt to Bangkok, and at the airport, haggling over the price of a city tour, they lose their camera, or perhaps someone just made off with it. Livid with Ben for not being more careful, Heidi storms off, until she realises she has nowhere to go. It's the Bangkok international airport. But that's not all. She comes back for a face off with her one and only, her shadow puppeteer, and he tells her that the film tapes were in the bag with the camera. The news pummels her. Heidi sinks down to the floor, cups both her hands over her face, and bawls. Tears bathing her cheeks like a wrung-out dishrag. This is just the shits, she blubbers. So unfair, what god has she offended? Ben hunkers down and cradles her. She sobs into his neck and the collar of his T-shirt becomes so damp he has to buy an emergency T-shirt to change into. He comes out of the bathroom wearing one that says, *This Guy Loves Muay-Thai.*

The worst is yet to come. Only on the return trip does Ben realise his passport has less than six months' validity, and the airline ground staff refuse to let him fly. Ben says she should go home first, that he'll join her as soon as he sorts it out. Reluctantly, Heidi acquiesces, but two days later, not only does Ben not turn up, there's no answer when she calls his cell phone and hotel room. Terrified that something might have happened to him in Bangkok—her mind roils from all the possibilities (seduced in a Patpong sex show? fell into the Chao Phraya?)—she frantically calls up the British Consulate in Bangkok, explaining herself incoherently to the officer at the other end, who responds frostily with, 'And may I ask what your relationship to said British national is?' The question stumps Heidi. Doesn't she love Ben, and yet why has the word 'love' never been uttered between them, why does the designation 'lover' feel like an ill-fitting suit of clothes? It's one of those things she can't bear to admit—are they together because Ben provides a link to that other 'home', a link never tensile enough, regardless of how accented her English is (not Singaporean, *haah,* as the taxi uncles ask). Rootlessness. The lack of an anchor. Where is home for hybrid people like herself, made up like a box of incongruities? Fluid identities that spill beyond boundaries, running like lines of flight, like ley lines that map and traverse different worlds? What lurks within the heart that no one sees, and when confessed, would it form bonds and communal links, as envisioned by Confucian philosophy? Would it create a safety net strong enough to hold her?

Ben finally calls. Over the static in the trunk line, he tells her he's back in London.

Heidi's utter shock: 'What in the world are you doing there?'

Ben's pause. 'I'm sorry luv.' The word 'love' used like this throws her. Her mind clouds over. Ben's sheepish regretful tone over the phone. 'I didn't know how to tell you, Heidi, but I just don't think I can continue with your project. I have no idea what I'm doing traipsing all over Asia, following you around like a hound dog.'

Her project? 'What do you mean?'

'I...' Then, the ultimate shaft. 'You remember Scott Pennington from film school, don't you?' Heidi has a vague recollection of this Scott Pennington—red hair, lots of freckles, a button nose, like Christopher Robin from Winnie the Pooh. 'He called me while I was in Bangkok. He's shooting a documentary all about ice up in Norway, it's quite an exciting project, and he says he could use another cameraman. I just thought...given...'

Heidi doesn't let him finish. She hangs up on him.

Time flows on. Life flows on too. A couple of months later, as she's on a flight to Guangzhou with three samsui women seated beside her—one of them Po Jie, but sans Katharine—she wonders if their initial framework for the project was flawed to begin with. 'Authenticity' is a gimmick, a façade, not to be confused with the 'real'. It wasn't a 'commemorative narrative' in the making, it was a comedy of errors. When 'home' as a concept is debunked or demythologised, what are you left with?

The eureka moment had occurred as she was scrolling through her Nikon just a couple of days after Ben's devastating phone call. She'd come upon a photograph of a Chinatown public mural of two samsui women in their iconic red headscarves and navy blue *samfoos,* squatting down on a pavement sharing a bowl of noodles. Ben, in typical impish fashion, had squatted down between them, and mimed eating a bowl of noodles with chopsticks, sticking out like a goat. Snap! Heidi took the picture.

They haven't spoken since the call, and the situation is not resolved, so they are back to their inception—the cat and mouse—hiding from each other. That's how certain things are: they don't end, they just hang.

The picture, though, had been like a nose tweak. Not 'roots', what a *dungu* she'd been, but 'routes'! She'd been reading a spate of recently published academic theories: Bhabha, Gilroy, Rey Chow. Being unhomed was the journey itself. It was as if the planet had opened up like the Hungry Ghost Festival, the gates of Hell thrown open, and all manner of ghostly half-realisations given a voice. Her role too became clarified: not creator, but witness. Like the movie houses on bicycles of old—partial glimpses, sneak peeks. Wasn't that, in the end, what memory making for those in the heritage industry is? Offering a series of windows into the past, and the past is a series of flows?

With that in mind, her focus changed. She filmed them doing their ablutions in the morning—Po Jie still using her Chinese rooster-design washbasin. The chamber pot as signifier. After all, official memory making sifts through what's worthy as myth, sloughs off the mind-residue without compunction, like so much body waste. She filmed them in a quiet moment: the restlessness on their faces. Also their capacity for stillness, just sitting, staring out the window, listening to the trill of birds. Cocking their ears to listen out for their neighbours in the HDB complex. Sticking incense into the urns of ancestral shrines. She filmed Katharine massaging Po Jie's knees, calves, wrists, arms and back with White Flower Oil. Her actions so thorough the moment was riven with tenderness. And the past was glimpsed through a sound her camera picked up: the cricks in Po Jie's joints and bones from a lifetime in construction. She filmed them at dinner with their families, the happiness that stole over their features when a family member nimbly picked up a slice of water chestnut or steamed abalone mushroom with chopsticks and placed it in their bowl of rice. She filmed them close-up, zeroing in on their interior journeys, until the iris dissolved into a counterpane of black criss-crossed with sparkings of light.

In China as well, she'll be a one-woman crew; her heart throbs when she thinks about the sights that await her. She wants to film them looking at decimated or newly done-over villages, tabulating the forces of industrialisation in their heads. She wants to film them being greeted by the young and old, relatives and friends they don't know they have, and how the generational divide is fielded through their gestures in between empty silent spaces. She wants to film them absorbing the sights and sounds of the welcome party the provincial government has planned to 'promote' these amazing, pioneering women full of grit and fire.

She wants to film the samsui women looking on.

Looking at.

Looking for.

Looking, looking, looking.

Awards and original sources

'Face' won First Prize in the Bridport Prize International Short Story Competition 2008 and is anthologised in *The Bridport Prize 2008.*

'Run of the Molars' appeared in *Cooked Up: Food Fiction From Around the World* (London: New Internationalist, 2015).

'Love, Nude' appeared in *Singapore Love Stories* (Monsoon Books, 2016), and the anthology was shortlisted for Best Fiction in the Singapore Popular Readers' Choice Awards, 2017.

'Florida Rednecks Loved Moo Goo Gai Pan' appeared in *Front Porch Journal,* June 2009, and also received an Honorable Mention in the Glimmer Train Very Short Fiction Award (2017).

'Confessions of an Irresolute Ethnic Writer' first appeared in *Unthology 10* (Unthank Books, 2018).

'The Coffin Maker' (in truncated form, and originally titled 'Tiffin Carrier') was longlisted for the Mogford Prize for Food & Drink Writing 2018.

'The Heartsick Diaspora' won Second Prize in the Bridport Prize International Short Story Competition 2018 and is anthologised in *The Bridport Prize Anthology 2018.*

Acknowledgements

THE HEARTSICK DIASPORA has been a long time in the making, from the initial story 'Face', which won first place in the Bridport Prize 2008, through to 'The Heartsick Diaspora', which won second place in the Bridport Prize 2018. This ten-year time frame, book-ended by the same literary competition, felt serendipitous, possessed of a hidden life meaning, to me. As I looked at how to order the stories I'd chosen to include in the collection, it became reflective of my own journey of 'nostos'—the root word in Ancient Greek for 'nostalgia', with the emphasis not so much on destination as on the act of searching for 'return'. Thus, to make manifest this journey of time crossed with place—Paul Gilroy's idea of diaspora as 'flows', that metaphysical space constituted by the tension between cultural 'roots' and cultural 'routes'—the cities of New York, London, Singapore, as primary places represented in the stories, became a symbolic order of my own journey of diaspora as 'homes' that have taken 'root' (this, despite manifesting Homi Bhabha's notion of the anxiety of being 'unhomed' for those displaced).

The historical stories in the collection, though fictional, have attempted to stay true in broad citation of facts and time periods, and thus, owe a debt to a variety of sources. Those with the most impact are credited below (any deficiency in nuance or imagination is mine).

There are many people to thank, without which this book may never have made the journey to publication. Writers Susannah Rickards, Susan Elderkin and Romesh Gunesekera read and suggested helpful edits on a couple of the stories in their early formation; writers Monica Ali, Karen Bender, Shelly Bryant, Vanessa Gebbie, Petina Gappah, Pippa Goldschmidt, Desmond Kon Zhicheng-Mingdé, Charles Lambert, Paul McVeigh, Dipika Mukherjee and Intan Paramaditha gave me encouragement and/or endorsements; and WordTheatre director Cedering Fox and the entire Edale crew were hugely supportive of my writing journey. Most of all, I want to thank the fabulous Bridport Prize (and Judges Helen Simpson and Monica Ali for choosing 'Face' and 'The Heartsick Diaspora' as winning stories), thereby throwing wide open the Gates of Opportunity in one fell swoop.

I want to thank Dan Raymond-Barker at New Internationalist Publications who introduced me to Myriad Editions, when I was enquiring about publishers of short story collections. New Internationalist is a publisher I owe much to, not just for publishing me in *One World*, but also for seeking me out to compile *Cooked Up: Food Fiction from Around the World.* These might be chance encounters, but in fact, chance encounters are the ones that have the capacity to turn your life around. I want to thank Candida Lacey, publishing director *extraordinaire,* Vicki Heath Silk for her trenchant, meticulous edits, Louisa Pritchard and others at Myriad for shepherding the book from draft form to tunnelling its way out into the world. I want to thank Gaurav Shrinagesh and Nora Abu Bakar at Penguin SEA for their enthusiasm and belief in the relevance of the collection's themes for Southeast Asia.

And then, there are the reservoirs of energy and emotional sustenance a writer draws upon for creativity and just to get her work done. The love of my husband, Sadiq, my kids, Teia and Zac, my brothers, Kean Loon (who took amazing publicity headshots, also Gisella Torres for headshots) and Kean Shyong (who provided his medical expertise for one story in the book), my dearest friends Gabriella (especially countless conversations forging meaning, identity and affect), Sigrid, Barbara, Jean, Manish, Peter, and our extended circle of friends who were supportive of my writing endeavours: Monica, Joan, Deirdre (especially in all my food explorations), Simon Ogus, Girish Kumar and Damian White. Many others were guardians, empaths, wise-ones, or a source of emotional strength, sometimes without them realising how much I drew upon their friendship and energy: the Currimbhoy clan—Sanu Bhaijan and his family, Amyn Bhaijan and his family (and all the sprightly, energetic young ones: Sana, Samiyah, Osma, Zoya), Bala and Ramesh at The Institute for Contemporary Arts, Pinky Lilani and certain members of her family, many writers, as well as the online community of fiction writers and journals who give me such validation and encouragement. I love you all.

Research Sources

Kurlansky, Mark. *Salt: A World History* (London: Vintage Books, 2003)

Kwok Kian Chow. *Channels & Confluences: A History of Singapore Art* (Singapore Art Museum, 1996)

Lee Geok Boi. *Syonan: Singapore Under the Japanese 1942-1945* (Singapore: Singapore Heritage Society and Landmark Books, 1st edition, 1992, 2017)

Low, Kelvin E.Y. *Remembering the Samsui Women: Migration and Social Memory in Singapore and China* (Singapore: NUS Press, 2014)

Tong Chee-Kiong. *Chinese Death Rituals in Singapore* (London and New York: Routledge Curzon, 2004)

Wong Hong Suen. *Wartime Kitchen: Food and Eating in Singapore 1942-1950* (Singapore: National Museum of Singapore & Editions Didier Millet, 2009)

About the author

ELAINE CHIEW is a writer and a visual arts researcher, and editor of *Cooked Up: Food Fiction From Around the World.* Twice winner of the Bridport Short Story Competition, she has published numerous stories in anthologies in the UK, US and Singapore.

Originally from Malaysia, Elaine Chiew graduated from Stanford Law School and worked as a corporate securities lawyer in New York and Hong Kong before studying for an MA in Asian Art History at Lasalle College of the Arts, Singapore, a degree conferred by Goldsmiths, University of London. She now lives in Singapore.